CORMORANT RUN

J. C. McKenzie

"Up!" she yelled. With a strong pump of her wings, she strained upward.

The bird-brained prince gaped at her.

Argh.

She swooped down, gripped a fist full of his hair and yanked.

Up! Up! Up!

"Up!" she screeched again, straining for the angry sky.

Ronin growled but listened, angling upward, and beating his powerful wings.

The tension from pulling his hair eased as he caught up to her.

"Stop pulling my—"

"Move!" she hissed and let go of his hair. The energy pooled in the depths directly below them. The monster was too close.

And too hungry.

"Move!" She beat her wings frantically. It wasn't enough. They weren't going to make it.

The Sea Beast burst from the ocean. Only his gaping mouth with rows of sharp jagged teeth and the dark depths leading to his empty stomach were visible. An ambush attack from below. The giant monster thrust upward from the ocean, driving his toothy mouth closer and closer toward them.

PRAISE FOR J. C. MCKENZIE'S BOOKS

Conspiracy of Ravens
"Raven is my kind of people. Half hot-mess, half bad-ass, all awesome... the story was had plenty of humor, action and mystery rolled up in a nice paced story."
~ Urban Fantasy Investigations

Nevermore
"The dramas, dangers, intrigue, and tension of NEVERMORE will have you glued to the pages, and when it is finished, Ms. McKenzie will have left you satisfied yet wanting more."
~ Fresh Fiction

Queen of Corvids
It has all the classic comedy, angst, and drama that I have come to expect from J.C. McKenzie, and then it piles on mystery and more interesting characters.
~ Lady with a Quill

The Call of Corvids
"This is a fascinating read that brings together a world that has been marred with fae wars"
~ Fresh Fiction

The Night House

"From the very first page till the very end I was hooked on this book and read it in less than one day...it had everything you could want from a story romance, secrets, lies, suspense, surprises and more."
~ Paranormal Romance Guild

Shift Happens

"SHIFT HAPPENS has excitement, intrigue and lots of danger. I love the whole cast of characters and how they played a part in the story" ~ Fresh Fiction

Beast Coast

"I loved this book as much as the first. There are secrets, surprises, and all manner of supernaturals."
~ Paranormal Romance Guild

Carpe Demon

"The story keeps the adrenaline pumping and spine tingling tension building throughout the story with well written scenes full of vivid details that capture the imagination and make it easy for the reader to become engrossed... ~ Literary Addicts Book Community

Shift Work

"It's a terrific series and if you like supernatural reads, with a side of romance, the sort with solid and intense plots, gripping and very real dangers, hard choices,

supernatural people some of whom can be selfish, cruel and bloodthirsty...You'll be hooked."
~ Jeannie Zelos Book Reviews

Beast of All
"This time out, J. C. McKenzie has outdone herself with high-velocity action, soul deep emotions and one of those finishes that you want to replay over and over!"
~ Tome Tender

Dangerous Dreams
"This new world promises to be an adventurous one full of snark, passion, thrills, romance, danger and wonderful characters and I can't wait to read the next one." ~ Stormy Vixen Reviews

Dangerous Liaisons
"Loved this story and loved Raf and strong, stubborn Lara and I can't overlook Lara's dragon who brought humor to this story." ~ Paranormal Romance Guild

The Good Griffin
"THE GOOD GRIFFIN is as addictive as a double shot of espresso, only without any of the withdrawal symptoms." ~ N. N. Light

BOOKS BY J. C. MCKENZIE

Cormorant Run

The Night House

Conspiracy of Ravens

Nevermore

Queen of Corvids

The Call of Corvids

From the Shadows

Shift Happens

Beast Coast

Carpe Demon

Shift Work

Beast of All

Dangerous Dreams

Dangerous Liaisons

Dangerous Decisions

The Good Griffin

Cormorant Run

Contact Information: jcmckenzie@jcmckenzie.ca

Cover Art: Eerilyfair Design

Publishing History:

First JCM Publications Edition, 2020

ISBN: 978-1-9992394-8-0 (print)

ISBN: 978-1-990143-34-2 (print 2022)

ISBN: 978-1-990143-09-0 (hardcover)

ISBN: 978-1-9992394-9-7 (ebook)

To my children, L and V
My two favourite reasons to smile...
And also my two favourite reasons for getting grey hair.

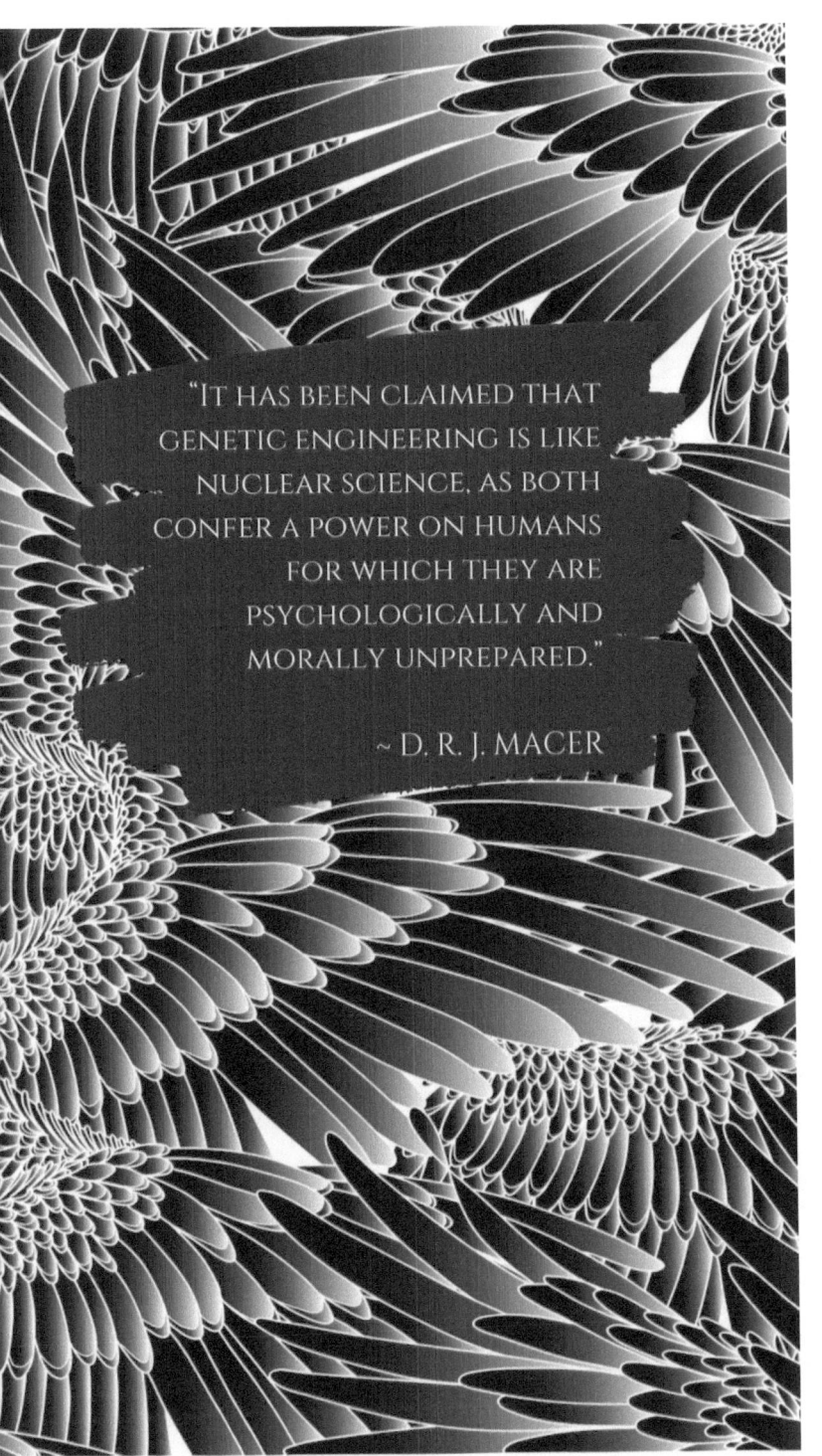

"IT HAS BEEN CLAIMED THAT GENETIC ENGINEERING IS LIKE NUCLEAR SCIENCE, AS BOTH CONFER A POWER ON HUMANS FOR WHICH THEY ARE PSYCHOLOGICALLY AND MORALLY UNPREPARED."

~ D. R. J. MACER

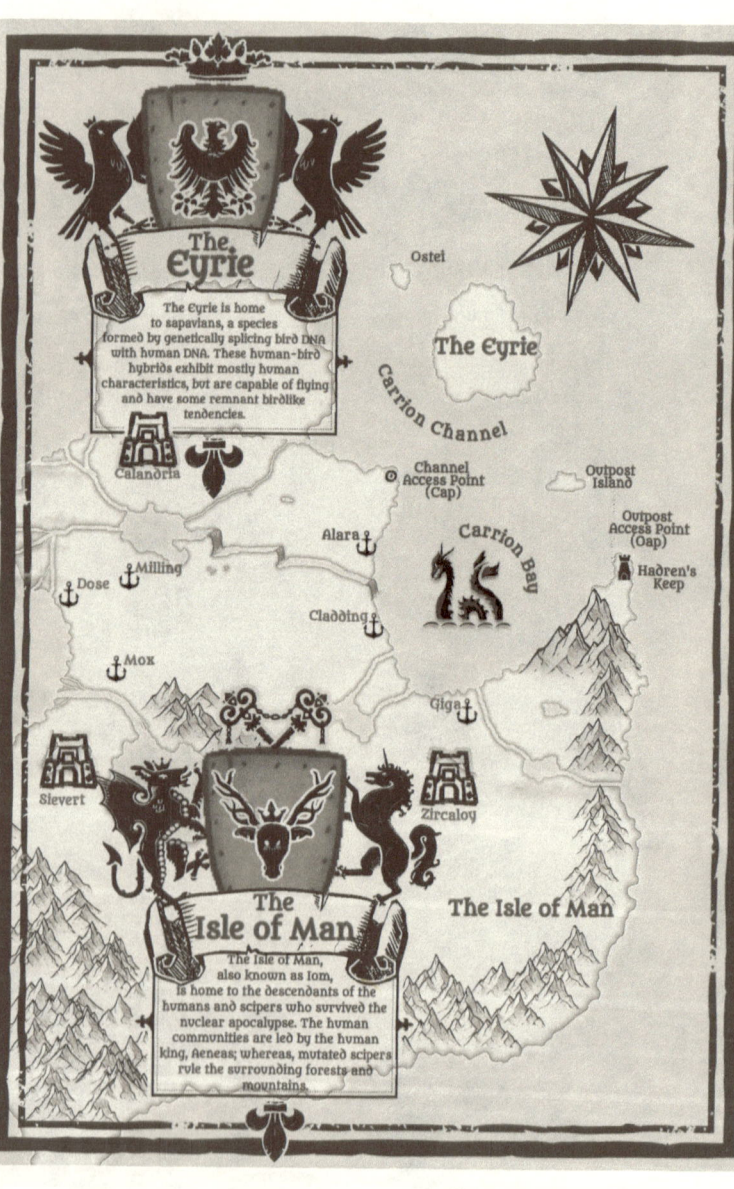

The Eyrie

The Eyrie is home to sapavians, a species formed by genetically splicing bird DNA with human DNA. These human-bird hybrids exhibit mostly human characteristics, but are capable of flying and have some remnant birdlike tendencies.

Ostei

The Eyrie

Carrion Channel

Calandria

Channel Access Point (Cap)

Outpost Island

Outpost Access Point (Oap)

Alara

Carrion Bay

Hadren's Keep

Dose

Milling

Cladding

Mox

Giga

Slevert

Zircaloy

The Isle of Man

The Isle of Man, also known as Iom, is home to the descendants of the humans and scipers who survived the nuclear apocalypse. The human communities are led by the human king, Aeneas; whereas, mutated scipers rule the surrounding forests and mountains.

The Isle of Man

1

"Oh, meltdown. It's one of these annoying buzz-words. We prefer to call it an unrequested fission surplus."

— MR. BURNS, *THE SIMPSONS*

A monster free flight. Things were looking up. The salt spray lifting from the churning ocean below slid over Cora's skin like a calming balm to her soul. She tucked her wings in and dove closer to the surface. Described by ignorant people as a cross between humans and birds, sapavians like Cora were neither, and both at the same time. She might have bird DNA running through her veins, but other than the giant wings protruding from her back and bird-like tendencies, Cora could pass as a human.

Not that she'd want to.

Ugh, humans.

She shuddered and dropped her arm to trail fingers in the ice-cold water. Finally, she was free to glide in the air flows on another run. The day-long journey had flown by. Pun intended. No dirty city filled with members of the Seagull Clan squawking at each other, no vultures haggling over prices in the market, no pigeons flapping around, getting in the way to deliver important messages, or hawks watching everything to report back to the king. And no eagles...well, no eagles being eagles. Pompous, self-righteous egomaniacs, the lot of them.

As a member of Cormorant Clan, Cora preferred the serenity of the ocean. If she had time, she'd dive below the surface and check for the pink run. They were later than usual.

The treeline of the awaiting shore loomed closer. Iom, the Isle of Man, led by King Aeneas. Humankind defied their name because there was nothing kind about them. The vicious beasts shot arrows at anything with wings. Humans had a wealth of land and other resources, yet loathed sapavians for their mastery of the ocean.

A flash of silver caught the fading sunlight. A jumper. The pink run had finally arrived.

Cora dipped closer, the salt spray coating the underside of her black wings and flying leathers.

Something cold sliced her shoulder. Her skin stung.

What the hell was that?

She patted the area with her hand. The cold sensation quickly turned to burning heat. She stared at her red fingers. Blood.

Blood.

Alarm bells screamed in her head.

She careened to the side. Another arrow shot past, narrowly missing her. She clenched her teeth and rode the surface of the ocean, weaving back and forth. She couldn't go skyward now. Without momentum, ascension took time. If the archer reached her over a kilometer from the shore, she'd become a pincushion if she tried to gain altitude right now.

Instead, she turned to the left, straight for the cliff. Another arrow flew into the sea directly in the path she'd travelled. Her heart pounded and her skin tingled. She needed to get out of range. She veered harder to the left. More arrows hit the water.

She strained forward, pushing her wings against the turbulent air to stay aloft and increase her speed. The sounds of arrows smacking the water's surface grew distant. Or was that hopeful projection?

The Cap Cliffs grew closer. With a great thrust, she angled up, flying leathers brushing the rough sandstone cliff as she flew along the surface and away from her would-be murderer.

Fucking humans.

They always scouted the Channel Access Point but getting shot at the Cap rarely happened nowadays. Bad luck? Or something else? Had they discovered her contact in the nearby village?

With the wind under her wings, Cora pushed forward and into the protection of the trees. Out of sight and out of range, she touched down. Her leather boots pressed into the dry summer soil and the wind caressed her back with sweet promises. *Just turn around,* the sea wind whispered. *Return to my sweet embrace.*

She tucked in her wings, the tips touching the sun-warmed path. The contact was more of an annoyance than a hindrance. She didn't like walking when she could fly. And she hated getting shot by an arrow even more.

Gingerly pressing against the wound, her fingers came away bloody again. Thankfully, the cut wasn't as bloody as before. The bleeding had eased, but a dull throb radiated from the injury. The arrow hadn't sliced deep as it whistled past her and it hadn't caught an artery or a wing. Just a nick, really. She'd been lucky. As long as she kept the wound clean, she'd mend. If she could take a dip in the ocean, she'd be even better.

Cora sighed, her wings drooping with the action. She needed to deliver the message to her contact and return home to report on the salmon run. Splashing around in salt water with humans actively hunting her would be irresponsible, and just plain stupid.

The sun dipped below the treeline and cast Cora in a world of shadow. The trip took most of the day and all her energy. She'd have to wait for the morning to return to the Eyrie across the Carrion Channel, but she had little hidey holes around the area. Even with the heightened danger, she enjoyed this time abroad.

As she walked, she stepped on fallen pine needles and stirred up the sweet smell she associated with the end of summer. The forest hummed with wildlife. Birds cooed and called from the branches. At one time, her people had been synonymous with the birds, but a nuclear tsunami in the aftermath of extensive genetic experimentation had changed that.

Cora continued down the forest path. The clank of metal, the groan of wood and the clamber of humans talking trickled up from the town through the trees. The townsfolk of the small fishing village would be busy finishing the day's work before they lost the light.

From all accounts, the humans had history books just like sapavians, which told stories of grand cities with all sorts of convenient amenities, many of which didn't require electricity. But a lot of humans believed if they started using the ways of the pre-cascade societies, they'd invite further ruin. The advance of technology had been the previous empire's downfall, after all. So instead, humans shied away from some of the ancient knowledge, embracing a practice they called, "the forgetting."

Complete nonsense. Dad always said, "Work smarter, not harder."

She took a deep breath and regretted it. Lack of technology also meant questionable hygiene and waste disposal for some of the smaller fishing communities. She struggled to tolerate the outskirts of town. Assuming she wasn't shot down first by an arrow-happy human, she'd never survive if she actually ventured in. If only she could practice her own form of forgetting.

Cora found the deteriorating stump and pulled out the candle and flint from the notch in the side. After making a small pile of dried twigs and grass, Cora knelt down and shielded her work with her wings. She struck the flint with the stone. Sparks shot out and the grass caught on fire. Cora leaned down and blew, coaxing the red embers to life. The twigs cracked and popped as the fire spread and warmed Cora's face.

Finally.

She dipped the wick of the candle into the small fire. When she first started making these runs, she'd tried to light the candle wick directly from the stone and flint. She'd failed, epically and repeatedly. Maybe she should've practiced more, but she found a method that worked and stuck with it.

Armed with her single flame, she stood and snuffed out the burgeoning campfire with her foot. Cora walked farther down the path to another open area. Similar to the previous one, this break in trees offered shelter from the coastal winds and a clear view of the town below. A single stump sat in the middle of the small clearing, close to the cliff's edge. Cora placed the candle in the holder sitting on the stump.

Well, that's done.

After leaving the candle to flicker in its protected location, Cora walked back to the woods and made her way to the meeting location. Hopefully, her contact looked out the kitchen window tonight. Once, it had taken days for her signal to garner a response. She'd gone through five candles and had to restock her supplies.

Cora enjoyed many things about her trips to Iom, but not humans or fishing villages.

2

"Someone didn't get the message about not shooting the messenger."

— CORA CORMORANT

A branch snapped and Cora pulled herself upright, withdrawing a dagger from her thigh-sheath in one smooth motion and waited. *This better be Ava.* If some numbskull stumbled upon her in the dark, the whole mission would be a bust and they'd have to figure out a new system and meeting place. Cora liked this one. The trees shielded her from the wind, and if she needed a quick getaway, she could take three lunges to the left and dive off the cliff to the murky ocean below.

The sounds of stumbling footsteps echoed in the dark forest and a woman hissed.

"Please, speak up," Cora whispered. "I don't think the whole village heard you."

Ava scowled under the moonlight and swatted a branch out of her way. "I hate this place."

"Really?" Cora rose her eyebrows and brushed her dark hair out of her face. "I think it's perfect."

"You're not the one facing imminent death if you walk two steps too far to the north or east."

"Please. With those stubby legs, you have at least four steps until you fall to your death."

Ava narrowed her dark, almond-shaped eyes at Cora and placed her hands on her hips. "If you weren't so generous with intelligence, I wouldn't be here at all."

Cora sheathed her dagger and brushed off her hands on her leather pants. She pulled the sealed letter from the pocket of her bodice. No crest covered the seal, but she recognized the smell and colour of the wax. Only one house on the Eyrie used this particular premium red wax. The same house Cora preferred to have nothing to do with.

But...orders were orders.

Ava reached forward, snatched the folded message from Cora's outstretched hand and stuffed it in her satchel. "Did you read it?"

"Of course not." Cora pulled her shoulders back. She didn't need to. Most of the communication from the royal family tended to put people in their place, scold those for perceived infractions or coerce others to do their bidding. With fancy words. Big, fancy words.

Plus, as a determined professional, Cora would never break the messenger code by opening sealed notes.

"And the salmon?" Ava asked.

Although technically not part of the deal—Ava would be paid well for delivering the message—Cora found it best to maintain a positive working relationship with a person from a community who would otherwise shoot her on sight.

Make yourself useful, Mom would always say. *And you make yourself indispensable.*

Cora smiled. "The pink have arrived. They're about a kilometre due north of the Cap."

Ava sighed and her shoulders dropped. "About time. They're late this year."

Cora bobbed her head. Late salmon runs tended to have catastrophic effects on towns like Ava's where the majority of families depended solely on the fish markets for their livelihood. "The Eyrie was also concerned. This will be welcome news for all of us."

Ava snorted, a guttural sound that contrasted with her delicate features. "Like any of us humans could compete with sapavians." Ava narrowed her eyes and she leaned forward. "You're bleeding."

Cora shrugged and instantly regretted the movement. The arrow wound still ached. "Just a scratch."

Ava pursed her lips but didn't say anything.

Instead, she straightened and lifted her chin. Her go-to body language for ending their little evening chitchats.

"Anything else?" Cora asked.

"Just—" Ava looked away.

Cora frowned and waited. Sometimes, Ava had information about merchant ships planning to come in and the Eyrie traders welcomed the news.

"Be careful."

Cora jerked back. "What's that supposed to mean?"

Ava glanced around the forest as if they stood at some town hall meeting and worried about an eavesdropper. A bit overkill. The trees told no tales in this forest. In any forest. The plant kingdom was one of the only living groups of organisms to emerge from the nuclear cascades relatively unchanged. "There's discontent among my people."

"That isn't new." She had the arrow wound to prove it.

"New, no. Different, yes."

"How so?"

"They've increased patrols along the northern cliffs and strangers are passing through town." She pursed her lips. "I've probably said too much already. You've always been good to me, though. To us. Change is coming. Be careful."

Cold prickled along Cora's skin. That didn't sound good at all. Despite the protection of the trees, the proximity of her escape route and the solitude of the night, Cora felt exposed. Her black feathers ruffled and the hair on the back of her neck stood up as if trying to spot the danger for her.

Time to go.

"May the winds be strong," Cora mumbled the traditional Eyrie farewell.

Ava flashed a small, sad smile and stepped into the shadows. "And always at your back."

3

"I could easily forgive his pride, if he had not morti-
fied mine."

— ELIZABETH BENNET, *PRIDE AND
PREJUDICE*

Cora moved through the Eyrie's busy night market, careful to keep her wings tight to her body. Though all sapavians of the Eyrie had wings, some were shorter than others and some just lacked general courtesy. Stepping on someone's wingtip was rude, avoidable and grounds for a legal knife fight, yet it still happened. In a busy marketplace, the perpetrator could easily disappear in the throng, leaving the hurt individual without anyone to spew curses at, much less take a stab at.

After taking the night to rest following the meeting with Ava, Cora flew across Carrion Channel to the Eyrie. Home. Her tired wing muscles ached, and her sore bones begged for her comfortable bed. She didn't want to shut herself away just yet. She'd visited the nurse first, got a stitch and then headed for the night market.

Though she disliked crowds and socializing in general, she found the square of bustling shoppers and loud vendors full of sapavians oddly therapeutic after her solitary trip. She wanted to feel like a part of a community.

She'd hate them all again tomorrow.

Father often remarked on Cora's "complexity," though he usually used coarser words. She wanted to be invited to parties she had no intention of attending and she felt lonely when alone but hated sharing her space.

Cora sighed and navigated through the crowd. She preferred it like this. Anonymous in a sea of people. Just another face. No obligations to make pointless conversation.

Too late to report to the Spy Master who coordinated the messages, Cora drifted through the marketplace, enjoying the throng of people and the smell of seafood. The Eyrie castle and surrounding town stood as a solemn reminder of the world of man before the apocalypse and the world broke apart. It wasn't really made for sapavians and it showed with its narrow streets and park benches. The ruling clan had ripped most of the benches out, but a few still stood as relics, reminders of a time long ago.

The Eagle Clan would probably have to remove those soon, too, for more room. A sign of overcrowding, the packed marketplace had become busier and busier. Sapavians were running out of space, and with angry, bird-hating humans populating the closest available land to the south, there wasn't anywhere to go.

Hopefully, King Edgar would figure something out —something that didn't involve mass extinction.

A familiar whiskey jack sapavian slipped a few quality *otos* to a merchant and leaned in for the Seagull Clan member to whisper something into his ear.

Cora cringed and turned to move the other way.

"Cora!" Jack yelled out.

She winced. Damn it. She slowly turned back to see Jack leave the merchant's stall with a wide grin. Whiskey jacks had the reputation for being the Eyrie's social butterflies, and it was a well-earned stereotype. Members tended to gravitate toward gossip, acting as town criers, and working as reporters for their niche in society.

Jack was gorgeous. One of those sapavians with naturally wavy hair that always looked like rumpled bedhead. Or maybe he constantly had nights filled with glorious sex. Cora didn't know and she never planned to find out. Jack might have a strong body that looked more apt for building towers with his bare hands than cutting down Eyrie residents with his harsh written words, but Jack's interest with Cora wasn't romantic.

"Hello, Jack," she said.

He rolled his beautiful blue eyes and dipped in a shallow, mocking bow. "For the hundredth time, my name is Marcus."

His name was Marcus Jack, but whatever. The more she remembered his role in society, and not how his bright white smile flashed in the moonlight, the better. Her heart had never been in danger around Jack, but her integrity and job security were. She had to guard her words.

Jack leaned in and sniffed. "Did you just get in? You carry a certain sea spray freshness."

What a lovely way to tell her she smelled. Thanks. "What do you want, Jack?"

He shrugged. "Word on the Eyrie is more sapavians are headed to the waystations to look for places to live. The albatross aren't returning home as often and you've been very busy."

"Are you watching me?" She left at the ass-crack of dawn yesterday. Surely, he didn't sit on the city walls to watch for her departure.

He shrugged. "More like noticing your absence."

"That hardly means I've been busy. I don't like crowds."

"No, you don't." He glanced around the busy marketplace and the sapavians weaving carefully around each other. "Yet, you're here."

"So?"

Jack examined his perfectly trimmed nails. "So, you tend to surround yourself with the very crowds you hate after you return from a trip. I figure you need to feel like you're not quite alone after such a lonely excursion."

She scowled at the whiskey jack. Not only were these birds full of gossip, but they also excelled at reading people. Exceptionally well, apparently.

She threw her hands up. "What does it matter?"

"The daughter of the Cormorant Clan leader always matters, despite what you might tell yourself."

Her scowl deepened. The rumours of Father's alleged betrayal never truly faded. This whiskey jack kept poking around trying to uncover some devious plot to confirm his conspiracy theories. And if he couldn't get that he'd happily settle for gossip or any tidbit of news to fill his column.

"What have you seen?" he asked.

"What do you think I've seen?"

Jack shrugged again. "I'm hoping it's either new land or salmon. I'd be happy to report either. An exclusive scoop would really help me out. What do you say?"

Cora's harsh response got lost in squeals of excitement. She surveyed the crowd and realized they were all watching something in the sky. With a deep sigh, she turned away from Jack to confirm what she already expected.

Sure enough, a male member of the Eagle Clan hovered above the Eyrie, holding hands with a woman from the Hawk Clan. Her long wavy brown hair whipped around in the air and the eagle's court armour.

"Who?" she murmured, not wanting to hear the answer.

"Lord Liam Eagle and Lady Azure Hawk."

Not Ronin.

She drew breath again, relieving the ache in her chest.

The eagle sapavian was the king's nephew, not the heir of the Eyrie.

The crowd cheered again as the couple embraced and fell toward the island. Everyone around her held their breath. When the couple broke apart above the rooftops to swing back up, the crowd screamed with delight and encouragement.

Cartwheeling.

The eagle mating ritual.

Coded in the very bird DNA that helped create sapavians a long time ago, members from the Eagle Clan retained the urge to complete this act when they found someone they loved.

Cora turned away from the spectacle and pushed

her way through the throng of sapavians and stopped dead.

A few feet in front of her, the crowd had cleared for another special viewing event.

Ronin Eagle, the Heir of the Eyrie, stood in front of her. Tall, strong, and built like a warrior, he wore the shiny silver and gold armour identifying his position as a member of the royal court. His brown hair had turned white during adolescence, marking him as a mature eagle.

With his angular face turned up to watch his cousin, the prince didn't see her. He wouldn't recognize her even if he did, despite the shock of white in her otherwise black hair and the scar running down her face. No, that wasn't quite right. He'd recognize her, maybe, in a flippant way, but she wouldn't elicit any emotional response. Recognizable or not, she was beneath his notice. Not even his hawk guards looked her way.

Being invisible wasn't a bad thing. In fact, it's where she needed to stay. Bad things happened to good people when the royals noticed them.

"Oh! The heir." Jack perked up. She hadn't noticed he'd turned with her. "Later."

The whiskey jack left her side to weasel his way through the other spectators, aiming for the prince. A number of "ladies" from the Hawk Clan and Eagle Clan already stood by his side, trying to fawn, hair-flip and eyelash flutter their way to his heart.

One day, Ronin would take his bride to the sky for all to see, completing the traditional mating ritual. Every girl in the Eyrie dreamed of being that bride at one point in their life. Some never gave up hope. Cora had dreamed, too, but hope and desire to be anything other than a messenger fled the day her mother died.

The couple plunged toward their death again, a tangle of limbs. The crowd cheered, roaring encouragement as they broke apart.

I'm done.

She turned away from the cartwheeling and her childhood crush and made her way from the night market to her small room in the cormorant house at the edge of town. Despite the melancholy ache in her chest, she dragged her feet. Cora constantly battled between choosing two undesirable outcomes. She could stay in the market and feel her heart crushed further, or she could return home and go to sleep where her recurring nightmare lay in wait.

Every night, dreams and memories plagued her. Ones where she relived her mother's murder. Ones of Ronin and his sister's rejection. Ones of flying low over the ocean's surface with the Sea Beast swimming underneath. But the monster never attacked in her dreams; instead, she found his presence comforting.

And that was the scariest thing of all.

4

"I love the smell of possibility in the morning."

— CORA CORMORANT

The morning market hummed with excitement from last night's events, yet an undercurrent of nervousness and danger kept the energy grounded. Cora stepped around a man with a rotund belly and slate gray wings.

He grunted and turned his bulging bird gaze on her. "Watch it, Crow."

Cora rolled her eyes. Like that was an original slur. Crows were not one of the founding birds used to create sapavians during the Scientific Experimentation Era, known as SEE in the crusty old textbooks in

Father's study. Instead, the intelligent birds sat along the rooftops and fences of the Eyrie and watched, mocking from a distance as if sapavians would've been better, done better, if crows had been included.

"Go peck yourself." Cora smiled sweetly to follow up the insult. She stepped into the nearby doorway and turned away from the angry hollers of the pigeon man. Her boots scuffed the cobble stones. She closed the door behind her, shutting off the incessant racket of the bustling marketplace. Not one to skip, saunter or glide like some sort of fairy drunk on pixie dust, Cora moved like an efficient machine down the hallway on light feet and made her way to the cormorant leader's office. Her father's office.

She trailed her fingers along the rough, stone walls, the familiar loamy smell and scratchy surface oddly comforting. She'd spent a lot of her childhood running through these starkly decorated halls.

Her footsteps echoed down the corridor and bounced back; cool air clung to the walls in spite of the heat outside. Though she didn't plan to travel today, she wore a clean set of flying leathers. The fitted pants, vest and vambraces might be hot for the late summer weather, but she never felt comfortable wearing civilian clothes. Besides, if she needed to cool off, she could always take a dip in the ocean.

Cora took a deep breath of dust-laden air and turned the corner. Two large double doors loomed ahead, the solid oak stained dark brown and polished to shine under the natural light streaming in through the open windows. Shear, off-white curtains billowed across her path and brushed against her soft leather pants.

The two cormorant guards standing on either side of the doorway straightened at her approach—Dax and Cam. The twins. She confused the two when she ran into one of them alone, but when they stood side by side like this, she could easily tell them apart. Honestly, as her cousins, she should do better, but they were called identical twins for a reason.

"Is he in?" she asked them.

Cam nodded.

Dax leaned over and opened the door, holding it open for her to pass through.

"Thanks," she said and walked into the office of the Cormorant Clan Leader, Master Fisherman. Those might be his official titles, but unofficially, he was the Spy Master of the Eyrie. Kane Cormorant orchestrated the delivery of overseas messages for anyone wanting to avoid the regular pigeon channels.

And to Cora, Father.

The old man looked up from the large oak desk he sat behind and placed his quill down beside the parchment paper he was writing on. Thick dark eyebrows rose slightly over brown eyes so dark they almost appeared to blend in with his pupil. His hair, once inky black, now had a splattering of white and the stubble on his face was growing in more gray than black. He rested his wings, folding them loosely behind his back. He wore the black leather livery identifying his position in the royal court. At one time, before his "fall" from grace, he wore the eagle pin on his shirt over his heart. Those days were long gone.

The door clicked shut behind her and she stepped forward. "Father."

The seriousness of his expression faded, and a genuine smile spread across his weather-worn face. He pushed away from the desk, unfurling his large black wings to stretch briefly before refolding them behind his back.

He held his arms out. "Coraline, my heart. Welcome home."

She walked around the desk and into his warm embrace. With a deep breath, she inhaled leather and parchment—the two smells she'd long-ago associated with her father. She squeezed him back before pulling away.

"How was the mission?" he asked.

"Successful."

"No return message?"

She shook her head.

"Something is going on over there in Iom and my contacts have grown silent. I don't like it," he said. His gaze drifted to the angry wound on her shoulder. He couldn't possibly see it through the neckline of her flying leathers, but her stitch itched as if his gaze had locked on it and gave it a tug. Those nurses must've told on her.

Her father reached out to cup her face. He ran his thumb along the scar that ran down her cheek from beneath her right eye to her jaw. His gaze flicked to the lock of white hair that rested along her shoulders. Sadness welled in his eyes. She knew the look. Memories of their past flooded his mind. Thoughts of a happier time. Thoughts of Mom.

His contacts went silent once before. They'd received no warnings and Father hadn't been there when the humans attacked the keep. The ultimately unsuccessful siege left Cora scarred and her mother dead. Moments like this proved her father still hadn't forgiven himself for not being there for them.

"A successful run, but not without problems," he spoke with a growl.

She nodded. "What trip across the channel isn't? Some enthusiastic scout on the bluff got a lucky shot. I veered east to avoid the archer and next time I'll approach farther to the west."

Father scowled.

"The pink run is in," she offered. "Feasting less than a kilometre off the cliffs."

Father straightened. "That's welcome news."

She nodded again.

"I wonder why the albatross didn't report them?"

She shrugged. Aloof and distant, the southern albatross preferred to stay offshore as much as possible.

They perched on rocky islands too small to live on comfortably and were almost as wild as the sea monsters. Too slow and moody to use as messengers, they still acted as Father's eyes and ears over the ocean by reporting fish runs and anything else of interest. Despite that, they often missed things, not out of incompetence, but out of ambivalence. Pointing that out right now wouldn't solve anything. Father already knew their personality quirks.

"There was something else," she said.

Father's brows rose. "Oh?"

"My contact—"

A knock on the door interrupted her. She clamped her mouth shut and turned to the door in unison with her father. She'd have to tell him about Ava's cryptic warning later.

"Enter," Father growled. He squared his shoulders and let his hand drift to the hilt of his dagger.

Cora took her place to the left and slightly behind her father and rested her hand on her weapon.

Both doors swung open and Cora caught sight of the twins' wide eyes and tense mouths before three intimidating figures walked into the room.

Oh crap.

Cora stiffened as she watched Edgar, King of the Eyrie and Leader of the Eagle Clan walk into the room, flanked by his son and daughter. No less spectacular than he appeared last night, Ronin always gave the impression he was above everything, unlike Sasha, who perpetually looked as though she smelled something bad and assumed it was you.

Cora clenched her teeth together.

"Edgar," Father said. "An unexpected surprise."

That was a nice way of saying, "I wish I could leap over this desk and stab you."

Daddy, the smooth talker.

"Kane," the king nodded and stopped in front of the desk. His gaze briefly flicked to Cora. Recognition flashed before he turned his attention back to Father.

Typical.

At one time, she'd run through the castle, tugging on his shirt hem so he'd slip her more candies. When Cora was little, their families had been close, often getting together and letting the children play. That was before Edgar and her father had a disagreement.

Cora never discovered the cause, but the result had been devastating.

She'd never forgiven the Eyrie leader for what happened next and judging from Father's stiff back and tense shoulders, he wouldn't either.

His hand remained on his dagger's hilt.

When they first returned from the outpost to the Eyrie, among whispers of betrayal, a number of the king's advisors publicly questioned his choice to bring back the Cormorant Clan Leader. Those advisors were now gone, dismissed from their positions. But they weren't the only ones confused with the decision.

Edgar wasn't one to surround himself with powerful sapavians who loathed or betrayed him.

The answer was simple, of course. Father never betrayed the king and provided an irreplaceable service. Though the king hardly confided his secrets to Cora, she could figure out that much on her own. Why the king and Father would allow the rumours to persist still mystified her, and why the king graced them with his presence today baffled her.

Cora took her direction from Father's stance and remained ready.

"At ease, Kane. I'm not here to attack you or your daughter. I'm here on business."

His son and daughter straightened and their gazes flicked to Cora in unison.

That's right, bitches. Here I am.

They hadn't recognized their childhood friend. She should've expected it. Hell, she had expected it. Yet a piercing pain still stabbed her heart. She really was nothing to them now. It made her question whether they were ever her friends to begin with.

Sasha quickly scanned Cora's face, came to some conclusion, and returned her attention to Father without breaking her dismissive expression once.

Being the same age, Cora and Sasha had been close friends, even braiding each other's hair and all that crap. Sasha had grown into a striking woman, her hair and wings retaining a tawnier colour, closer to the hawk genes from her maternal line than an eagle. Her golden, almost yellow gaze still held their piercing focus, as if she shrewdly saw through all the bullshit. Her expression held no warmth for her childhood friend. Assuming it ever did.

And Ronin...

Her face grew warm. Well, Ronin had grown up to be just as stiff and arrogant as his father and not at all as dashing as her girlish heart and dreams had imagined him to be. The heir's striking golden gaze had paused on her face, most likely taking in the scar and streak of white in her otherwise black hair. At least that's what she assumed the look of pity was for.

Father relaxed, but rested his hand on his belt, still close to the dagger strapped to his side. "How can I help you, King Edgar?"

Edgar scowled at the title. He glanced at his grown children and hesitated.

Sasha nodded. Ronin remained a statue.

"I need my son escorted across the channel to the Cap."

Kane stiffened. "Why?"

As a servant of the court, Father shouldn't question the king, yet the other man made no attempt to reprimand him.

"He will attend a meeting with the humans."

Father's hand tightened on the belt and the leather creaked from the stress. "I'm a fisherman. I run a fish scouting service, not bodyguards. If you don't want to send your own men to guard your son, use the hawks.

If you want a message delivered, the pigeons will be more than happy to assist you. Unless you want to know the location of the pink run, I can't help you."

"Cut the crap, Kane. You work for me, remember? I've already briefed Ronin and Sasha. Everyone in this room is aware of your alternate role in society."

Father's wings ruffled and resettled. "I'm hardly the vigorous youth I once was, and we don't make outings across the channel. It's too dangerous. Even the waystation route holds a certain risk."

Edgar leaned forward and placed both hands on the flat surface of the desk. His hair, long turned white from age, fell in front of his amber gaze. "I ordered you to cut the crap. You have at least one messenger that makes it through. My guardsmen have seen them."

Cora silently cursed herself. She'd gone too close to the curtain walls of the palace along the coast. She knew it.

"I'm not suggesting you accompany my son," Edgar continued.

Ronin whipped his head to the side to stare at his father.

"I want the best," Edgar said.

Oh no.

The King of the Eyrie turned his yellow eagle gaze to her. "I want Cora."

5

"I love fools' experiments. I am always making them."

— CHARLES DARWIN

Every muscle in Ronin's body tensed at his father's proclamation. Why hadn't Father said something? Ronin was risking his life for this possible alliance. Peace between the two warring realms would allow the Eyrie to prosper and provide new land for their expanding population to grow into. He was willing to risk his life to save the kingdom from suffocating. He hadn't offered to go in Father's stead just to throw his life away with an inexperienced guide.

Cora's head snapped back as if Father had slapped her. She glanced at the spymaster. Fisherman, his ass. Everyone feared Kane Cormorant. His own daughter was something to behold as well.

Cora had grown into a striking woman. Without the jagged scar running down her face, she'd look too perfect, like some sort of figurine with pixie-like features. The scar and streak of white in her hair made her appear real, and dangerous.

Maybe she wasn't an inexperienced guide.

One thing Ronin was certain of—this wasn't the cute little girl who'd followed him around and played dolls with his sister.

She'd changed.

And whose fault was that?

He hunched his shoulders and looked away when she turned to him.

"My daughter?" Kane whispered. "Haven't you taken enough?"

Father snarled and straightened. "I'm risking my own son. If I thought this mission was hopeless, do you think I would send him?"

Kane pressed his lips together while Cora shifted from foot to foot. Deep bags underlined her eyes. She looked tired. What had she been up to?

"She just has to get him across. From what I hear, she does the trip more often than you let on. What's one more crossing?" Father asked.

"Going alone is a lot different than taking someone...unused to the physical demands of such a crossing." Cora's lilting voice had just enough rasp to prevent her from sounding like some sort of damn fairy or woodland elf. Her words slid over his skin and then the meaning woven within them punched him in the gut.

He ruffled and resettled his wings while he pinned her down with a glare. "My physical stamina has never been and never will be an issue."

She blinked. "And how about taking orders, Your Highness? Do you still rebel against them?"

"I'm here, aren't I?" he growled.

She leaned forward and smiled. It was not a warm or welcoming smile. "Will you listen to me? A girl? A subordinate?"

He let his gaze travel down her body. Though lean and chorded with muscle, she still had all the wonderful womanly curves. "There's nothing girlish about you."

Her cheeks grew rosy and she curled her hands into fists. She probably wanted to punch him. Bring it.

Father looked back and forth between them and finally settled on turning to Kane. "Will you do it?"

"Absolutely not," Kane said.

"Yes," Cora said at the same time.

The father and daughter exchanged a look. The flat expression on Kane's face melted into something soft and tender.

"You don't have to do this." He reached forward and gripped his daughter's shoulders gently.

"Yes," she said. "I do."

6

"If the ocean can calm itself, so can you. We are both salt water mixed with air."

— NAYYIRAH WAHEED

Cora swore under her breath the entire walk home. *Yes, I do?* That's what she said? She had to escort that stuck up snob across one of the most treacherous stretches of the Carrion Channel? What the bird-loving hell was wrong with her? Why had she said yes? Why had Ronin's challenging gaze dared her to say yes when she should've said no?

Argh.

"Cora! Wait up." Ronin's deep, charismatic voice shouted from somewhere behind her.

Cora cringed. Unlike the pigeon from earlier, she couldn't tell the heir of the Eyrie to go peck himself.

Oh, it would feel good, though.

Could she hide behind her wings? Disappear into the brick wall lining the narrow walkway? She couldn't even disappear into the crowd. The path was empty. No one travelled along the outer path willingly except Cora. That's why she chose to go this way.

She'd never regretted her choice until this moment. A fawning crowd of simpering women to latch onto the prince would really come in handy right now.

She quickly checked for an escape route. On one side, the brick curtain wall of the castle rose to the towers above, and on the other, a sheer cliff with a one hundred foot drop off to the icy ocean below. She could escape, but it would involve literal fleeing and only provide extra ammunition for Ronin to think less of her.

A cormorant squawked at her as she kept walking.

"Hello, cousin."

The birds squawked again and launched off the path. Lucky beast.

"Cora!" Ronin growled.

Hmmm. Ignoring him wasn't working too well.

She sighed and turned around. Some loose pebbles fell from the path and ricocheted against the cliff face before hurtling to the ocean. Lucky dirt.

"What do you want, Ronin?"

The tall warrior brushed his white hair from his

face and stopped a few feet away. The leather and metal fighting gear fit him perfectly, the gold and silver armoured shoulder and leg plates glistened under the sun. He probably had a page with the sole responsibility of shining his gear.

"What do I want? I don't know. Maybe a few moments of your precious time to plan our trip, or maybe, and this is extreme, get an advanced information session so I can prepare myself physically and mentally for this potentially deadly trip."

Oh my. He was angry.

"All of which we can cover tomorrow," she said.

Ronin took a deep breath. He looked as though he wanted to strangle her.

Try it, Pretty Boy.

"We leave tomorrow," he said.

"Exactly. The information will be fresh. You always struggled with long term memory retention."

"Coraline Evangeline Cormorant," he growled at her again.

She straightened at hearing her full name. She couldn't help it—years of conditioning. He wasn't just angry, he was furious.

"I need time to gather and pack my things," he said. "How will I know what to bring if we don't discuss it first?"

Ugh. He was making valid points. And she was being petty and purposefully obtuse, which made her look like the nitwit. Double ugh.

"Pack light," she said. "Bring only what you can't live without. Ditch the flashy armour."

"Weapons?"

"Small and sharp. There's no use for pretty swords over the seas."

He gripped the hilt of his sword, his fingers squeezed, then released the leather binding. "What about on land?"

She frowned. "I don't go inland. My understanding was that I had to bring you back and forth. You'll have a better idea as to what you need once you get to the Isle of Man. Surely, your meeting will be held on the coast."

"That's still your mission, but I'll have to go inland."

She recoiled. "That's suicide."

His smile widened. "You almost sound worried."

"Of course, I'm worried," she hissed. "If you do something stupid like die, my father and I are as good as dead." And there it was. The real reason she couldn't say no. Ronin's visual daring might've spurred her into agreeing to this death trap despite all the warning bells in her head, but after she left Father's office and thought through the possible outcomes and consequences, she knew she made the right call.

And it made her angry as hell.

Cora didn't like being manipulated, but the king had maneuvered them like pawns on a chessboard. If they'd said no, the punishment would have been swift.

The king couldn't allow them to know about the meeting and roam free. That's why he hadn't reprimanded Father for questioning him. He provided the extra information, telling them the purpose of Ronin's trip and sealing their fate. Cora and Father had no choice. Not really.

And now that Cora had agreed to take Ronin, failure wasn't an option either.

Something flashed across the heir's golden gaze.

"Yeah. You didn't think about that, did you? As if your family hasn't done enough. Now you're truly trying to end us."

"I'm trying to save the Eyrie."

What in the bloody bird hell did he mean by that? She waited expectantly, but he shook his head and the set of his jaw said he didn't plan to elaborate.

Ronin crossed his arms and his mouth turned down. "Why did you agree to take me?"

"Because, unlike my father, I'd already accepted the fact that we had no choice. We've already experienced your father's particular brand of punishment when he's displeased. At least this way we have a chance of avoiding it." She didn't wait for a response. She spun on her heel and continued on the path.

Ronin didn't follow.

Her pillow and bed called to her. She needed to rest and recuperate before the mission tomorrow. Normally, she had at least a week for turnaround before another channel crossing. Not this time.

Tomorrow, she had to escort her childhood crush across the dangerous Carrion Channel that had claimed more sapavian lives than any other cause, whether they flew above the clouds or below. And somehow, she had to keep her secret of survival from Ronin.

7

"The devil is already at the door, cleverly disguised as an engineer."

— JEREMY RIFKIN

Cora looked up from her pack on the bed when someone knocked lightly on the wooden door to her room. Seriously? Surely, Ronin would leave her alone after their chat on the ocean path. If he thought he could follow her home and tell her off, she had a few more choice words for him. She took the three steps needed to cross the room and opened the door.

"If you think—" she started.

Instead of Ronin standing at her door, cutting off

the light with his imposing body, his sister leaned against the frame, tawny wings tight to her back, arms folded, and eyebrows raised. "Expecting someone else?"

"Maybe."

"Are you going to invite me in?"

Like hell she'd invite this woman into her humble home. That would be akin to finding a rattlesnake and trying to play with it. Cold and indifferent, Sasha wasn't her childhood friend anymore. Was she ever a real friend or had it all been an act? "We can chat here."

Sasha looked around the hallway of the brick building and shrugged. "Things really have changed for you, haven't they?"

Cora's family had lived inside the royal palace at one time. Now they took up a small brick building on the edge of town. At least they had a place to live, which according to Jack, wasn't something every resident could boast nowadays.

"What do you want?" Cora asked.

"I want to make sure you understand the importance of your mission."

Cora frowned. "Why wouldn't I?"

"Things haven't just changed for you." A brief look of pain streaked across her expression.

Well, maybe it was pain. Maybe it was indigestion. Sasha wasn't prone to making emotional displays or having feelings.

The princess stepped onto the threshold of Cora's room, crowding Cora's personal space. Cora refused to budge or allow the princess entry into her home.

"If anything happens to my brother, you and your father will pay," Sasha said.

Did she think Cora didn't know that already? Why in bloody bird hell would she make a special trip down to Cora's slum to point out the obvious? "I'm well aware of the consequences of failure. Did you come here to add to my stress, or do you have something more helpful to say?"

"If you don't come back with Ronin, you may as well not come back at all," Sasha said instead of answering her question. She paused to peer over Cora's shoulder, scanning the room for something. "What happened to you?"

Funny, Cora wondered the same thing. The cold regal woman standing in front of her was not the same person as her childhood friend. Cora blinked at the princess.

"All those years ago," Sasha prompted.

Ice travelled along Cora's skin. Images of an angry ocean and large jagged teeth flashed in her mind. Is that why Sasha had come? To try to dig into Cora's past? "I don't know what you're talking about."

"The attack at Hadren's Keep. You went missing for a week. They found you washed up on the shore nearly dead."

Cora ground her teeth. She knew exactly how they found her. Half-drowned and incoherent.

"How did you survive?" Sasha narrowed her eyes and leaned in as if her question would somehow cause Cora to spill all her secrets.

The sad thing was, there weren't any secrets to spill save one. And Cora would take it to her grave. "Luck, I guess," she lied.

Sasha scowled, probably detecting the lie as soon as it left Cora's mouth. Without another word, the princess turned from her position in Cora's doorway and walked down the hall, leaving a sense of foreboding in her wake.

Cora wasn't one to prescribe to signs or omens, but if Sasha's visit and Ronin's attitude were any indication of the trip ahead, Cora was in for an unpleasant time. She just hoped she survived.

8

"The pessimist complains about the wind; the optimist expects it to change; the realist adjusts the sails."

— WILLIAM ARTHUR WARD

Cora clasped her custom travel sac to her back and let the wind wash over her face. The bag nestled snuggly between her wings didn't rub or impede her range of motion. It had been a birthday present from her mom.

She saw her father this morning, sharing Ava's warning and then sharing a moment of silence. Not one for prolonged goodbyes, Father had held her briefly in his crushing hug and told her to come back to him. Their farewells were always the same—short but full of love.

Cora stepped up beside Ronin who intently glared at the clouds above.

"A storm is moving in," Cora said. "Can we delay a day or two?"

"Absolutely not."

"How did you arrange this meeting without going through my father?" She toed the loose gravel and watched the small stones fall off the cliff edge.

"We did," he said.

So, the last message had been from the royal house as she suspected. "But not all the time. How else?"

"Waystations." He named the rocks that acted as little hops, skips, and jumps to cross the Carrion Channel. They led to the Waystation Access Point, or Wap, on the Isle of Man. Considered neutral territory, there was an unspoken truce and understanding that sapavians kept to the north side of the constructed wall and the humans remained on the south.

"Isn't that dangerous?" she asked. "Anyone could've intercepted the message. The Waystations are filled with scoundrels."

His brows lifted. "Scoundrels?"

"You know what I mean."

He grunted and buckled his pack in place. He'd actually listened and left his shiny breastplate and embellished boots at home, opting for black leather pants and vambraces, and a breastplate with matte black metal and leather trim. He looked just as powerful and lethal.

And arrogant.

Ugh.

He peered off the cliff edge and sneered. He wasn't afraid of heights, she knew that much. As an eagle, he was accustomed to soaring at higher altitudes than she was. Rumour had it, the eagles snuck out at night to mate during their cartwheeling—joining in the act and plummeting to their death but breaking from the free fall at the last moment. The cartwheeling in public was all hugs and kisses, but according to some spicy gossip, eagles liked to do it in the air.

Cora had never worked up the nerve to ask anyone if it was true.

But the height couldn't be why Ronin scrunched up his face and eyed the ocean below with distaste.

"What is it?" she finally asked.

"I don't like flying low."

"Well, go ahead and fly high. If the dragons and thunderbirds don't get you the moment we leave the protection of the Eyrie, the *scoundrels* who pirate the clouds will. And if you somehow miraculously survive, go ahead and announce your arrival to the humans with bells and whistles since you apparently have a death wish."

He scowled harder in response.

She stepped forward and jabbed his metal armour. "We fly low and in tight formation. If I shout anything, you do it. You don't ask why. If I change direction, you follow. You don't hesitate. I'll answer whatever questions you have on the other side when we safely arrive. Until then, keep your mouth shut and follow orders. Got it?"

He smirked and saluted.

Ass.

Without another word, she launched from the cliff's edge and dove toward the thrashing surface of the ocean.

Ronin cursed somewhere behind her.

Before she hit the churning water, she unfurled her wings. The updraft of wind licking off the surface of the water pushed against her wings and she leveled out above the cresting waves. Sea spray splattered her flying leathers.

"Show off," Ronin growled somewhere above and slightly behind her.

Sure enough, the big lug had pulled up sooner, a lot sooner, and now angled down toward her.

"Do you always—"

"Hush!" she hissed. "The monsters hear us. No more talking unless necessary."

He snarled at her, raising his lip and showing his teeth, but luckily his mouth remained shut.

This would be a long trip. She hoped for all their sakes, he stayed quiet and kept up.

9

"What would an ocean be without a monster lurking in the dark? It would be like sleep without dreams."

— WERNER HERZOG

Rain hammered against Cora's back and wings. She swiped her soaked hair from her face and pushed forward.

"Is it always like this?" Ronin drifted closer, looking no less god-like despite white hair plastered to his skin and his drenched clothes. He looked like the God of Thunder swooping in to rain vengeance on his wayward follower.

Was it always like this? Did he not remember a few

hours ago when she asked him to delay the trip? Yup, he still struggled with memory retention.

"Do you always talk when ordered not to?" she bit out through clenched teeth. Now was not the time to strike up a conversation. The Sea Beast had stirred. Cora felt his energy rising and vibrating in her bones.

Ronin said something, but she tuned out his deep rumbling and focused on the beast. His hunger was so strong, it was palpable. Her stomach rumbled. The feeling intensified, growing stronger.

And stronger.

And closer.

And closer.

"Up!" she yelled. With a strong pump of her wings, she strained upward.

The bird-brained prince gaped at her.

Argh.

She swooped down, gripped a fist full of his hair and yanked.

Up! Up! Up!

"Up!" she screeched again, straining for the angry sky.

Ronin growled but listened, angling upward, and beating his powerful wings.

The tension from pulling his hair eased as he caught up to her.

"Stop pulling my—"

"Move!" she hissed and let go of his hair. The

energy pooled in the depths directly below them. The monster was too close.

And too hungry.

"Move!" She beat her wings frantically. It wasn't enough. They weren't going to make it.

The Sea Beast burst from the ocean. Only his gaping mouth with rows of sharp jagged teeth and the dark depths leading to his empty stomach were visible. An ambush attack from below. The giant monster thrust upward from the ocean, driving his toothy mouth closer and closer toward them.

Ronin cursed.

Cora veered to the side, still angling upward. The monster moved with her, following the change of course.

Why fight, little one?" His creepy gentle voice spoke in her mind. *Come with me. Feed my soul.*

"Never!" she yelled over her shoulder. She changed direction again and dove toward the ocean, streaking past the Sea Beast's long scaly neck.

Ronin shouted something. Whatever. As long as he kept moving up, he'd be fine.

The monster screamed in her head.

She leveled out before crashing into the waves. With a pump of her wings, she used her momentum to swoop up toward the dark clouds again.

Lightning shot through the sky followed with the crack of thunder. The ocean raged below. Too big to maneuver as quickly as Cora, he wouldn't catch her now. The Sea Beast fell back into the water with a giant splash.

Cora swiped at the cold sweat now mixed with the rain pouring down her face. She flew to where Ronin hovered near the clouds at a safe distance from sea level.

"What did you yell at me back there?" Ronin hollered over the crash of the waves and thunder.

She hadn't been yelling at the prince, but she could hardly admit to talking with the Sea Beast. She shrugged. "Trying to direct you out of danger."

"Danger? That was more than danger." Ronin glanced at the sea again. "What the fuck was that? Was it the...?"

She nodded. "You finally met the infamous Sea Beast, Channel Monster Number One."

"Number One?" His brows shot up. "How many more will we meet?"

She shrugged. Every trip was different, but over the years she tended to run across less nuwaps each time she crossed.

Hundreds of years ago, before the nuclear revolution, scientists had begun to experiment with altering the human genetic code, enhancing it with other animal DNA to make super humans. The result were called scipers—scientific experiments. The scientists never refined their pursuit of perfect humans, and their tampering with the genetic code left it temperamental and unstable. DNA sequences once highly conserved with few errors, began passing on more and more mutations. This led to rapid radiation and divergence from the original scipers. A number of new species evolved, including the sapavians.

Then the nuclear apocalypse happened.

Nuwaps, or the nuclear warped, were the result of uncontrolled radiation from the nuclear explosions on scipers with volatile DNA. Sapavians emerged from the nuclear cascades relatively unharmed or altered. Not all scipers could boast the same result. Some lost all touch with their once present humanity.

During the nuclear cascades and radioactive fall-out, humans survived in bunkers on algae and bottled sunlight. When they finally poked their heads out, decades later, they arguably suffered no adverse changes as a species save their attitudes. Or maybe that was always an issue. Hard to tell.

When humans discovered what survived the radioactive fallout, they made it their societal mission to eradicate all the scipers, whether warped or not. They found only mild success and a lot of resistance.

"Surely, you know what lurks in these waters," Cora said to Ronin.

"Of course, I know what's been spotted out here, but reading and experiencing are two different things."

"He's the only one of his kind. At least in the channel." Too mean and hungry, he would be unlikely to cohabitate, even with a mate. "But as you know, there are other monsters in the channel."

"What else should I expect?" he asked.

She almost lashed out with a comment that he should've asked before they left, but then she recalled her behaviour from yesterday. She clamped her mouth shut. He had asked. He had tried to find out all this information before, and because she was pissed off with how things transpired in the meeting, she'd hoarded the information.

"What else?" he asked again.

She glared at him, more out of anger for her own actions than his. But still. What did he not understand about keeping quiet?

"Thunderbirds." She scanned the clouds. "Usually, the beast is first. They sense each other somehow and the birds are too dumb to keep their distance. Instead, they hover nearby and try to steal the meal or pick up the leftovers. Keep your eyes open. They're strong, but slower and can't maneuver as quickly."

Thunderbirds were a distant cousin of sapavians. Once created as weapons, the nuclear cascades had turned them into mindless killers. They survived solely on instinct, killing, and consuming whatever they could find.

She nodded toward their destination and set a path. Ronin fell in line with her, easily coasting with his giant beautiful wings.

"You could have told me sooner," he said.

He was right. She could have, but what would the knowledge have changed? He still needed to listen to her. "I haven't been attacked for the last three crossings."

He glanced at her and frowned.

That's right, big boy. Make the connection.

"You think it's me?"

He got it in one. "They can detect life energy somehow. We're a bigger target together."

"You want to split up?"

She shook her head. He wouldn't survive without her. Whatever had happened that night years ago had changed her—made her into something different, something more...something like *them*.

She angled back toward the ocean's surface. Ronin's eyes widened.

"Split the difference," she said, holding her finger to her lips. Halfway between the threats from above and the ones below, they might have a shot at surviving.

Ronin looked like he'd explode with questions, but instead of breaking the silence, he nodded.

Not even halfway across the channel, this would be a long ten-hour flight. Cora's wing muscles already burned from her previous trip and her evasion tactics from the Sea Beast left her weary and dreaming of her bed at home.

More lightning streaked through the sky, the branches of electricity burning a path through the gray.

They'd attack soon. They always did. The Sea Beast's energy trailed behind them, keeping pace, and tracking their progress. Did he sense her like she sensed him?

One day, little cormorant, you won't get away, his voice vibrated in her skull.

She squeezed her eyes shut. That couldn't be good. He was talking to her in coherent sentences now.

Maybe she should say something back?

She focused inward, reached for his energy, and formed words in her head. Would this even work? *What do you want?*

The Sea Beast's energy pulsed, but he remained silent.

Well, now she felt stupid, thinking thoughts at some deranged sea serpent intent on eating her. He probably couldn't hear her.

I want...

Thunder rocked the night, drowning out his voice in her head.

"Move," she hissed, diving to the right just as thunderbirds broke from the cloud cover, lightning fast. Sharp talons snatched at the air where she'd been seconds before.

A deranged off branch from the evolutionary tree to sapavians, the thunderbirds appearance alone revealed their origin. Created by scientific experimentation and twisted during the nuclear wars that started the apocalypse, thunderbirds retained very little of their human features. They had snarling, malformed humanoid faces with black bulging bird eyes. Instead of a mouth and nose, their features had fused together over time to form something like a beak. They had tiny forearms about half the length of Cora's and massive wings.

"Slow?" Ronin barked, diving out of the way of a thunderbird twice his size.

"Slower." She swung to the side, and another bird flew past.

In a deadly game of chase and evade, Cora and Ronin dodged, ducked, and dove out of the way. Six thunderbirds continued to pursue them through the lightning streaked sky.

"There are too many." Ronin cursed and drew his sword.

He was right.

And wrong.

"Ronin! No!" She turned toward him, now facing all six thunderbirds as they barrelled toward them. He hovered in the middle of the sky, the light flashing off his sword, like a defiant hero defending some hopeless twit.

What in the bird-loving hell was he thinking?

She put her chin down and shot toward him, unsheathing her dagger as she flew through the air.

The thunderbirds screeched; their calculating gazes triumphant.

Cora barrelled into Ronin, knocking his large muscled body out of the pathway of imminent death. At the same time, the surface of the ocean broke open.

The Sea Beast burst from the waves below, opened his enormous mouth and engulfed all six of the thunder-birds in one gulp. He twisted and slammed back into the water like a breeching whale. His toothy mouth curled up at one end.

Was that a smile?

Waves rolled over the spot where the Sea Beast disappeared, hiding any answers.

Why, she sent to the beast. Why had he spared her and taken the other birds instead?

Better meal, he answered.

That was reassuring.

And you're mine. Not theirs.

Yeah, that wasn't what she wanted to hear either.

"You can let go of me now." Ronin's deep voice vibrated against her ear.

Oh crap!

She'd clung to Ronin the whole time she'd hovered over the ocean's surface, glaring at the murky depths for answers.

Suddenly, all too aware of his proximity and how this must look to him, she let go and pushed back, hovering a foot away. "You brainless turkey!"

He raised a brow and sheathed the sword, the steady beat of his wings synchronized with hers. "I'd prefer to go down fighting, not as a coward."

"I'd prefer not to go down at all."

He raised his eyebrows, a smile tugged at his lips.

Grrrr.

She jabbed a finger into his chest. "You're not allowed to die."

He looked down at her finger poking his armoured breastplate and frowned. "I'm surprised you care."

He really did have a memory problem. She ground her teeth. "About you? Not particularly. Your whole family can go peck itself."

The dark clouds thinned out, lightening the sky around them.

He flapped his wings, blasting her with air, and moved away from her.

"My father will pay for my failure. It's a price I'm not willing to pay," she continued. "He's all I have left, so you will listen, and you will live. Do you understand?"

The sun broke through the thinning clouds and bathed Ronin in a spectacular beam of light. All emotion fled from his face. "Perfectly."

10

"The Law of Probabilities: the more things you try, the more likely one of them will work."

— JACK CANFIELD

Cora held her breath as they approached the shore to the west of the cliffs. With any luck, they'd reach the bank and she'd deliver the Royal Pain in the Ass safely. He'd complete whatever princely mission he was tasked with and they'd leave Iom unscathed.

Wishful thinking.

A high whistle cut through the crisp afternoon air.

"Dive!" She pulled her wings in and dove toward

the water. Without hesitation, Ronin followed. They levelled out before impact and veered to the side.

A flash of metal was her only warning. She careened into Ronin and knocked him out of the arrow's path.

Thunk!

Piercing pain erupted in her wing. The force of the arrow driving through her skin rocked her balance. She dipped sideways. The tip of her wing trailed in the cold ocean water. She cursed and pushed, righting herself.

They rounded the curving shoreline. Unless the humans had more scouts set up farther along the coast, they'd be safe as long as they kept moving.

"What the fuck?" Ronin let out a string of curses.

She glanced over at him. He'd curled his giant hands into fists and his chest heaved with each deep breath.

"Are they always this hostile toward sapavians?" Ronin asked.

She shrugged and instantly regretted the additional strain on her wing. Pain radiated from the arrow wound. Her muscles tensed, threatening to cramp. They needed to land soon. "You bring out the best in people."

He scowled but thankfully stopped asking questions. They landed on dry soil near the cliff's edge. From the sweet smell of the surrounding evergreens, it still hadn't rained. That couldn't be good.

Her wings sagged behind her. Pain radiated through her entire body. The relief of setting her feet down on land eased some of the tension in her shoulders, but her body still vibrated with adrenaline. She needed to calm down. *Breathe.*

Without speaking, they moved in unison to the protection of the trees. Once engulfed in the shade, Ronin turned to her with the deep frown she'd come to expect from him.

"You're injured."

Oh, that was so not the topic she anticipated. She'd expected him to fault the approaching course she set, not concern.

"Mere flesh wound." She purposefully didn't look at the arrow protruding from her wing. Unlike the last time she was shot at, she hadn't been as lucky. An arrow in the wing was one of her biggest fears, but an arrow through the wing bone was even scarier. At least she avoided that.

Ronin's frown deepened.

That couldn't be good.

"How did they know?" He narrowed his gaze.

She scowled at him. Screw the mighty prince for implying she somehow colluded with the humans. She took an arrow to the wing, not him. Had he thought this through? She found out about this trip yesterday. As the fastest messenger in Father's arsenal, even if she wanted to betray Ronin, the earliest the humans could have found out about this trip with her as the source was right now.

Breathe.

Control your response.

Don't punch the prince.

"Last time I came, they were waiting for me, too." She forced the words out smooth and even. "I veered east toward my destination. I assumed they'd move more to the east in anticipation of my return."

Ronin's glare softened. "So, they anticipated that you'd anticipate them."

"Pretty much. Or they just set up on both sides."

He leaned in, his handsome face unbearably close. "The question is how did they know to wait for you in the original location the first time? Who tipped them off? And how? You're the only messenger capable of crossing the void to the Cap."

She shrugged. "Apparently, my trips across Carrion Channel haven't been as covert as I thought." Hell, the entire royal family knew about them.

"Besides the obvious arrow-toting humans…" He leaned to the side and examined the arrow-wound. "Why do you say that?"

"You knew about it."

Instead of answering Ronin stepped forward, his arm brushing her shoulder and gripped the arrow.

"Don't—"

Snap!

He broke off the tail-end of the arrow, reached behind her wing and pulled the rest of the shaft out by the arrowhead. Pain streaked along her wing bones and down her back. Tension seized her shoulders.

"Mother—"

"Shh." He ran his hands along the humerus bone and gently pulled to extend her wing. A dull ache thrummed through her body. "Think you can fly?"

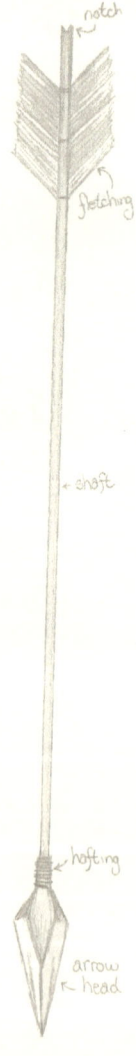

"I flew with it in, didn't I?" She glared at him over her shoulder. The arrow had punctured the elastic fold of skin that aided in aerodynamics, avoiding bones and major arteries. Like an earlobe after an ear-piercing, the membranous patagium hurt from the arrow, but didn't bleed significantly. The wound didn't even need to be patched. But the injury and resulting pain annoyed her, and it would mess up her balance in flight.

Ronin frowned, his golden gaze flicking to her briefly before reassessing the damage. "I think I should continue on alone."

Though he only reiterated the plan already provided to Cora, she never intended for him to leave her sight. Not when her life and Father's hung in the balance. Her plan was to follow him to the meeting and keep him alive.

Cora clenched her hands into fists. "I think that would be unwise."

Ronin released her wing. The warm pressure of his hands was replaced with cool air. "I've been raised my whole life as a warrior and a leader. You're now a liability and still need to get me back across the channel. The plan was always for you to stay here."

Mmhmm. Sure. She'd let him keep thinking that. She pulled her wings in and turned to face him. How was he still standing so close to her? "Your family won't be executed if you don't survive."

He narrowed his gaze and leaned down, now unbearably close, his powerful build even more imposing. He could loom all day, she wasn't backing down.

Cora straightened her spine and lifted her chin.

"Cora, the meeting is inland."

An invisible fist slammed into her stomach. She'd expected them to hold the meeting closer to the shore. Inland? She shuddered. That didn't change anything, but the idea of losing access to the ocean sent a wave of unease through her body.

Cormorants, both her bird cousins and sapavians, didn't fare well amongst the dense trees and rolling hills with no ocean in sight. They were shore birds and thrived near and on the sea.

"My contact is expecting me alone," Ronin added.

She sighed. His words made sense, but his logic and reasoning did little to unravel the twisted feeling in her gut. Why would they agree to meet on foreign soil without a guard? This whole thing felt off.

"How long?" she asked.

Ronin glanced at the sky. The sun travelling toward its apex. "The meeting is at sunset. I should be back in the morning."

"You're going to fly at night?"

"Would you prefer me to bed down with the humans?"

She recoiled.

He nodded again. "Travelling at night will provide better cover. Besides..." He stepped forward, only an inch separating his hard body from her own. If she breathed deeply, her chest would brush against his.

He reached out and gathered the strands of white hair that had escaped her braid. "I wouldn't want you to worry about me."

Argh.

He tugged her hair gently before releasing it and stepping away.

"Where's your meeting location?" She somehow managed to speak.

"Why?"

"If you're not back by noon, I'll come after you."

A slow smile spread across his face. "I'm touched."

"Don't be. This is purely self-preservation."

He sighed and pulled out a rolled piece of parchment from one of the leather pockets on the inside of his sword belt. He held out the paper.

She snatched the parchment from his hands and unrolled it. A map. "Won't you need this?"

He tapped his head. Without another word, he turned and walked from the cover of the trees to the cliff edge.

Words bubbled up her throat, words she wanted to say and words she wanted to suppress at the same time. Ronin was flying to a secret meeting inland across enemy occupied territory. She might never see him again. She stepped forward to follow.

Ronin launched off the cliff, caught the wind and soared into the sky. He didn't turn back. He didn't look over his shoulder. He left his good little soldier where he ordered her to stay and continued on the mission alone with no further thoughts of her.

Cora swallowed her words and turned back to the forest. She needed a safe place to make camp and get some food. If she weren't so far up on the cliff, she'd try venturing down to the water. But how many men stood in her way? How many humans lay in wait with their sharpened arrows?

Cora shuddered.

Piercing through the feathers and skin, the arrow wound wasn't too bad. Her healthy wing would have to compensate for the compromised integrity of her injured wing. Flying would hurt and sap her strength. If she did end up going inland after Ronin, she'd need her energy.

Cora shuddered again and settled in for the long wait.

11

"Sometimes the road less traveled is less traveled for a reason."

— JERRY SEINFELD

Ronin cursed his stupidity as he flew over the treetops. He'd left her. He'd left Cora alone and injured.

He really was the jerk she thought he was.

Ronin cursed again before scanning the terrain. Up too high for human eyes to detect, the tension in his muscles should've faded away by now. Instead, unease gnawed at his brain and constricted his breath. Tactically, he made the right choice. Cora needed to heal and rest. Flying inland had never been her thing growing up and seeing her face pale at the mention of it confirmed she hadn't changed her opinion. She'd always had a strong connection with the dark waters surrounding the Eyrie. More so than most cormorants, and especially after the incident.

Still.

Ronin enjoyed flying beside her. He liked her company. He looked forward to her snarls and bark, and her heated looks when she thought he wasn't paying attention.

Too bad so much history existed between them and their families. Some good. A lot bad. Cora hated his family, including him, and he didn't blame her, yet he couldn't forgive or forget what her family had done as well.

Maybe he should've said something before he left.

Maybe he should turn around?

His father's stern face flashed in his mind. No. Some things were more important than his feelings. This mission took priority. The Eyrie before the individual.

He'd see Cora tomorrow and maybe then he'd confront their past.

Right now, he needed to focus. So much was at stake with this meeting. If they could broker a peace with the humans, they could form a more formidable force against the monsters, commerce would improve, and his people would finally have room to expand. With the way the population grew on the Eyrie, they'd run out of space with the next generation. They needed room to grow and the humans had it.

We could take it. A memory of his sister's voice bounced in his head. So bloodthirsty. When had she become like that?

Father had explained how the humans were too spread out for a single attack to devastate them and too numerous to take on in a lengthy war. In short, sapavians would likely fail.

Sasha had remained unconvinced.

"Remember what happened at Hadren's Keep," Father had said.

How could they forget?

The sun continued its slow decline toward the horizon, casting colourful rays of light and painting the puffy white clouds in pinks and purples.

Almost there.

He'd arrive on time, too, thanks to Cora.

Tucking in his wings, he swooped toward the treeline. Air blasted past his face and his eyes watered.

The meeting location crystallized with perfect clarity.

No signs of anyone.

Fucking humans. Figured they'd be the ones to stand him up.

At least he'd have a chance to scout the area first. He circled the clearing, using his heightened eyesight to detect movement. Nothing. Where were they? Had he gotten the timing wrong?

And where would he land? Surveying the area yielded no feasible options. With a wingspan of almost twenty-two feet, he needed space. Branches could be such a bitch.

Unease prickled his skin.

If he landed in the clearing, he'd place himself at a tactical disadvantage and possibly find himself in a trap. If he landed farther away and walked into an attack, he'd have no room to maneuver or launch back into the sky. And if he didn't land at all, there'd be no alliance. He'd have to fly home and either make up an elaborate story or admit cowardice.

That's why they chose this location.

He circled again. Were they here? Were they hiding?

Lower and lower he circled. With superior eyesight, he could spot a hare over three kilometres away, surely, he'd catch the awkward and ungraceful movement of humans in a forest.

The sun's rays weakened with each circle of the clearing.

He might've arrived before them. They might've stood him up. This might be a trap. So many maybes and only one way to find out.

Ronin unsheathed his sword, swooped in, and landed in the centre of the clearing. Long grass gently swayed and brushed against his leather pants. His boots pressed into the dry soil.

He slowly turned and surveyed the clearing. Nothing.

He kept his sword ready and walked toward the cover of the trees.

Something sharp pricked his neck. He reached up and swatted at the skin. His vision swam. He held his hand in front of his face. Nothing.

He staggered and swung his sword out. No contact.

He looked at his hand again. Through his wavering vision, he made out a little speck of blood on his fingertip. They darted him.

Where were they?

Cowards!

The drugs latched onto his mind. Everything tilted. He lurched to the side. Darkness crept into his vision and he fell to the ground.

12

"Distance makes the heart grow fonder."

— NOT CORA CORMORANT

That pampered prince wasn't coming back.

The awful thought kept cycling through her brain all day as she sat on the edge of the cliff, dangling her legs over the side. Rocks and pebbles dug into her butt through the thick flying leathers. Earlier, she'd been tempted to dive off the cliff and into the ocean. But unlike her cormorant cousins, she couldn't launch easily from the ocean, and a quick dip and the following hike back up to the meeting spot would leave her exposed and vulnerable. Common sense prevailed, even though the arrow wound continued to burn, and salt water would help it heal.

Casting the angry ocean in shades of dark blues, purples and pinks, the sun dipped below the horizon just as it had last night after Ronin left. A pretty sunset. And completely at odds with the turmoil inside.

Where in the bloody bird hell was Ronin?

If he left the meeting and flew through the night, he should've made it back by dawn. If he waited for first light, he should've made it back to her by noon at the earliest and sunset at the latest. At least that's what she calculated. She'd told him she would look for him at noon, but she kept putting it off, hoping the next minute would see him flying over the copse of trees.

Maybe the meeting went long? Maybe they extended negotiations? Maybe he went back to their place?

Cora bit her lip and eyed the treeline. She had to face the facts. Something happened.

Something bad.

And she'd have to fly inland to find out.

A cold shiver racked her body. Her feathers puffed out and she shook the invisible ice from her limbs. Cora didn't have the same vision capabilities as those from the eagle or hawk houses, and she wasn't the descendent of a nocturnal species, but that didn't mean she was blind, weak, or helpless.

Cora picked up her bag, swung it in place between

her wings and with one more look at the fading horizon, she crouched down and launched into the darkening sky. Her black wings caught the wind and she soared up and over the treetops. A dull ache vibrated through her injured wing with each push of air. Not enough to impede her flight, but persistent enough to annoy her. She might have to rest sooner than she'd like, and she'd have to fly low.

Over the land.

She cringed.

At least the trees would camouflage her as much as they would the angry mob of sapavian hating, arrow-toting humans who probably prowled in the shadows.

The cool air pressed against her face and ran down her flying leathers.

Inland.

Fucking inland.

If Ronin lost track of time knocking back brews with the boys, she'd kill him.

If he were already dead, she'd find a way to revive him and kill him all over again. How dare he die and endanger her and her father's lives. He should've taken her.

As the almost imperceptible treetops blurred below in the fading light, the dull ache of her injured wing bloomed into a full, brain-numbing throb. She grit her teeth and pressed on.

There! The clearing loomed ahead, marked by giant red cedars positioned like the points of a compass.

She swooped down and hugged the treeline. If they had spotters, she had a better chance of blending in with the night. She needed to blend in. Be stealthy, like some sort of sky ninja. With her injury, she couldn't maneuver in the air as well as she liked and had no ambition to play, "Dodge the Arrow."

With her heart pounding, she drew her short dagger. The matte onyx blade wouldn't reflect the moonlight like her long dagger, allowing her to maintain near-invisibility in the cloak of darkness.

Where the hell would she land?

She couldn't circle the clearing multiple times and look for signs of life. Not unless she wanted to act as a dart board for arrows.

She pursed her lips. Was she being too paranoid?

Better to be overly cautious than dead.

What should she do? She couldn't land in the middle of an open field like some sort of turkey, fattened and stuffed for the oven.

She scanned the trees lining the approaching clearing. Her gaze snagged on the dark outline of the tall red cedar.

That would do.

The red cedar in the northern position would block her from anyone's view in the clearing and was large enough to support her weight.

Cora drew close to the top and pulled her wings back and out. At a near stall, she reached out for the rough bark. Once she wrapped her hands around the large branches, she pulled her wings in and clung to the tree. Gravity tried to pull her down, but she held on, moving with the giant tree as it swayed from her landing.

Now the tricky part.

With her breath caught in her throat, Cora pulled her wings to her back as close as possible and scaled down the tree, branch by branch. The rough bark bit into her hands, the needles stabbed her skin and the sharp cedar smell burned her nose.

Her spine tingled and her scalp prickled. Climbing trees and frolicking on the ground with no open sky was unnatural. Only humans did this crap for fun.

When her feet landed in the soft dirt below, the tingling sensations eased.

Where are you, Ronin? If you have me mucking around on the forest floor for shits and giggles...

She surveyed the field from the edge of the tree-line. The grass in the middle was trampled in a large circle with a path of more trodden grass leading to the other side of the clearing.

Had he walked through the clearing on his own to meet someone at the forest's edge? Or had he been dragged?

The tingling sensations returned. Ronin might be a giant brute of a warrior, but he moved with grace, finesse. The pattern of broken grass blades suggested a struggle.

Cora cursed under her breath and picked her way

around the clearing. Pain continued to throb through her injured wing. Maybe she should rest it.

She'd be no good to Ronin if she found him and exhaustion made her collapse.

Her lip curled up from her teeth in a silent snarl.

And Ronin was no good to her dead.

She pressed on.

Metal glinted near the base of the southern cedar, catching a sliver of moonlight. Cora narrowed her eyes and ducked behind a tree.

A lookout.

Placing one foot in front of the other, she clutched her onyx dagger and made her way slowly around the clearing. She'd never make it all the way to the spotter without him hearing her. Unfortunately, she wasn't one of those stealthy warriors from her bedtime stories.

She crouched behind a thicket of bushes. Now closer, and with the moonlight helping, she could make out the man's profile.

She'd have one shot at this. One attempt.

If she messed this up, she'd die, leaving Ronin to his current fate and Father to a public execution.

Not acceptable.

Gripping her dagger, she leapt, launching over the bushes and diving forward. As if flying over water instead of sun-hardened soil and grass, she snapped out her wings and caught the wind enough to float over the ground. No footsteps, no sound. Silent like an owl. Deadly.

The man turned when the gust of wind from her wings hit the side of his face. Too late, she was already on him, with the sharp edge of her blade pressed against the soft tissue of his neck.

"Where is he?" she asked, keeping her voice low. Though she hadn't detected any other lookouts, that didn't mean there weren't any.

The man sneered and raised his chin, jutting it out in defiance.

Cora wasn't a killer by nature, but she wasn't above it. She'd kill if needed. No one crossed the channel and kept their halo squeaky clean. Hell, no one kept a halo at all.

She pressed the dagger forward. Blood pebbled along the edge.

The man winced and raised his arm to point down the trail from the clearing and his lookout position. When Cora glanced down the path, the man shifted under her blade. She turned and pivoted in time to avoid the dagger the man had thrust upward to gut her. As she stepped behind him, she ran her dagger across his neck. Blood soaked her hand. The man gurgled and dropped the weapon. He slumped against her. She caught his body with two arms around his torso and lowered him to the ground. He wasn't light and she wasn't graceful. The body thumped on the dirt and grass. His hair spread out and covered his face. The wound she'd inflicted gaped open and blood coated his jawline, neck, and the leather jerkin. She took a life.

Cora squeezed her eyes shut and took a number of deep breaths. Her hand shook but she forced herself to kneel and clean her dagger. Then she checked the man for supplies and money. She didn't know what the future held, but she might need human coins.

She'd killed someone and now she looted his corpse.

Deep breath. Save the panic attack for later. Ronin needs you.

The scout didn't have a lot, but Cora pocketed the money before turning toward the trail. She gulped. Walking would be cumbersome and place her in a vulnerable position should she run into humans. Flying wouldn't eliminate the danger, because she'd have to fly within arrow range to follow the trail, but she had to do something.

Cora trusted her wings more than her feet, even injured and away from the shore. Decision made, she launched back in the air and started tracking the path from above. She had to find Ronin, and he better be alive. If she failed, everything she loved was forfeit.

13

"He who is outside his door has the hardest part of his journey behind him."

— DUTCH PROVERB, DEFINITELY
NOT CORA CORMORANT

I t took the rest of the night for Cora to catch up to the party of human warriors who'd captured Ronin. The sky had lightened to a dark blue, but the sun hadn't crested the horizon yet. Bound and gagged, Ronin rested against the tree he was chained to, head tilted back on the rough bark. His chest rose and fell evenly. Still alive. Guess she wouldn't have to revive him to murder him all over again. His white hair had fallen from his face, revealing the dark bags under his eyes, his swollen jaw and cut lip.

In addition to shackling his arms behind him, the humans had pulled his wings back to cover the tree trunk and wrapped a rope around Ronin, his wings, and the tree. Ronin's wings were stuck in the extended, bent-backward position. Ouch.

Somehow, captured and vulnerable, Ronin still managed to scowl at his captors around his gag and glare at them from behind his dishevelled hair as if they were pesky ants under his boots.

Condescending and self-righteous to the end.

Cora passed the campsite and found a tree to scramble down to the ground. As soon as her feet touched the spongy moss on the forest floor, dread raced along her spine. She shivered. Closed off from the sky and ocean, walking on the ground wasn't a comfortable feeling for a cormorant. Knowing a gang of human warriors rested mere feet away wasn't a comfortable feeling for any sapavian. She couldn't take them all on in a fight or defend herself. The key to Ronin's release was stealth.

Cora's wings trailed along the path, being skewered by random branches, and bruised by rocks.

Progress was slow. Cushy, sound-absorbing moss didn't cover the entire forest floor. She took her time, fully aware of the rising sun and her dwindling time.

Her heart punched against her ribcage. Her breath

consumed her hearing—how did they not wake up from her ragged breathing?

Each step felt like it took an eternity to make.

Ronin shifted his weight and glanced over his shoulder. She quickly reached forward with her wing and trailed her black feathers on his face and shoulders. She didn't dare say anything or shush him. Ronin wasn't stupid—pigheaded and arrogant, sure, but not an actual turkey, though she liked to think of him as one. He'd know silence was key to their survival, too.

Ronin's shoulders relaxed and she made the final steps to reach the back of the tree to access the ropes and chains binding him. She pulled the gag loose first, letting it fall around his shoulders before moving to a better position to tackle the locks.

She stepped down on a branch. The wood snapped. Loudly.

Cora froze.

Ronin stiffened.

One of the men in the clearing rolled over and grumbled in his sleep. About twice as wide as Cora, with arm muscles as thick as her waist and hands larger than her face, he intimidated her from his bedroll.

Stay asleep.

Cora waited. The sky continued to lighten. She supressed a growl, crouched down and extracted pins from one of her pockets to pick the lock on the shackle around one of Ronin's wrists. They really didn't want him to escape. Most of this was overkill.

Unless they expected her.

The men began to stir, shifting on the ground, rolling over, grumbling, in that hazy pre-waking moment before they had to greet the day.

"Hurry," Ronin hissed.

Right, like she wasn't aware of impending doom. The reminder was so helpful. She'd snarl at him, but the additional sound would only make matters worse.

The lock clicked open. Cora carefully returned her pins to the inside pocket of her flying gear and slipped the shackle off Ronin's wrist. He immediately brought them to his lap and started rotating his hands.

Cora glanced at the restless sleepers. They didn't have time for her to remove the other shackle. Instead, she gathered the chain that linked the two wrist shackles and placed them in Ronin's open hand. She stood, shook her legs out to prevent the cramp threatening her muscles and drew her blood-crusted dagger to start working through the thick rope binding Ronin's body and wings to the tree. Her blade sliced through the course material and the rope fell to the ground.

Cora glanced at the men. Still asleep.

Ronin stood slowly, refusing her offered hand and gingerly folded his wings forward. He winced. Everything about his movement looked stiff and painful.

She jerked her head toward the path she'd taken to reach the campsite. It headed in the wrong direction, but anywhere except here was preferable. And sneaking through the campsite was just a bad idea.

"My sword," Ronin whispered.

She glanced around the campsite and spotted the weapon a few feet away from the circle of sleeping men. If it were her choice, she'd leave the stupid thing here, but it was the Sword of Eyrie. King Edgar had gifted the family heirloom to Ronin on his twentieth birthday in front of the entire kingdom. She'd witnessed the celebration amongst the market crowd, no longer important enough to garner an invitation to the private ceremony that took place afterward.

She had to get the stupid sword. It meant something to Ronin.

With sweat trickling down her face and her throat raw from sucking in the cold morning air, Cora made her way to Ronin's sword, tiptoeing past the warrior with gigantic hands.

The sword rested in its sheath against the base of a large red cedar. Fingers shaking, Cora gripped the hilt and swung the weapon into both arms. *God, this thing weighs a ton.*

She picked her way back to Ronin's side, ducked under his wing and latched the sheath to his belt.

Ronin stared down at her fiddling with his belt, the corner of his mouth tugged upward. If they were anywhere else, if death weren't sleeping a few feet away, she'd bet money he'd say something completely inappropriate right now.

He must be feeling better already.

Cora straightened and nodded toward the path again.

When Ronin stepped forward, his leg buckled. She lunged forward before he crashed to the forest floor. Holding his heavy body against hers, his hard armour dug into her flying gear, and his breath fanning her cheek and neck. God, he was heavy.

One of the men in the camp rolled over and stretched.

Cora's heart lodged in her throat. Ronin regained his balance. Slowly, they turned in unison toward the path. Ronin pulled away from her hold. They needed to get high enough to launch or reach a large enough clearing to take off. And quickly.

She looked back at the campsite over her shoulder. The guard had settled back into his makeshift bed, a dreamy smile on his face.

Cora draped Ronin's arm around her shoulder and helped him stumble away from his abductors.

14

"Adventure is just bad planning."

— ROALD AMUNDSEN

Cora and Ronin launched into the sky from the giant red cedar they had climbed when a cry of alarm erupted from the nearby campsite. Men cried out and hollered, and then silence.

The silence was far scarier.

It meant they'd spread out to track them.

"This way," Cora hissed.

"South?" Ronin's voice sounded rougher than usual. With a shackle still locked around one of his wrists, metal glinted under the morning sunlight. His large white wings spread out to catch the wind. Eagle

Clan members excelled at soaring, but he wavered every now and then, and his face had grown pale.

"Do you want to fly over your abductors? Maybe flash them a sign or tell them which way we plan to go? Rattle your shackles? Drop them a little love note to meet us at the Cap Cliffs? Hmm?"

"We'll gain altitude," he said. "They won't spot us if we're high enough."

"Not with your wings."

He grimaced. "My wings are fine."

"You're allowed to admit they're sore, Ronin. I'm the one who untied them, remember? They must be stiff. I know it hurts. I can see it in your face. Braving the stronger winds at the higher altitude right now is ill-advised."

He scowled at her and said nothing as he turned south, away from the men. Away from home. And toward the centre of Iom and the rest of the humans.

"I take it the meeting went well?" She bit her lip.

"Don't."

Her mouth snapped shut and a flash of guilt staved her in the stomach. Then, she remembered the danger his actions had placed her in, placed her father in, and the guilt faded away. "Oh, I think I will. Had you died my family would have received a death sentence. You should've brought me. You should've been more careful."

Ronin clenched his jaw and drifted away from her. He wavered less and his colour slowly returned to his face. Handsome, healthy, and still a complete asshole.

"I mean, it wouldn't be the first time your father attempted to kill us," she continued, showing no mercy. He didn't deserve it. "I guess we should be honoured to attract the attention of the king."

An image of her mom popped into her memory. Cora clung to the sight of her silken black hair and mischievous eyes. It had been years since she saw her mom and the memory of her had faded to the point where Cora couldn't always recall what she looked like. This image was so clear. All the details—how she had dimples, how her nose crinkled when she was teasing, how her bronzed skin glowed under the sunshine. Cora clung to the sight until Mom's face faded away.

"What was the meeting about?" she asked after collecting herself.

"None of your business."

"It is now. In case you haven't noticed, we're flying farther into enemy territory." Not for long, of course. As soon as they put enough distance between the angry humans, they'd swing around, giving the clearing and the human's last known location a wide birth.

"In case you haven't notice, I'm the heir of the Eyrie and don't owe you anything."

She rolled her eyes. Except his life.

Instead of acknowledging her efforts, though, he pulled rank. So typical. "We're going to have to find place to hole up until we heal enough to make the trip back across the channel. You're going to have to drop the airs, *Your Majesty*."

"I'm not a king yet."

Cora shrugged. Majesty, highness, excellency, eminence, grace. She never cared for labels or using them correctly, though she could if she had to. What did it matter? It didn't change Ronin from being a royal pain in the ass.

"And I'm fine," he said, managing to throw in an extra special glare.

"You very well might be fine, but I need time."

"I can go by myself," he grumbled.

"You can try."

He glared at her and she glared right back. He wanted to leave her, alone and injured, on the Isle of Man after she risked her life and saved him from an unknown, but probably very unpleasant and short, future.

He wanted to abandon her.

Just like his family had abandoned hers years ago. Just like he'd abandoned her when she needed him most. Why did she think it would be any different now?

"Like father, like son, I guess," she said.

Ronin flinched. His glare lost its heat. "It's not like that. I need to get back."

A strong gust of wind lifted them and separated them, rustling the green forest below. They drifted back to each other, flying close enough to continue talking without getting their wings tangled.

"Why?" she asked.

The glare returned. That was getting old.

"I'm risking my life. I need to know why," she said.

Ronin drifted closer to her, his brilliant white wings and hair glinting in the sun.

"The humans reached out asking for an alliance."

Shock slapped Cora in the face. "Couldn't you have sent your rejection by letter?"

"I came to negotiate terms, Cora."

"W...why?" Why would they even consider agreeing to peace with the people who killed her mother?

"Haven't you noticed how packed the Eyrie is? How there's no room? Bird folk have started to make homes on the waystations, but even those are becoming crowded. We need space and the humans have an abundance of it."

"What do they want in return?"

"Food. Transportation. Fishing partnership. Things we don't struggle for."

It always came back to fish.

King Edgar didn't hold any love for the humans, and it had little to do with her own mother's death. For the King of the Eyrie to respond positively to a cessation of conflict and agree to an alliance meant things truly had gone bad.

"Doesn't look like the humans want an alliance."

"No, it doesn't, does it? This was a classic set-up."

"You knew?"

"I should have." His face contorted with emotion. Anger, but something else as well. Disappointment? Regret? Shame? Whatever it was, it was gone in an instant and Ronin's stony expression returned to face the wind.

In that moment of vulnerability, she'd wanted to reach out, to say something, do something to take the look away and make Ronin feel better. And that was the danger with Ronin. He could seduce her in a moment of weakness without even trying. Heaven forbid if he ever tried. She'd forget the anger and hurt he caused.

A long arrow sped through the air from the forest below and struck Cora's wing. Bone crunched. Pain exploded. Cora spun through the air from the impact, flapping her other wing. The air whistled by her. Panic slammed into her mind. She hurtled toward the treetops.

Pain consumed her wing. A direct hit. Her luck had run out. She strained and it kept hanging, unresponsive. She couldn't catch the wind.

She wasn't going to make it.

This was how she died.

Sheer agony cramped her entire wing and the other one was already injured. Even if it were in perfect working order, it wouldn't be enough.

Ronin's body slammed into hers. Strong arms grabbed her waist and pulled her against his armour.

What was he doing?

She'd drag him down.

"Drop me. You can't—"

He growled in her ear. "Hold on."

She wrapped her arms around his neck, her legs around his waist and buried her face into the heat of his neck. Their only hope was a rough landing. She pulled her wings in and winced—only one wing listened. The other stuck out with a large javelin-sized arrow protruding from the middle section. Not ideal. The newly injured wing created an uneven drag and pain throbbed through her whole body.

The wind blasted past them as they sped toward the trees. The air jostled her injuries. She gritted her teeth and tucked her chin, pushing her face against Ronin's neck.

He needed to level out. They were going to crash.

Ronin spread his wings, catching the air. They slowed, levelling out a little more. They were still going too fast, heading toward the treeline at a break-neck speed.

"Let me go, Ronin." He needed to save himself. He had to live.

Ronin held her tight and strained upward. Pushing his giant white wings against the air rushing past them.

The treetops loomed ahead.

He flapped his wings. Again. Once. Twice.

They slowed, levelling out some more.

And then they reached the forest. They barrelled into the treeline. Branches and twigs snapped as they flew past. Ronin pulled his wings in so he could maneuver around the larger trees. Before impact, Ronin wrapped his arms and wings around her and flipped them over. He hit the forest floor first. Cora slammed into him. Dirt shrouded them as they bounced and slammed into the ground again. And again. Until they finally slid to a painful stop on a patch of moss-covered soil.

The sounds of the forest faded along with the pain as Cora's world turned black.

15

"I'm afraid to lose you and you're not even mine."

— DRAKE

Cora opened her dirt-encrusted eyelids slowly. The overwhelming throbbing sensation burned her senses. Her raw skin chafed as if it were on fire. The javelin arrow had broken off from her injured wing at some point during the crash, but a small chunk still stuck out like a piercing gone bad.

She groaned and moved through the pain to push off the ground. Nothing else was broken—just the injured wing. Luckily, her flying gear had protected the majority of her body from getting covered by road rash and Ronin had broken her fall.

Ronin.

She managed an awkward sitting position with her pierced wing jutting out at an uncomfortable angle.

Ronin lay in a heap of white feathers and limbs a few feet away from her with his glorious wings spread, one bent unnaturally.

He wasn't moving.

"Ronin?" *Oh, no. No, no, no, no, no.* He did not get to save her life only to die. This couldn't be happening. He wasn't allowed to die. Especially after she saved him. He should've dropped her. Why hadn't he dropped her?

She staggered to her feet and lurched over to where he lay, careful not to touch his wings. "Ronin?"

Somehow managing to tuck both her wings in so they didn't hit the tree she passed, she knelt by his side. If he was breathing, it was too shallow for her to tell with his armour on. Despite the broken wing and the bruised face covered in scratches, he looked peaceful, eyes closed, expression relaxed.

Cora reached out and hesitated. No. She needed to know. Delaying the inevitable only succeeded in wasting time. It never lessened the blow.

She pressed two fingers to his throat above the carotid artery.

Nothing.

She pressed harder and angled her fingers for a better position.

Still no—

There!

A big gush of air escaped her lungs.

She kept her fingers in place to feel each pump of his heartbeat—each thump against her fingers calmed her nerves and released tension from her sore muscles.

He was alive. And that meant she'd live, too. And her father. At least for now. She didn't want to think about the long list of challenges that just got added to their list.

First, she needed to assess the extent of Ronin's injuries. Just because he was breathing and only appeared to have a broken wing, didn't mean he couldn't be harbouring other serious injuries, such as head trauma or internal bleeding.

Ronin had managed to slow and ease their descent, but he'd still taken most of the impressive impact when they landed. She brushed his white hair from his face. Flipping her around to protect her had been the dumbest thing he'd done on this trip. And because of it, he'd saved her life.

The moment Ronin regained consciousness was evident in the changes in his expression—his brow furrowed, eyes creased, forehead rippled, and mouth turned down in a full-face grimace. A low moan escaped his full lips.

She brushed the hair from his face again. "Ronin?"

His eyes fluttered open and, in that moment, when their gazes connected without any guarding, she saw more than pain and relief. Something almost akin to longing and it stole her breath away.

"How are you feeling?" she asked.

His brows furrowed farther. "Who are you?"

"Not funny, Ronin." He better be joking.

"Who's Ronin?" He stared at her blankly.

She blinked at him. He couldn't possibly be serious.

"Are you an angel?" he asked.

She snorted. Now she knew he was messing with her. Sapavians weren't angels. They were the result of scientists trying to create something in their image. "Nice try."

"Cora." His deep voice rumbled and caressed her skin. With his gaze still locked with hers, he reached out toward her face. His hand shook.

She tensed and jerked back.

Ronin dropped his hand. His gaze shuttered, guarded once again, and still creased with pain. He cleared his throat. "Are you okay?"

"Yes, thanks to you." She scanned his body for more injuries. His armour appeared largely undamaged—dents and scratches, but nothing glaringly obvious to indicate the armour was compromised or they should worry about internal injuries.

"How are you?" she asked.

"Alive." He rolled to his feet, wavered, and shifted

to adjust his wing position. "Wing's broken."

She stood from her kneeling position and dusted off her pants. "Your skills of observation and self-assessment are impressive."

He had the nerve to wink at her. "That's not all that's impressive."

Her mouth dropped open. She shut it right away, but it dropped open again. She shook her head. "The only thing that's impressive about you is the thickness of your skull."

"Are you calling me dense?"

"Catastrophically."

He jabbed his chest with his thumb and flung his other hand out to point to the forest. The shackles still attached to his wrist clanked with each movement. "I just saved your life."

Really, he should point up since they came from that direction, but that was the least of the issues with this conversation. "You said yourself you couldn't wait for me to heal. Now you're injured, too. And that little stunt could've ended a lot worse than it did."

"Little stunt?" Anger flashed in his gaze. If she were smart, she'd take the hint and a step back.

She did neither.

"You ungrateful brat. Remind me not to save your life next time," he said.

She stepped into his personal space and lifted her chin. "Unnecessary. There won't be a next time."

"For someone who's been hit *twice* with arrows,

you're awfully full of bravado."

They stood, toe to toe, seething at each other. Now was not the time to mention this attack was actually the *third* time she'd been hit with an arrow in less than a week. The ache of her newly injured wing started to beat out the rage.

They fought like two seagulls over a dead crab while injured and stranded in the middle of Iom. The severity of their situation slapped Cora in the face and the rest of her anger fled.

"We're fucked," she whispered.

Ronin's shoulders drooped and the tension in his face eased away. He broke his gaze to survey the surrounding woods. "I know."

"We need to move before those hunters come to claim their prize."

Ronin nodded and stepped back, taking the heat of his body with him. He raised his hand and twirled his fingers.

She turned around and clenched her jaw. This wasn't going to feel good.

"Relax." Ronin skimmed his hands along her injured wing. A shudder wracked her body.

"Go peck yourself," she said, without any heat.

"That's no way to talk to your saviour." Ronin tsked while probing the skin around the arrow. "This doesn't look good."

"I tried to stop an arrow."

"The bone is injured. It's sitting straight, but the

swelling makes it difficult to tell whether it's shattered instead of a clean break."

And the good news kept coming. This was by far the worst run yet.

Ronin's hands stopped their exploration. "The arrow needs to come out."

She had expected as much, but that didn't make hearing the news any easier. The challenge would be finding a way to stem the bleeding and bandage the injury. Unlike the nick to her shoulder or the puncture wound through the patagium on her other wing, this injury was serious, the ulna bone damaged, the main artery potentially severed.

"I have a mend kit," Ronin said.

Or at least that's what she thought he said. Instead of focusing on his words, she became hyper aware of his hands on her wing. Not sexual awareness. More like one of impending pain. He'd have to grasp her wing to pull the arrow out and her whole body was already tensing in anticipation.

Warm, large hands smoothed the feathers near the wound. Without warning, Ronin clamped down on the metacarpus of her wing with one hand and pulled out the remaining portion of the arrow with the other.

Pain flared down her wing and spread across her back. She yelped in pain and tried to arch away from the source.

"Shh," Ronin's hand maintained his grip on her wing. "I'm working here."

Little pricks of pain punctuated the intense throb emanating from her wings.

"The arrow missed the cornu artery but splintered the ulna and possibly the radius bone. Shouldn't need a splint as long as you don't fly and keep movement limited and controlled. In about five to six weeks, it will be healed enough to fly," Ronin continued.

"Across the channel?" Flying the gauntlet across the most treacherous stretch of the channel with less than perfect wings would be a fool's mission.

"Probably not," Ronin said in agreement. "You'll need more time to regain your strength and endurance. That will add at least two weeks."

"Do we have two months to wait?"

Ronin resettled his wings behind his back. The broken wing didn't sit properly and jutted out. His face paled and he wavered on his feet. He would've adjusted his wings by instinct, forgetting the injury. From his tightly compressed mouth and deep frown, though, the injury just reminded him how unwise that was.

Ronin visibly swallowed before answering her question. "I don't think we have much of a choice. My wing will take the same amount of time to heal or more. I've had some of my men sustain similar injuries."

"But your father..."

Ronin jabbed her with a needle from his mend kit. Most likely a dose of antibiotics laced with pain meds. It sent a jolt through her body.

"My father will have to wait to learn of the humans' duplicity. He will likely figure it out when we don't return home as scheduled." Ronin spoke as he worked, stitching together the wound.

If the king could wait, why was he planning to leave her behind before they got shot out of the sky?

"We could send a message," she suggested. She wasn't the only messenger. Others made it across using the waystations.

"We will, but it will have to go through the Wap." Ronin echoed her own thoughts and continued to work on her wound.

And with the additional time and handlers, privacy couldn't be assumed or assured. Cora's contact, Ava, was the fastest, surest route to deliver messages, but without Cora, there was no messenger.

"There." Ronin smoothed her feathers down once again before applying the Eyrie gauze made especially for wing injuries. It would help slow the bleeding. "All done."

Cora nodded and turned around. Ronin's anger and despair from earlier had faded away His gaze appeared tender, concerned even.

Wow.

Shock must've set in.

She peered up at her bandaged wing. "You do some good work. If you don't make it as a prince, you have a calling for the medical profession."

He dipped his chin. "Field dressing was a part of the specialized training I received."

"Of course, it was."

His open expression snapped shut and the cold statue returned.

Hmmm. Cause and effect. She definitely brought out the worst in him, and vice versa. Why was she being so snarky? He didn't deserve it.

"Your turn." She raised her hand and twirled her fingers in the air, imitating his earlier gesture.

"Take this off first." He raised his arm and waved; the shackles clanked.

"Injuries take priority."

He shook his head. "I need this off first. Please."

Lines etched around his golden eyes. So, the prince didn't want a reminder of how vulnerable he'd been. Well, who would? She couldn't tease him about that. Instead of saying anything, she quickly picked the lock and removed the shackle. It fell to the ground in a clatter.

"No more stalling," she said, as if that had been his reason. "Time to assess that wing."

He scowled at her and turned around. Without her asking, he knelt down so she could examine the break better.

"Can you hand me one of those needles from your med kit?"

He tensed. "There was only one."

And he used it on Her. Cora's chest constricted.

"Turkey," she muttered under her breath.

"It had antibiotics in it," he said. "You needed it more. A puncture wound is more susceptible to infection than a broken bone."

She turned her attention back to his wing. The humerus appeared to be completely broken.

"This doesn't look good." She bit her lip.

"I tried to stop a tree."

She shook her head, tempted to swat him, but she didn't hate him that much. He must be in an incredible amount of pain—it showed in the tension of his shoulders and the crease of his brow. And he pushed it all to the side to patch her up and banter with her.

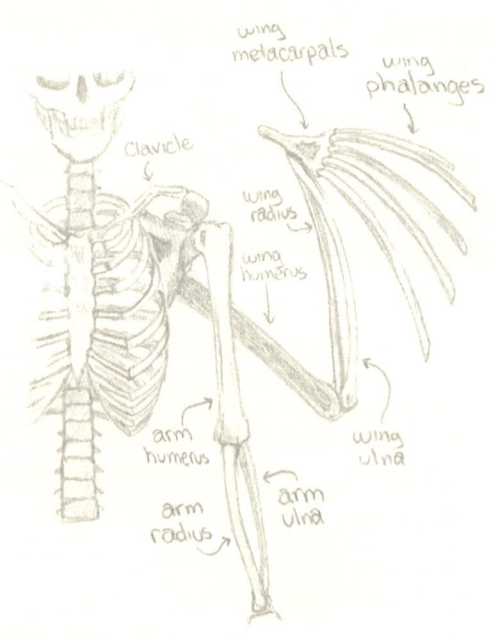

"Thank you," she said.

He grumbled and hunched his shoulders. She gripped his wing, one hand on each side of the break and jerked, hard.

Ronin cursed. The bone slid back in place.

She ignored Ronin's heavy breathing and pressed around the tender skin. It felt realigned, but the swelling made it hard to tell. Hopefully, it wouldn't require a healer or resetting.

"We need a splint." His voice wasn't as growly as normal. His gruff words, a command.

Ronin and his damn pride.

She turned away and left him at their crash site to find a straight stick. The gnarled branches of the nearby trees laughed down at her as she stomped along the mossy forest floor. Having rescued Ronin at dawn, there was plenty of daylight left. They needed to put more distance between Ronin's abductors and whomever shot them from the sky.

At least the abductors were most likely headed in the wrong direction. They would assume Ronin and Cora flew straight home.

Maybe they should've made a break for the shoreline instead of heading farther south into Iom. If they had, though, they would've ended up at the cliffs with Cora too injured to fly and Ronin not experienced enough to cross the channel on his own. They would've been cornered with nowhere to go and no place to hide.

No. They had to hole up and heal without humans detecting their presence.

Cora scanned the forest. Who'd shot at them? Where were they now? Had the humans seen where they landed?

She sighed and continued to search for something straight enough to act as a splint. Each step sent pain racing through her body and her head throbbed. Her wing tips trailed against the forest floor and though the moss was soft and cushy, the drag applied pressure to her damaged wings and made her stomach twist with the pain.

The twig snapping was her only warning she wasn't alone. She spun and flung her wings out, blocking the attack. Metal flashed and a dagger went flying. Cora faced a man with leather skin and a mean smile with more gum than teeth. He wore hunting gear. No bow or quiver. Not an archer, then.

The person who shot her down still lurked in the forest somewhere. What a lovely thought.

The hunter sneered and pulled another dagger from his vest. "I told the boys we went in the right direction."

She pulled her wings back and unsheathed her own dagger, the longer, shinier one. Another quick scan of the dense woods didn't reveal anyone else, but human hunting parties typically had four members and were known for their stealth. She'd never interacted with hunters, but Ava had mentioned the Hunter's

Quad before, and her father had warned her to look out for them.

"Did the large brute with you survive?" the man asked.

Like she'd tell him.

"He must be around here somewhere." He held his dagger in front of his body in a hammer grip and surveyed the trees as if expecting Ronin to jump out at any minute. If only he knew the truth—the heir of the Eyrie was injured, most likely easily incapacitated, and a mere walk away.

Cora lunged forward with her dagger.

The man turned, deflecting her advance with his leather vambrace.

Cora clenched her teeth. Heart pounding, she stepped sideways and spun, dodging the hunter's counter strike. His arm shot past to where she'd stood moments ago. She grabbed his extended arm, continued to spin, and slashed out with her dagger. The sharp blade cut into his back and ran diagonally down, slicing open his leather vest and the skin underneath.

The man howled, arching back.

Cora didn't wait. She couldn't afford to wait. Completing her spin, she reached out, clamped her hand on his shoulder and drove her dagger into his lower back, right where his kidney was. She yanked the weapon back and drove it in again.

And again.

And again.

Blood sprayed from the wounds and splattered against her hand and flying gear.

The man jerked with each strike and barked out a cross between a scream and a groan.

She pulled him closer, sliding her hand from his shoulder to cover his mouth and kept plunging her dagger into his side. Blood was everywhere. Her hand was slick with it. Her grip slipped off the dagger hilt, leaving the weapon stuck in his side.

The man slumped in her hold. She released him as he sagged to the forest floor. The blood had tainted the healthy green colour a dark red.

The sounds of the forest returned. During the struggle, her awareness had focused on the man, tuning out her surroundings. Now, the birds chatting in the trees and the gentle wind playing with the leaves thundered in her ears.

Oh, God. She'd killed two men in two days. Now she was a serial killer.

Studying the man at her feet didn't relieve the shame twisting her gut. Pain had creased the man's face, but now the expression eased. More blood pooled from his body.

Cora swallowed. Not the best way to die. Not the best way to kill. If she had more skill, she should've gone for the heart or neck. Next time...

Her stomach twisted more, and she staggered to the side to retch. Nothing came out.

Next time? There better not be a next time. Cora might've killed channel monsters in the past, but killing a man was entirely different.

She paused. Not all sapavians would agree with her. Would Ronin?

Ronin!

She gripped the slick handle of her dagger and yanked it from the hunter's side. She didn't have time to dwell or get sick. This hunter hadn't travelled alone.

She hesitated before plucking his discarded weapon from the ground. She sheathed it in an empty compartment in her flying leathers before flicking her own dagger to get rid of the excess blood. Using the dead hunter's pants, she wiped off the rest.

The birds seemed to find the show highly entertaining and increased their chatter to one another. Cora ignored them and walked back to where she'd left Ronin. Careful not to make more noise than she and the hunter had in their struggle, she placed each step softly on the mossy path. When she drew near the crash site, she spotted Ronin's brilliantly white wings spread wide and glistening in the sun like a bright beacon. And target.

She stepped from the trees. "We need to move."

Ronin turned and drew his uninjured wing back. Three men lay in a heap at his feet. The sword clutched in Ronin's hand dripped blood from the tip.

They wore the same hunting leathers as the man she'd fought.

"You don't say." Ronin's dry tone made Cora wish she stood closer so she could punch him.

Blood drained from her face. She grew light-headed and her stomach lurched.

Vaguely aware Ronin started talking again, his deep voice vibrating along her skin, the sounds around her faded again. Her heartbeat took over the surrounding sounds until she heard nothing else.

You're mine, the Sea Beast's voice, though faint, was unmistakable.

Why could she hear him? Even now? Even on land?

"Cora?" Ronin's heavy hand clamped on her shoulder and ripped her from her thoughts. "Are you okay?"

"I killed a man," she said. "I've killed two men."

Ronin's face contorted. His brows drew in and his gaze flashed as if they contained their own lightning. He glanced down at the dagger she still clutched in her hand. She needed to clean it better, blood still crusted the base of the blade and hilt.

Ronin tightened his grip on her shoulder. "Where?"

"One was yesterday—a scout from the meeting place. The other..." She jerked her chin toward the path behind her. "Do you think there are more?"

He shook his head. "Hunters usually travel in packs of four for big game hunts."

She nodded, his words confirming her earlier

thoughts.

"We should still move," she said. "We don't know if another group saw us." Her lip started to tremble, and her skin grew cold. Had the temperature dropped? Why was she shaking?

Ronin studied her face and pulled her forward. She stumbled into his arms.

Oomph. "What are you doing?" She mumbled into his chest. She shouldn't find this soothing. This was so wrong.

"Shhhh." He closed his arms around her. "I'm trying to comfort you."

She stood rigid. "I'm not some weak fainting flower—"

"I know. I know." He cut her off. "You're a total badass. Very independent."

She pressed her lips together and shifted her weight in case she needed to knee him in the junk.

"You're also in shock," he said. "Let me hold you for a minute."

His actions and words might've been for her benefit, but for every second he held her, tension eased from his muscles. Did it really matter what his motives were? He was right. She was in shock and the only thing keeping the cold away was the heat emanating from Ronin. Maybe this once, just for a little bit, she'd relax.

Cora sank into Ronin's embrace and let his warmth chase away the cold.

16

"Silence isn't empty, it's full on answers."

— UNKNOWN

Ronin tightened his hold on Cora as she sagged into him. For the first time during this entire ill-fated trip, he wished he didn't have his armour on. He wished he could feel the warmth of her body pressed against his. He'd have to be content with this. And he was. She was here and she was safe.

Something odd stirred in his chest, not entirely uncomfortable, but not exactly pleasant.

He ignored it and rested his chin on the top of Cora's head. Her hair had tangled and knotted, resembling a hastily constructed bird nest more than the black silken hair he always associated with her. She'd looked so fierce stomping out of the forest, clutching the dagger, flying leathers splattered with blood, injured wings drooping behind her. The scowl and gaze flashing with worry and anger made her striking. Beautiful.

He wanted to gather her in his arms the moment he saw her, yet she wouldn't have welcomed him then. Even now, he held her on borrowed time. He'd enjoy it while he could. He'd let the comfort of her body pressed against his armour work the tension away from his muscles and ease the palpable fear that had wracked his body when he realized he'd only killed three hunters, not four.

Despite what Cora believed, he wasn't a turkey. He could count to four and that meant another hunter must be out in the woods where Cora searched for a splint. He'd cut down his attackers with quick, brutal efficiency, hoping to make it to her in time. But he hadn't been fast enough. She'd been in danger and he hadn't been there to protect her.

Turned out, she hadn't needed him. Like the trouper she was, she proved she could take care of herself.

Cora sighed against his chest and her wings lowered.

God, if she ever realized the effect she had on him, he was doomed. Hell, he hadn't realized anything until he saw her spiraling out of control with a javelin sized arrow sticking out of her wing. He didn't think it through, he reacted.

When she told him to let her go, his heart ached. If he'd followed Father's teachings, he would've released her and let her fall to her death. A king should never risk his life for a servant of the court.

Total bullshit.

If Ronin wouldn't risk his life for the people, how could he ask them to risk theirs for him? He never would've come to this godforsaken place if he'd believed in Father's ideology.

And Cora was never just a servant.

He'd convinced himself over the years that he kept tabs on her whereabouts out of curiosity at best and mistrust at worst. Her father had betrayed his family. He couldn't let that go. He couldn't stop wondering how much Cora knew. She'd been a teenager at the time, so he could forgive her complacency, but could he ever trust her?

Apparently, his heart had already answered that question. But his heart didn't get the ultimate say, his brain did. This moment wouldn't change anything. Cora hated him and despite what he might feel for her, he was the heir of the Eyrie and had responsibilities. He couldn't afford to trust the daughter of a traitor, much less give his heart to her. If he were a wise man, he'd let her keep her distance. He'd let her continue to push him away. He wouldn't pursue this painful ache in his chest.

Ronin might not be stupid, but he never claimed to be wise.

Cora took a deep breath and pushed away from him. He instinctively tightened his grip for a quick second, not wanting to let her go, but in the end, he let his arms fall to his side.

Cora stepped back. "What now?"

"Splint my wing and find a place to hide." He looked at the sky to give her a moment to collect herself.

Hell, Ronin needed some time, too. He itched to reach out and pull her back into his arms. That was all sorts of wrong.

"Any suggestions?" he asked instead.

Cora turned to consider the forest which made little sense. She'd find no answers there.

"There are three access points to Iom that have a manageable flight path back to the Eyrie. The channel crossing is the closest, but after your abductor's botched kidnapping attempt, they'll be watching for us there and we're injured. The Cap also appears to have gained additional archers over the last few runs. We have to assume capturing you will be too good an opportunity for them to ignore and there will be men waiting for us there. The Waystation Access Point is the second closest, but it's also the most heavily guarded in both directions and as it's the easier flight path, there will be tons of regular traffic."

Ronin's mind ran ahead of her thoughts once he realized where her reasoning took her.

"No, Cora. We don't have to go there."

She shook her head. "Is there any other option?"

The third access point, nestled away from humans behind a wall of mountains and perilous cliffs, housed Hadren's Keep, the outpost where Cora's mother had been murdered and Cora narrowly escaped with her life. How she survived remained a mystery, but Father had been the one to send them there in the first place.

"It's the farthest access point from us," he said. "It will take weeks for us to walk there instead of flying and that's not factoring in injuries and off-path travel to avoid humans."

Officially named the Outpost Access Point, the Oap was roughly a four to five-day flight from where they currently stood and if they didn't have any other choice, he'd gladly avoid the keep nestled there.

She stepped forward again, invading his space and angling her face up to him in challenge. "Is it too scary for you?"

"Minx. You know it's not."

Her eyes widened. "You can stay here. We'll find a cave and I'll throw you some food and cover you with leaves."

He growled.

"Look at us." She threw her hands up. "It will take

weeks for us to heal and this way we'll be on the move and less likely to be caught flat-footed. It's the last place they'll expect us to go."

"They will still send a few men to the Oap. I would in their shoes."

Her gaze clouded with a thunderstorm of emotions. "Of course, they will." She licked her lips and looked away.

"We should've headed north after you freed me." He grumbled.

"Well, we didn't," she snapped. "I had no way of knowing how many men were involved. No idea whether they had already sent men to the Cap in case you brought backup. There were already men on the cliffs trying to shoot us down when we arrived. You didn't look capable of flying across the channel straight away. And resting where we would've been surrounded by humans intent on gutting us didn't seem like a good idea."

She was gorgeous when she was angry. He folded his arms across his chest and waited for her to finish.

"I made a decision under duress and I stand by it," she growled. "We can't reverse time, so we may as well accept that we went south and got shot down, and deal with the situation we now find ourselves in."

"Are you done?"

Her face turned red and she visibly shook.

"Thank you for saving my life. You're right. My wing was cramping before you got shot with the arrow.

Attempting the channel crossing would've been suicide and they likely would've captured us had we stayed to rest."

She jerked her chin in a tight nod. If he reached out now, she'd probably bite his hand off. Feral beast.

"What route should we take?" His mouth twitched. He knew her answer before she whispered it.

"The coast."

17

"Sleeping next to a woman presents a greater radioactive risk than camping beside a nuclear power station."

— PILE BOTHA

Cora nearly ran into Ronin's wings when he stopped abruptly on the deer trail.

His shoulders rose with a deep breath and he peered up at the darkening sky. "We need to make camp."

Cora shivered and glanced around. "Here?"

After finding a suitable branch to use as a splint, they'd bound his injured wing and started off toward the coast. They hadn't gone far when Cora suggested a detour.

They were still in the northern forest, somewhere to the south of Ronin's ill-fated meeting.

"We won't make your fishing village even if we march all night," he grumbled.

"It's not *my* fishing village." Cora kicked a pinecone. The sudden motion sent a streak of pain down her wing. *Ow.*

"We're both injured. I'm not sure about you, but the adrenaline has worn off and all I do is hurt. Besides, we need to wait for nightfall to signal your contact anyway. I'd rather time it so we aren't camping beside a village full of sapavian haters, either right before or after we meet with Ava, who may or may not try to kill us or send her bloodthirsty townsmen after us."

"Or women."

The weakening light made it hard to read his expression, but if she had to bet money, she'd place it on a sneer or an eye roll.

"Or women," he muttered. "I think you're missing the point."

"Oh, I got it." She studied the forest again. A gentle breeze flirted with the leaves and the open skies had provided lovely weather for daytime travel. The lack of cloud cover now, however, promised a cold night.

She hugged her arms again. Why couldn't they get closer to the coast? The ocean waves always had a way of calming her and right now she was a ball of nerves from running through all the possibilities. Normally, overanalyzing meant she prepared well for channel crossings. Now, it almost drowned her to the point of suffocation.

Warm hands gripped her arms and dragged her thoughts kicking and screaming from her own head. Since their crash landing, he'd voluntarily touched her on numerous occasions. Almost as if he looked for an excuse to soothe her.

Cora frowned.

Had he hit his head as well as his wing?

"It will be okay," Ronin said.

Why did he have to be so unbearably handsome with that confidence and growly voice? After Mom died, she'd returned to the Eyrie broken and beaten and he'd turned his back on her.

Cora scowled at him now, but that seemed to encourage him. His mouth twisted into a small smile and he rubbed her arms before letting go. "How much food do you have left?"

"Not much." She pulled out the package of dried meat from one of her sealed pockets. "I only brought enough for three days." The original plan involved travelling to Iom, staying the night, and returning to the Eyrie the next day. She'd brought more than she needed "just in case" and thought it overkill at the time.

The smell of beeswax tickled her nose as she unwrapped the dried meat, broke off a piece and handed it to Ronin. They'd already eaten a day's worth on the trip over and she'd snacked on some more while waiting for Ronin to return from his meeting. They needed to find more food, or they'd run out after tomorrow.

Cora chewed on her share before rewrapping and stuffing the remaining food back in her pocket. The dry meat stuck to her teeth and she used all her spit to wash it down. Water would be nice right about now, but they'd have to wait until they found a stream or river.

"We need to make camp," Ronin repeated, wiping his mouth with his vambrace.

She didn't like the statement the second time around either. "In the middle of a deer trail?"

Ronin studied their surroundings and frowned. "You're right. We should get off the path a little and spend the rest of the light we have finding somewhere more tolerable."

Without a word, he spun and walked into the woods, giving her the choice of tramping after him or staying on the path. Cora grumbled and followed. The forest didn't offer much in the way of "tolerable" accommodations. They had a choice of rocks, sticks, dirt, moss, or a number of combinations for their bedding. When Ronin found a large patch of spongy moss, he called a halt to their searching.

"Should we risk a fire?" she asked. Though the sun

hadn't fully set, yet the night chill had already seeped in to scare off the lingering heat of the day.

"Too risky," he replied. "Those hunters won't be found for a while, but my would-be abductors are still around somewhere."

"They would've headed to the Cap," she said with more hope than certainty.

Ronin's dark look said enough. He wasn't willing to risk it. "Not all of them."

She didn't want to argue, especially when Ronin was probably right. But a fire would be really nice right now. Instead of picking a pointless fight, she nodded and lay down to curl up on her side. She rested her damaged wings out behind her instead of folding them in. The pain had subsided to a dull constant ache. Maybe the throbbing hadn't lessened. Maybe she had just became accustomed to it.

Ronin didn't move to copy her actions. Something flicked across his expression as he looked down at her on the moss. Interest?

Her breathing stopped. She wasn't prepared for that. Not now. Not after all this time. Not when she was literally the only option available.

He unstrapped his sword belt and placed it in front of Cora before he stretched out on the moss, facing her. In the darkening light, his eyes resembled two deep pools of black. Without a word, he stretched his broken wing out to cover her, cocooning her in feathery warmth. The white feathers softly caressed her face and the considerate gesture made her want to cry. Cora wasn't prone to tears.

"Come here," he said.

Cora stiffened.

"I can hear your teeth chattering from here."

When she didn't move, Ronin scooted closer so only a few inches separated them. He reached out and pulled her into his arms, tucking her head under his chin and wrapping his damaged wing tighter around her. The splint helped brace his wing and prevented her from getting smothered.

She should've called him a fool. She should've pushed him away. Instead, she nuzzled into his warmth and let the exhaustion take her into its dark depths.

18

"Genetic engineering is to traditional cross-breeding what the nuclear bomb was to the sword."

— ANDREW KIMBRELL

A branch cracked and Cora snapped awake. Moisture from the moss had soaked into her flying leathers, leaving her skin cold and damp.

Ronin's arm tensed around her, his hand splayed over her back and his breath fanned the top of her head. He was awake and he'd heard it, too.

Another snap.

Ronin pulled her closer and shook his head.

Cora itched to leap from the ground and launch

into the pre-dawn sky. Knowing how stiff and injured she was, she'd probably flail before collapsing on the moss in a giant body cramp instead. Overriding instincts weren't easy. She lay tense and shook with the need to move.

Something large roamed the forest nearby. Ronin must think they remained undetected, otherwise he'd grip his sword or dagger instead of her.

The next branch snapped closer.

And closer.

Cora held her breath,

Another snap, even closer, near the edge of their makeshift campsite.

Ronin released Cora, his hand drifting to the dagger strapped to the waist of his armour.

Cora gripped her own dagger's hilt and eased it from the worn sheath. Her mouth grew dry and the sound of her heartbeat thundered in her ears.

The rest of the forest remained silent, as if waiting with bated breath to see how events unfolded.

Ronin withdrew the wing he'd covered her with, his feathers trailed down her arms and along her face. The cold air washed over her, and she missed the heat of Ronin's wing immediately.

Slowly, Ronin folded his wings behind him. The grimace creasing his face said he was just as sore and stiff as she was. Their odds didn't look good. Something fell heavy against the ground near their feet.

Ronin surged up. Cora scrambled to follow. A

wave of light-headedness spread through her and she stumbled to the side.

Ronin gripped her arm and steadied her. When Cora's vision cleared, she almost fell over again.

"I thought they were a myth," she whispered.

Standing in front of them stood a magnificent unicorn. Rumoured to be a result of genetic testing and radiation prior to the cascades, unicorns were categorized along with sapavians as scipers—products of scientific experimentation. Until this moment, Cora didn't believe unicorns survived the nuclear apocalypse. Some myths said the scientists' quest to create unicorns caused the first cascade.

Cora had only seen sketches from history books. Larger than the horses humans rode, both in height and width, the unicorn was far more magnificent. The white coat and wavy white mane glistened under the predawn light, giving off a sparkly light of its own to the point it made the beast appear to glow. Intelligent purple eyes studied them from a few feet away and the golden horn with flecks of silver protruding from its forehead looked more like a deadly weapon than a magical item rumoured to cure any wound.

Ronin leaned down. He still gripped her arm, but whether he did so to continue supporting her or to reassure himself was unclear. "No sudden moves."

Hah! Like she could move right now. Even if her muscles weren't locked in a full body cramp, Cora had no wish to be the first known sapavian skewered by a magical unicorn. Her lip curled up and Ronin chuckled.

The unicorn snorted a puff of condensed air from its muzzle before bouncing its head up and down. The mane rippled like a waterfall, mesmerizing.

Maybe death by unicorn was the way to go.

"Beautiful." The cold seeped into Cora's bones and her limbs ached. She wanted to curl into the heat of Ronin's body under the shelter of his wing, but she also didn't want to break this moment.

And die. She didn't really want that to happen, either.

The unicorn bobbed its head again, this time angling its head to the side. Ears pinned back, the unicorn whipped its tail and opened its mouth to reveal sharp, jagged, blood crusted teeth.

Cora flinched. Ronin stiffened beside her.

Another branch snapped deeper in the forest and they all turned toward the sound. A gust of wind brushed the side of Cora's scarred cheek. When she turned back to the unicorn, the beast was gone.

Ronin frowned at the empty space the unicorn had occupied moments ago. "I'm not sure if that was a good omen, or—"

Screams erupted in the night. Clashes of metal, thrashing bushes, jostling branches, cracking and wails of agony bounced around the dark forest.

Cora's blood turned cold. Those men had been so close. Too close. The humans would've found their trail when the sun rose and set off again. Instead, a unicorn feasted on their flesh. They'd never go home to their families, but they also wouldn't take down Cora and Ronin.

The cries and whimpering faded away, consumed with an eerie silence. Cora swallowed. Should she feel relieved? Thankful? Scared?

Yes, fear seemed appropriate. She willed the tension from her shoulders and turned to Ronin who still held her arm in an iron grip. She would've said something catty—as if she'd run off after that thing—but she found the near-painful pressure reassuring. "It didn't eat us. I think it's a good omen."

A higher, shriller sound than a horse's nicker echoed through the trees.

"It hasn't eaten us, *yet*." He hesitated and released her arm. "Why didn't it attack us?"

"Do you want to stick around and ask it?"

"Fuck no." He cast a wary glance at the forest again. "I'd still like to know why."

Cora shrugged and collected her belt and extra dagger from their sleeping spot. "Maybe it feels a kinship with other scipers?"

"Would be nice if the Sea Beast and thunderbirds afforded us the same courtesy," Ronin muttered.

Cora chuckled and then clamped her mouth shut.

"Too late." Ronin leaned down, impossibly close. "I saw it."

"Shh. It's nerves. Let's get out of here before the

unicorn realizes it left behind two tasty snacks and gets peckish."

The humour drained from Ronin's face and he plucked his sword from the spongy moss. She followed him as he stumbled from the clearing to find the deer path.

The unicorn had moved so quickly and so silently, it could sneak up on them at any time. Instead, the fabled beast had stomped around their campsite with little attempt to mask its presence. Did that mean the fellow sciper found sapavian flesh unpleasant? Or was there another reason?

Cora really didn't care to find out either way.

19

"Anger, if not restrained, is frequently more hurtful to us than the injury that provokes it."

— LUCIUS ANNAEUS SENECA

The sun dipped below the horizon and Cora scrambled to her feet to stretch. After a long, tense day of hiking along deer trails and goat paths, they made it to the place where Cora exchanged messages with Ava. The unicorn hadn't returned to gnaw on them, but they spent most of the journey looking over their shoulders and flinching every time something snapped in the woods. The unicorn was by far the most magnificent and scariest thing Cora had ever faced.

Along with the pain from their injuries, they arrived at their destination with sore necks and tense shoulders. Since they made it to the meeting place by midday, they decided to nap and rest. They had to wait until dark to signal Ava anyway and needed to conserve their energy in case the meeting went poorly.

Ronin stepped up behind her and placed his large hands on her shoulders. He kneaded the knots from her sore muscles. God, that felt awesome.

No. She couldn't do this. She couldn't stand here and pretend like he hadn't treated her like garbage, or that his father wasn't responsible for her mother's murder, or that she hadn't been manipulated to escort the prince on this hot mess mission.

She tensed and ducked out of his hold. With a deep breath, she tried to calm her racing heart before turning back to face him.

Ronin stared down at his hands and frowned. "What gives?"

Cora shrugged and pain shot through her body. She winced. *Let's not do that again.*

He dropped his hands to his sides. "No, that's not good enough. Why are you pissed off at me?"

Really? He wanted the list? "Besides you walking into a trap and placing my life and that of my father's in danger?"

Ronin tried to knock her over with his glare.

She lifted her chin.

"Yes, besides that. You've been a ball of hostility

before we left. We were friends once."

Ah, yes. Friends.

"Was it because my father sent you and your family away? Is that it? Do you blame him for your mother's death? I'd get that, but this feels like something more. This feels like it's directed very much at me and I had nothing to do with that order."

"Of course, I blame your father," she hissed. "He was the reason we were there."

"He saved your life."

Cora rocked back on her heels. "What are you talking about?"

"Your father was a traitor. Normally, he would be sentenced to death and the family cast out. My father couldn't bring himself to tear your family apart, so he sent you away instead."

Cora clamped her mouth shut. A traitor? Never. Did Ronin actually believe the lies he'd been dished? Had the king even bothered to give details of the alleged betrayal or had Ronin bought it on his word alone?

"I can't believe you," she whispered.

Ronin's expression softened and he stepped forward to grip her arm, the warmth of his hand chased away the cold on her skin.

"I know it's a lot to take in, but—"

"No, you fool. I can't believe you bought that crap."

Ronin's hand fell to his side. "What?"

"My father is not a traitor."

"Yes, he is."

"No, he's not. Think about it." She tapped the side of her head with her finger. "Why else is he allowed to live on the Eyrie to command the largest known spy network with your father's knowledge? Why would your father allow that? Why would a king trust him if he were a traitor?"

Ronin stepped forward again, waggling his pointer finger in the space between them as if to lecture her with the facts. He hesitated and then clamped his mouth shut.

She waited.

He rocked back on his heels and dropped his hand again. "Why then? Why would he send your family away only to take you back again?"

"I don't know." She turned away to stare at the ocean from the safety of the trees. She yearned to dive from the cliff into its icy depths and feel the water as a healing balm on her skin.

"Your father never said?"

She shook her head. "My mother said once that your father betrayed mine when my dad's only fault was blind loyalty."

Ronin stepped up beside her to look out at the same ocean scenery. The wind tussled his white hair. They stood there for a long moment, silent and watching the ever-moving ocean before Ronin spoke again. "Sounds as though your father isn't just a keeper of spies."

She nodded. Knowing where his reasoning took him because her own mind had travelled the same path. "He has a secret."

Ronin nodded.

"A secret your father would've killed a lesser man for having but banished us instead."

Ronin's hand rested on the hilt of his sword. "What changed?"

"Maybe your father took pity on mine. Maybe he realized the hurt he caused. Maybe he grew a conscience and tried to right a wrong. Or maybe he realized how much he needed my father on the Eyrie."

Ronin peered down at her, his face encased in shadows from the setting sun. "Is that why you hate me? Because the pain my father caused?"

"I don't hate you," she whispered, though she had at one time. Grief, anger, and hatred in high doses tended to swirl together and become indecipherable.

"Is that why you're angry at me, then?" Ronin continued to study her, gaze intent, body tense as if he'd release a world of violence at the wrong answer— not on her, but everything around her.

She shook her head, trying very hard to let the dying light over the ocean transfix her instead of Ronin. "I'm not angry at you or Sasha for your father's actions. Not anymore, anyway."

"What then?"

She clenched her hands, letting her nails bite into her palms.

"Cora!" Ronin growled.

"I'm pissed at the two of you for abandoning me." She whirled toward him. "Even if my father was a traitor, I wasn't. You were my friends. I was sixteen years old. What could I have possibly contributed to this alleged betrayal of my father's? You didn't even give me the common courtesy of questioning me about it."

Ronin's head jerked back as if she'd slapped him.

"You two acted as if I was tainted. I lost my home, then my mother and then my only friends. I returned injured and scared, drowning in grief, confusion, and anger. And I had no one. My father was lost in his own grief, and you...Our friendship meant so little to you, I meant so little to you, I wasn't even worth checking on. I was so alone."

"Cora—" Stepping in, he reached out.

She backed away and held her hand out. "Don't."

Ronin shook his head again and closed the distance.

She ducked under his arm and struck out, jabbing at his solar plexes. Her fist slammed into his armour and pain shot down her arm.

Goddammit. She marched back toward their bags, shaking her hand.

"Cora!"

"It's time to light the signal," she growled over her shoulder. It was time to focus on surviving instead of ripping off bandages from old wounds.

20

"You can have data without information, but you cannot have information without data."

— DANIEL KEYS MORAN

The night wind wound around the old trunks and teased Cora's hair. Her mind drifted as she stared into the forest and waited for Ava to arrive. Her mother's screams echoed in her memory. She struggled to remember Mom's face, but she could always recall the fear in her voice when she told Cora to run, and how she'd clutched her dagger and turned away from Cora to face the humans.

It happened nine years ago. Cora had turned sixteen a few days before the humans ambushed them.

She'd raced through the house with Mother to find a way out, a window or balcony they could launch from to fly away. The nearest accessible window was on the second floor but had bars across it. Meant for protection, those same bars acted as a prison instead. Cora had fumbled with the key. She'd nearly dropped it. When she finally swung the iron barred gate away from the window, it was too late for her mother. It had almost been too late for her as well.

Cora raised her hand to the scar running down her face. If only she'd been faster. If only she hadn't hesitated or fumbled.

Branches snapped and cracked on the path. Cora squeezed her eyes shut for a brief moment, willing her eyes to stop stinging and for the hollow feeling in her chest to go away.

Ronin studied her from a few feet away, his hand drifting to his sword hilt. They'd removed their bandages and Ronin's splint, forcing their wings into the folded position. Ava might not be an enemy, but she wasn't exactly a friend, either. Cora didn't know what Ava would do with the information if she found out about their injuries.

"What are you doing?" she hissed.

"You said she'd come alone."

"She is alone."

Ronin frowned and turned toward the path, flinching at each crunching step. "Doesn't sound like it."

Cora's mouth twitched. Ava's graceful nighttime forest walks hadn't improved. Cora wouldn't have it any other way. The loud stomping allowed her to locate her human contact at every point of her way up the path.

Ava panted through the forest and made it over the final steps. She leaned over and rested her hands on her knees. "Have I told you how much I hate this meeting place?"

"Only every time we meet."

Ava wheezed out a laugh and straightened. Her attention snagged on Ronin. Her whole body tensed, but her gaze continued moving, raking over his body.

"Hello, handsome." Ava relaxed with the fluidity of a woman who wanted to do naughty things with someone else.

Cora squashed the urge to grab Ronin or verbally warn Ava away. Completely irrational. Cora had no claim to Ronin, nor did she want one. Instead, she swallowed and forced her expression to remain neutral.

Ava's eyebrows shot up into her hairline before she turned to Cora. "With men looking like this." She waved her hand at Ronin as if he couldn't hear or see her. "Why would you ever leave to come here?"

Ronin grunted and somehow straightened more. Did he just push his chest out a little? Dear lord, his ego was big enough.

Cora snorted. "Trust me, if you knew this one, you'd want to get away, too."

Ava grinned but didn't take her gaze off Ronin. "Do you have a message for me?"

Cora slipped the sealed message Ronin had written earlier from her pocket and held it out. Ava plucked the folded paper from her hand, read the label, and frowned. "The Eyrie?"

Cora nodded. "Via the Waystation Access Point."

"The Wap?" Ava's frown deepened. "Why don't you take it back yourself?"

Cora resisted the urge to flutter her damaged wings. They had the lack of light and Ava's poor eyesight on their side, but if she started asking questions and studied them closer, she'd figure it out.

"Time," Cora said.

Ava's lip curled. "You don't have time? Are you staying in Iom for a bit?"

"It has something to do with timing." She shrugged. "I don't know the contents or the motivations of the sender. I was equally confused. My guess is they want the message to arrive delayed and to appear to have come from Iom."

Ava's shoulders relaxed, she pocketed the message and withdrew another one. This one had a black seal Cora had seen before. Most of the messages she'd returned to the Eyrie lately had the same markings.

"Your timing is impeccable." Ava held out the message. "I have one for you, too."

Cora took the message and slid the sealed paper

into one of her pockets. If she refused to take it, Ava would wonder why.

Ava folded her arms and waited.

Cora copied the motion.

"Well?"

"Well, what?" Cora asked.

"Aren't you going to show off and leap from the cliff, now?"

Cora smiled, hoping it covered her unease. She normally left first. Showing up with Ronin already broke her habits. Ava couldn't become suspicious or her questions might place Cora and Ronin in even more danger.

Ronin stepped in close and draped a lazy arm over her shoulders. Pain shot through her wing. This couldn't be comfortable for Ronin either. Cora shifted a little to ease the pressure, leaning into Ronin's body. Her vest opened and the silver butt of her newly acquired dagger popped out.

Ava's gaze dropped down.

"We thought we'd change things up. There's been a lot of hunters along the coast lately." He glanced at Cora. The heat in his gaze nearly knocked her breath away. It said he wanted to see her naked and sent all sorts of ideas racing through her mind. His gaze also left little doubt to any onlooker what his intentions were.

Great.

Now Cora's credibility as a top-notch messenger

would be forever tainted. She was *that girl* who brought her boyfriend along on missions to bang.

Ugh.

Should she be worried about her professionalism right now? Though important, living through this botched mission held the highest priority.

Double ugh.

Cora leaned in and use the motion to readjust her vest and hide the dagger hilt.

Ava hooted with laughter. "Well, I'll leave you love birds alone to *change things up*." The humour fled from her face. "Just...just be careful, okay? We've had two hunting parties go missing. There have been rumours of a beast tearing travellers apart between here and Milling."

The unicorn.

Both the hunting parties hailed from Alara. Ava undoubtedly knew them.

Cora shouldn't ask. *Don't ask.* "Were you close to any of them?"

Why did she ask?

Ava looked down at her hands. "My fiancé was in one of the parties."

Cora's stomach sunk. Which one? The unicorn party or the one Ronin and Cora had taken out after they shot her from the sky?

"It was an arranged marriage. He was older and cruel, but my family counted on the union."

"Are you okay?"

Ava stopped twisting her fingers together and met Cora's gaze with her own. "I don't know, yet. I don't know what to feel." She attempted a smile, but it was more of a grimace. "I'll leave you guys, now."

They waited until Ava's thrashing through the forest grew distant before picking their own way through the trees on the path leading south. Though Cora knew she shouldn't feel guilty for the hunters' death, it still ate at her gut alongside the unease over the journey ahead.

Ronin turned to Cora, his mouth twisted down. "Do you trust her?"

"Of course not. She's human."

Ronin cocked his head. "You seemed friendly."

"Friendly and friends are two different things. Despite what you might think, I'm not an asshole. I like Ava. I think she tolerates me for the sake of our business transactions and the fishing tips I give her. If she had to choose between sheltering me and helping her people, though, I would be plucked and strung up in the town square in a heartbeat."

The moon shone from above, dappling leaves and the underbrush with its silvery glitter, but true darkness waited in the shadows.

"They're not all bad," Ronin said.

"I didn't say they were. But it's dangerous to forget where a person's allegiance lies, and I'll never forget what they did to my mother. Nor should you. If it makes you feel better, I also trust very few sapavians."

His eyebrows shot up, the question clearly playing with his mind and teasing his tongue. She would answer him truthfully and he wouldn't like what she had to say.

Don't ask.

Ronin jerked his chin toward her pocket. "What's the message?"

Cora shrugged.

"Really? I'm the heir of the Eyrie. Open it."

She shook her head. "It's not for you. I'll deliver it to the intended recipient when we return."

"You're not going to read it?" His eyebrows rose.

That's right. Not even for you. She folded her arms. "I'm a professional messenger. I take my job seriously. I don't snoop and read other people's messages."

"Fine." He paused walking long enough to hold up his hands in mock defence. He could order her to open the message, technically, but he had to have reason for such an invasive action. An important reason. Not just curiosity. "She saw your dagger's hilt."

"You caught that, too?"

He nodded.

They turned in unison and made their way down the other trail. They'd place the splint back on Ronin's wing once they made it far enough away. With any luck, if Ava raised an alarm, they'd assume Cora and Ronin flew away from the meeting place. Ava was perceptive. She picked up cues and kept a poker face, but the night was dim, and they'd kept their movements minimal. Hopefully, the human hadn't deduced their injuries.

Hopefully.

A lot of their plans hinged on that concept. A word and feeling Cora had no time or patience for.

"I can hear your mind clanking over there. Can you think quieter? We're trying for stealth," Ronin whispered the last word and theatrically tip-toed over exposed tree roots.

Would it be too much to ask for him to trip right now?

"Oh, no. Not the snarl." He resumed walking and heavy silence settled between them.

She wanted to curse him, but any anger she possessed this morning had drained away. She didn't have the energy to be snarky right now. She just wanted a soft bed and a full night's sleep. Proper food. She'd get neither. They needed to make it to one of Cora's hideaways. There was one prepped just south of the town and it would take all night and all her patience to get there.

21

"I have found out that there ain't no surer way to find out whether you like people or hate them than to travel with them."

— MARK TWAIN

"If you ask me if we're almost there one more time, I'm going to break your other wing," Cora growled.

"Harsh." Ronin's wings tensed as if they had a mind of their own and didn't appreciate her threat.

At least some part of her companion realized her words weren't completely idle. She was hot, hungry, thirsty, tired, and injured. She didn't even care for a soft bed now. She just wanted to flop down somewhere, close her eyes and pretend none of her problems existed. The moss on the side of the road looked really good right now.

"How much longer?" Ronin asked.

She glared, not appreciating his new wording to ask the exact same thing. "Seven hours."

"But you said seven hours last time I asked," he gruffed. "And the time before that."

My, my, my, the prince's tone bordered on a whine. "And it will remain seven hours until it is not."

"I've been tramping through the forest and on this road all night," Ronin growled. "We're out of food and we're out of time. The sun is rising, and travellers will be out soon. We need to get off the road."

"We will," she said.

"Soon."

"We will."

He glowered.

"While very impressive, your brooding looks will not make this process any faster. It will only serve to irritate me further. By all means, keep pushing. You might like to remember I'm your best chance for survival and getting home alive."

"And you might want to remember I'm the future king of the Eyrie. You're my subject and if I don't make it back alive, neither will you."

They stopped and glared at one another. A fly buzzed around her ear and she swatted at it without breaking eye contact.

Ronin grunted and turned back to the road. "And I don't brood."

"You do, too." She focused on placing one weary step in front of the other. The roar of a nearby waterfall urged her forward. "Do you remember Gabriel?"

"He's the captain of my personal guard." Ronin kicked a rock and scowled. "Of course, I do."

"Okay, well, look what happened at the aerial trials."

Ronin's lip curled up to show his teeth. "What about them?"

"You were so angry he scored better than you in the final event, you stood to the side, folded your arms and glowered at anyone who dared to come near."

"I did no such thing. I am the paragon of diplomatic poise."

Cora bit back a laugh. "My father sent me to check whether some mage infiltrated the Eyrie to create a storm cloud just for you."

"You're making this up."

"The last part, yes. But I still had to check to see if you were poisoned or under someone's control."

Ronin scowled.

"You wouldn't talk to Gabriel for a month. He was your best friend," she said.

"I'm the crown prince of the Eyrie. Second best isn't an option. I didn't talk to anyone during that month. My priorities changed. I focused on training so

I would perform better. Gabriel beating me was a wake-up call."

Cora tried to hide her smile and failed. "So, you made Gabriel your captain?"

"Of course. If I can't be the best, I need to surround myself with the best."

"I'm surprised he let you out on your own."

"He didn't know."

Her eyebrows shot up. "He's the captain of your personal guard. How does he not know about this trip?"

"Caleb got injured on the last salmon run, so I gave Gabriel time off. Besides, no one knew. We kept my trip top secret. Only my family and yours know about this mission."

They followed the curve of the road, the trees to their left thinned out to reveal the ocean while the path led to a wood bridge spanning a chasm. A swift flowing river rushed under the bridge, spraying out into a spectacular waterfall to the raging ocean over a hundred feet below. The Edge of Iom.

This section of the mainland ended in a sheer cliff drop off and was a welcome sight after a long night of walking.

"Gabriel and Caleb?" Cora picked up her pace. "I always thought Gabriel had a thing for Jerome."

"Oh, he did." Ronin grimaced. "That ended."

"Ended how?"

"Spectacularly."

Huh. She hadn't heard a thing about the relationship. Then again, she'd distanced herself from the royal court as much as possible after they made it clear she was unwelcome. "I never liked Jerome, anyway."

"I remember."

And he would. Jerome called her an ugly turkey when they were in school because she didn't agree with him. Ronin had overheard and ended up coming to her defence, punching Jerome below the belt. That pretty much sealed the deal on her childhood crush—as far as adolescent Coraline Cormorant was concerned, the heir of the Eyrie could do no wrong and the sun rose and fell on his shiny perfect hair and beautiful face.

Whooo boy.

She had it bad.

"You'd left for training on Ostei." Ronin interrupted her walk down memory lane. "I'm sure you would've heard about Gabriel and Jerome otherwise."

Cora almost stopped walking. Sheer adrenaline and the knowledge that if she stopped now, she wouldn't start again kept her going. Exactly how close did Ronin keep tabs on her? The training she'd left for on Ostei, the first of the Wayfair Stations, was over five years ago. He acted so indifferent yet kept track of her movements around the Eyrie. Or did he track all of Father's messengers?

"Are we—" he started.

She held her hand up. "Don't."

He snapped his mouth shut.

"We're here."

Ronin's frown was almost comical. Whose brain clanked around now, huh?

"Cora?"

"Yes, Your Majesty?"

He faltered and scowled. "There's nothing here except a cliff, a waterfall and a bridge."

"That's what you and every human sees from the road." Cora walked off the path to the cliff's edge. The early morning sun broke across the horizon and cascaded Cora in golden light. She brushed aside the bushes that thrived in the sea air and nutrient poor soil.

"Those stone berries aren't going to tide us over for long," Ronin growled, his voice devoid of any patience.

"You sound nervous." She glanced at him over her shoulder. "Does His Majesty fear for his life?"

"That's not my proper title and you know it."

She ignored him and gripped the two bars embedded into the rock. His scowl brought a smile to her lips. She pushed off the rock and swung in the air over the side of the cliff.

"Cora!"

Holding onto the bars, she faced the cave she'd found years ago and silently thanked her planning. Over the course of multiple runs, she'd installed bars and stored dried food in case of emergencies—injuries or skewed timing where she needed somewhere to hide. Her toes touched down on the ledge and she let go of the bar with one hand to grab another one near the cave's entrance. A gust of wind pushed her off balance. She clung to the bars and ground her teeth.

Normally, she enjoyed the play of the ocean wind, but not today. Not when her wings were unlikely to save her from plummeting the hundred feet to her death on the rocky shore below.

She waited for a lull in the wind and regained her balance before letting go of the safety bars.

The cave was exactly as she left it. The roar of the waterfall to the left of the opening droned continuously. If she extended her arm from the cave's mouth, she could catch the freshwater thundering over the cliff edge. A locked wooden chest sat in the corner. Dry. Lock still in place. No rodents. An invisible weight lifted off her shoulders.

Oh, thank god.

A shadow passed over the cave's mouth. She whirled around. Ronin stood at the entrance of the cave, blocking the early morning's light. Shadows danced along his chiseled features but did little to hide the thunder in his gaze.

The cave suddenly felt very, very small.

"That wasn't funny." His deep voice filled the cave.

She held up her hand, leaving about an inch between her finger and thumb. "It was a little bit funny."

Murder flashed across his expression.

"It would've been funnier if I got to see your face."

Ronin squeezed his eyes shut and took a deep,

pained breath. The tension in the air eased. "What is this place?"

"My safety cave."

Ronin blinked at her.

"I have a number of hidey holes around the Cap. Sometimes, I need to rest before returning to the Eyrie, especially if I get injured. The idea is never go to the same place twice in a row. I always change my resting location. This cave is one of my spots, but I rarely use it, keeping it for emergencies only."

Ronin studied the cave, mouth working, but no sound coming out.

She gently tapped the box with her foot. "Every few months, I change out the supplies. There's about three months' worth of dried food in here for one person. So, this can feed us for about a month and a half at the most. With your excessive energy-sucking muscles, we're probably looking at closer to one month. Hopefully, by then we'll be healed enough to get our own food." She jerked her chin toward the river. "And fresh water."

Ronin still didn't say anything. She was damn proud of her safety cave and preparedness. Why wasn't he saying anything?

Ronin burst forward, gripped both her arms, and pulled her into his body for a bone crushing hug. "I could kiss you."

Cora wanted to sag into the heat of his body and let his words and her heart carry her away from the reality of their circumstances and respective positions in Eyrie society. Her brain said, "Nope."

"Please don't kiss me," she said. "Your breath is awful."

Ronin chuckled, his chest rumbling against hers and his hands searing into her back. "You're no spring flower yourself."

He released her and stepped away to study the cave.

As if a giant had scooped out a chunk of the cliff face like it had the consistency of butter, the cave was a rounded, open-faced blemish in an otherwise sheer rock face. Using her own height and wingspan, she determined the space was about eight feet high, twelve feet wide and thirteen feet at the deepest point. Not enough space for Ronin to fully extend his wings, but enough for the two of them to cohabitate, and more than enough for any accumulated heat to escape.

"We can't stay here."

"I know. Too cramped and cold, but we can for now."

Ronin grimaced. "We'll lose our lead. If Ava's townspeople, the men who tried to abduct me or the hunters who shot us down are after us—and we have to assume they all are—we risk getting sandwiched in between the groups." Whenever he mulled over something serious, he squinted as if someone had just punched him in the nads and he was debating how to punish them without puking. He had the same look on his face now. Guess some things never changed.

"Do you honestly think we'd maintain our lead with our injuries and our very obvious, hard-to-hide tracks?" Keeping her wings off the trail was almost impossible on a good day, and obscuring the tracks took more time than they had.

"No," Ronin agreed. "But I don't want to be caught in the middle of three blood-thirsty, sapavian-hating groups."

"We could wait more than a few days," she offered.

Ronin grimaced. "It's going to get awfully awkward if we stay here more than a day and popping in and out of the cave would increase our chances of getting caught."

"There are bar-holds that lead to an area under the waterfall from here." She nodded at the entrance. "Not only does sprint mint grow along the sides, we can use the area to bathe and take care of private matters." She hesitated. "It's too wet for sleeping though."

Ronin grumbled.

"If we delay for a week or more, we can regain our energy, let any potential tail get way ahead of us and take our time once we head out." She hugged herself against the breeze. "We might want to consider staying here the entire time instead of trekking across the coastline to the Oap. By the time we're healed, the heat at the Cap should've cooled down and we can make the return crossing we originally planned."

"It's too populated here. That food will not last us more than a few weeks, not if we're trying to regain energy and heal. We need exercise and food with sustenance, and it's too busy here to risk venturing out to hunt on a regular basis."

She sighed, knowing his assessment of their predicament was spot on—she'd thought similar things as well, but part of her didn't want to leave the safety of the cave. If it were just her, she'd hole up here for a month and then risk the channel crossing.

"Fine," Ronin said. "We'll stay, but for no more than a few weeks."

She perked up.

"And fires are out."

Her smile turned into a scowl.

"Okay, maybe a little fire."

If he made some cheesy line about keeping her warm, she'd slap him.

"Of course, there are other—"

Slap! Her hand stung, but it was totally worth the pain.

22

"I want to touch with my mouth. His mouth, with my mouth. Maybe his neck, too. But first things first: Make him aware I exist."

— LAINI TAYLOR

Cora tensed as a shadow fell over the opening of the cave. She whirled around to find Ronin standing by the entrance and a sense of déjà vu settled over her.

Water dripped from his bare chest and his underwear clung to his powerful thighs and left little to the imagination.

Oh my.

Her mouth went dry.

"Are we out of food already?" he asked, gaze flashing.

Huh? They'd been here for two weeks and she had to endure daily sightings of near-naked Ronin and nightly cuddles to stay warm, but food wasn't an issue yet. "We have a couple more weeks."

A grin spread across his face.

"Why do you ask?"

"You look hungry." He picked up his shirt to dab his chest. Usually, he moved with quick efficiency, but today he took his time, running the shirt over his hard muscles. Was he flexing?

Grrrr. "You're such an ass."

His grin could melt the panties off a nun. "Interesting choice of words."

Do not take the bait. Do not ask.

He waited.

Why me? She sighed and threw up her hands. "And you say this because...?"

He pulled the shirt over his head and let it hang loose around his back. It clung to his still damp skin. If history repeated, he'd sit at the cave's entrance, dangle his legs over the edge and let the sunshine dry his underwear before pulling on his pants and buttoning the back of his shirt up.

"The way you've been looking at my ass makes me think being called one isn't an insult." He stepped away from the cave entrance and crowded her personal space. He opened his wings behind him, blocking the early morning light.

She tensed under his scrutiny. It didn't matter what her feelings were or how attractive she found him or what she wanted to do with him and to him. None of these things altered the reality that he was the arrogant crown prince from the ruling Eagle Clan whose father's orders inadvertently resulted in her mother's death and she was a lowly messenger spy from the cormorant family. At one time, when she'd followed him around believing them friends, he'd thought of her as a little sister at best and an inconvenient doe-eyed follower with a massive crush at worst.

Damn it.

She didn't want him to sense her attraction, her weakness for that smile or heated gaze. A little dignity to walk out of here after their isolation would be nice.

Ronin studied her from a foot away, his predatory gaze softening into something unreadable. "I can hear your brain clanking around again."

Great. Call me stupid. Real charming. "Your game needs some work."

"You must be thinking about something hard."

Her mind nose-dived into the gutter. Her gaze drifted to his groin area to salivate over how the wet cloth clung to his...Argh. She snapped her gaze up. He did that on purpose. "I'm not thinking hard about anything. Just looking for the exit." She stretched up on her tiptoes to look over his shoulder.

Ronin ruffled his wings. He was healing well, a few days ago he wouldn't have made that move with his injured wing. Hopefully in a few more days, they could remove the splint and try gliding. Long distance flying was still out for both of them.

"Nervous?" Ronin asked.

"No. A little worried. You've obviously slipped and hit your head. Or maybe you sustained a concussion during our crash landing. We might have to alter our plans in light of you clearly becoming delusional."

His white teeth flashed in the shadows.

Why did she suddenly feel like prey?

"I think..." Ronin reached out and trailed his fingertips along her arm.

"Shocking."

He grinned and carried on, his fingertips sending thrilling little pings along her arm. "I think you're thinking about us together. What it would be like. How it would feel. How I would taste."

Oh my. How was it suddenly so hot in here? He wasn't wrong, but that wasn't the point. "Wow. How do you manage to fit in this cave with that ego of yours?"

He stepped closer, so close the coolness from his waterfall shower reached out and licked her skin. "You're as red as last night's sunset."

Her cheeks grew warmer. This was ridiculous. She

was a badass messenger, one of the few capable of navigating the Carrion Channel. She refused to get all swoony and flustered from a strutting peacock of a prince who decided he needed some female attention with the absence of his admirers.

She pulled herself upright. "I think you're homesick."

"Is that so?" He remained standing a few inches away. "First delusional and now homesick?"

She ignored his quirked brow. "You're obviously in withdrawal from feminine affection and have zeroed in on your only option."

His head jerked back. Sore point. "Is that what you think of me?"

"Oh, you're so much more than that."

His gaze flashed in warning. Bottled rage vibrated in front of her. He leaned in, almost brushing her lips with his own. "Is that so?"

If she were smart, she'd take a step back and placate him. He'd had enough. Instead, she lifted her chin. "Of course, *Your Majesty*. You're also arrogant, conceited, ru—"

He pressed his lips against hers and she lost her train of thought. She'd expected anger or sarcasm, an outburst, not a tender kiss. Not a gentle touch that asked for more with the tease of tongue. He folded his wings tightly against his back, letting the sunshine stream in to bathe the cave in golden light.

She could bolt. He left her an opening.

"You're so beautiful." He pulled back to catch his breath and cradled her face in his hands. When she leaned in for more, he smiled and kissed her again. His tongue flicked out and licked her lips. He tasted of spring mint and forbidden nights.

She moaned into his mouth and that was all the encouragement he needed. His hands moved from her face, one tangling in her hair to grip the back of her neck and the other travelling down her body. She arched into him, wanting, teasing, and kissed him back, hard.

His hand gripped her butt and pulled her into his hard erection—hard to miss with only a thin layer of clothing between them and just...hard.

A low ache throbbed in her core. Almost painful, the need for Ronin grew as he deepened the kiss and she answered. She wanted him inside her. She wanted him rocking into her.

She moaned into his mouth again and ran her hands down his back to the hem of his underwear. One tug and she'd release him from his clothing. A couple more seconds and she'd have her clothes off. If he sat back, she could impale herself on his hard shaft and ride him, grind against him, and release this agonizing pressure that continued to build.

"I want you so much, it hurts." Ronin moved from her mouth to kissing her neck, tasting her skin as he tugged at her clothes.

"Well, I'm telling you, Derek, this fucking sucks." A deep voice thundered down from the cliff's edge over the roar of the waterfall.

Cora and Ronin broke away in an instant. She drew her dagger and Ronin eyed his sword a few feet away.

"That bird-loving bitch said they looked injured." Another man shouted back, probably Derek. They must be standing right at the cliff's edge. They had to yell at one another over the waterfall.

"And we followed their trail to here. The scouts we sent forward on horses haven't found a thing. The trail never picks up again. I'm telling you, they took off. They're sapavians. There's no telling how far they went. They're probably back at the Eyrie laughing their asses off. Ava must've been mistaken."

A shiver wracked Cora's body. If they'd continued on instead of holing up in this cave, they would've been chased down by those hunters on horses. Cora could defend herself, and Ronin was a trained warrior, but fighting injured, tired and on foot against prepared hunters? The outcome could've been disastrous for them.

Ronin's grim expression said he rolled through the same scenario and reached a similar conclusion.

"Or she lied, Andrew. We'll just have to beat the truth out of her."

"Again?" Andrew said.

Cora hissed quietly.

Ronin glared.

Oh, give it a rest. If those men hadn't heard their heavy panting and make-out session over the rushing water, they certainly wouldn't hear her little hiss.

Those men.

They'd beaten Ava. Any heat remaining from Ronin's kiss fled her body. Her almost-friend had been caught and beaten for information on them.

"Yes. Again," Derek said. "I know you have a soft spot for the girl, but we need to find these two before Aeneas' people do."

"I don't think she lied. You scared her thoroughly. She told the truth," Andrew said. "I don't think we needed to tie her up."

"You heard her. She liked the messenger. We couldn't risk her running off to warn the creatures," Derek grumbled.

Cora was beginning to really hate Derek.

"And if she didn't lie, where are they?" Derek asked.

Silence settled over the men.

The waterfall continued gushing freshwater to the ocean below. The waves lapped the shore and the sea looked calm—a complete contrast to how Cora felt.

Had the men moved away from the edge? She remained frozen in place. Though a feather ruffle, hiss, or heated kiss wouldn't likely give them away, she didn't want to risk it. The silence stretched and the tension in her body faded away. She relaxed and moved to sheath her dagger.

"There's a number of caves along this shoreline. Cory is arranging a boat," Andrew said.

Ronin bit off a curse.

"They're risking the ocean?"

"We are, yes. The shoreline is relatively safe, and these villagers make their living on the water."

"But the Sea Beast has been spotted in the bay near the shore," Derek said.

Ronin tensed at the mention of the monster and glanced at her. Why? Did he want confirmation? Why did he think she could add anything to this information? She shrugged and went back to waiting.

"Pfft, rumours. They're always saying that. It keeps the competition away."

"What are we going to do then?" Derek yelled. "Wait here?"

"You'll have to hold off on your torture fetish. We'll stay here and signal to the boat to let them know where the trail went cold. If they're hiding in some cave, we'll find them." The man's voice faded as he presumably walked away from the ledge.

Dirt fell from the ledge and sprinkled down to the cave's entrance. The men's boots must've scuffed the earth as they walked away.

Ronin turned to Cora and whispered, "Is the cave visible from the ocean?"

Cora shook her head. "Not if they hug the shoreline. They have to be far enough offshore and armed with either good eyesight or binoculars."

"Then why do you look worried."

"They'll realize the same thing when they try to locate those men. And there's still a chance they'll see the handles, either from the boat or from the edge. We're really lucky those two turkeys didn't look down very closely."

Ronin's expression darkened. "We have to move."

She nodded. "But we can't gracefully pop out of the cave without alerting them."

A slow smile spread across Ronin's face, not a nice smile, a smile that promised pain and death. A chill ran along Cora's spine.

"We'll wait for nightfall," he said.

"And until then?"

"We pack and rest. There's still a chance they'll discover us before we get to them. We have to be ready. The cave is easy to defend, so if they decide to investigate, we'll have an advantage."

"Unless they know we're here and decide to wait us out while we starve."

Ronin sighed. "That's a possibility. They haven't found us yet, though. We can't dictate what the future will hold, but we can prepare for the possibilities."

"So we wait," she said.

How remarkably perceptive of him. Then again, Ronin had demonstrated cool, logical thinking under duress already. The king had trained him well. "We wait." His gaze sparkled. "And you'll need to keep your hands to yourself."

She snorted. The road ahead held many possible challenges, but none greater than resisting the urge to throttle the prince.

23

"The best defense is attack."

— ITALIAN PROVERB

The scrape of metal against stone woke Cora from her nap. She jerked awake, ripped her dagger from the sheath and bolted upright. A dark shadow near the edge of the cave moved.

Cora bit back a scream.

Ronin stepped close enough for her to make out the familiar contours of his face, the set of his shoulders, the intimidating armour and the shockingly white wings folded behind him. He raised his finger to his lips. The moon played with his expression and a twinge of longing struck her chest. A different time, a different place, a different life. She and Ronin were not meant to be.

And what totally ridiculous and pathetic thoughts to have at a time like this. *Focus, Cora.* There would be plenty of time to lament the loss of a relationship when they made it home. It certainly wasn't the time to mourn something that didn't exist. Cora almost snorted, but that would be dumber than her thoughts.

"Be ready," Ronin whispered. He drew his dagger and placed it between his teeth.

What?

Before she could question him, he was up and out of the cave in one swift fluid move. The gentle whisper of his feathers against the stone was the only sound and she had to strain to hear it over the waterfall.

She grabbed Ronin's sword and the bag with the food and set them by the entrance.

A grunt and a thud punctured the roar of water. Cora held her breath. Her heart pounded. Should she go up there and help?

More smacks. Scuffling feet on dry dirt. Crunching rocks. Another grunt.

Cora adjusted her grip on the dagger and squeezed. She'd be ready for whatever came over the edge.

A man hollered, the sound cut off with a gargle.

She squeezed her eyes shut. Please let that be Derek.

A dark shadow flew past the entrance toward the ocean. A body.

Cora stuck her head out and looked down in time to catch the dark ocean swallowing the body in its infinite darkness.

Dirt crunched again. A long, low grating sound followed. Another shadow sped past her, only a foot away. A blast of air smacked her face in its wake.

Body number two.

"Could you stick your head out a little more? I might manage to hit you next time."

Cora swivelled up to find Ronin standing at the cliff edge looking down, his dagger flashing under the moonlight as he cleaned it with a cloth.

"Do you have a third body handy or are you just making idle threats?"

His white teeth flashed. "Come out, princess. The boys left us some gifts."

Princess? She'd been called many things in her life, but that was not one of them.

She shoved both arms through the bag straps, wearing it against her chest and slung the belt for Ronin's sword across her body and along the back of her shoulders above the wing sockets. She scrambled up the bars. Princess? More like pack mule.

Ronin gripped her forearms and pulled her over the ledge to place her on solid ground.

Instead of letting her go, he slid his hands up her arms

until he clutched her shoulders. His gaze captured her own and though night descended hours ago, the moon cast enough light for Cora to see Ronin's fierce gaze.

"We have horses," he said.

Not what she thought he'd say.

As if picking up that the weird humans with wings were talking about them, two horses lifted their heads from where they chomped on a patch of grass near a make-shift campsite.

Cora raised her eyebrows. Sapavians and horses rarely mixed. They didn't have any on the Eyrie. "Horses?"

Ronin squeezed her shoulders before letting go.

"Do you know how to ride?" She certainly didn't.

"How hard can it be? Sit on the saddle and give them a nudge with your heels."

She hesitated. The one who looked as though a child chucked a couple buckets of white paint on a black canvas looked at Cora sideways, while the other one with a pure black coat went back to munching the grass.

Ronin leaned in. "I get the all black one."

"Why?"

"Everyone knows the hero is more badass when he's riding a black stallion."

She waved her finger back and forth between them. "Are you the hero?"

"I happen to recall saving you from falling to your

death." He pulled his shoulders back. "Of course, I'm the hero."

She ignored the way he puffed out his muscular chest, walked closer to the animals and bent to peer under them. "Well, I think your dreams of riding into battle on a black stallion will have to be waylaid."

Ronin scowled. "He will be a fine steed."

"He's a she, hero." She patted his chest.

Ronin snapped his mouth shut and glared. "You're just jealous you have to ride the cow horse."

"Just call me the dream crusher."

Ronin stepped up to the horses and looked under them. "They're mares. Why would those men choose mares?"

"Why not?"

Ronin straightened and gaped at her, for once appearing speechless.

"Because..."

"Because having a penis makes it better?"

He scowled at her. "Just because, okay."

She laughed softly and shook her head. "Maybe, the humans who live and work with horses on a regular basis know a tad bit more than either of us about the beasts, hmm?" She held her hand out to the cow horse. The animal ignored her and joined her friend to eat more grass. "I read somewhere that mares and geldings are preferred because they have better dispositions for riding."

"Huh." Ronin ran his hand along the neck of the

black mare. "Let's go, *Dream Crusher*. We can put more distance between us and the other groups now."

Cora hesitated again.

Ronin sighed and turned to her. "You want to go after Ava, don't you?"

"They tied her up and tortured her."

"You hate humans. You owe her nothing."

"I don't hate Ava. I like her, I just didn't trust her to choose us over her own kind. There's a difference."

"And you were right, weren't you? She betrayed us."

Cora shook her head. "No, she didn't. Just as I don't owe her anything, she doesn't owe me or you any sort of allegiance. She was loyal to her people, and you heard the men, she didn't want us harmed. She did what she thought was right and they beat her for it."

"This isn't our problem. You should leave her to her fate."

"We killed her fiancé," Cora whispered. "Probably the only connection that ensured her protection. She tried to withhold information to protect us. I can't just leave her there. Not when she spoke in our defence." She looked away from the thunder in Ronin's gaze. "I can go on my own. You should stay safe and get back to the Eyrie."

Ronin didn't respond. When the silence became unbearable, she turned to find him glaring at her. She opened her mouth and then shut it again.

Why was he so angry? Because she told him to stay

behind and stay safe? Oh for goodness sake. "Or you could come with me."

"Of course, I'm going with you."

Warmth spread through her chest and the tension gripping her body faded away. "I'm so honoured to have the company of the most majestic hero on his trusty, badass, black mare." She fluttered her eyelashes.

"Shut up."

She grinned.

"I'm only going with you because Ava might have more information on these men and King Aeneas." His words were cold and harsh but even with the limited moonlight, she felt the heat of his gaze still on her.

"Liar."

He grunted and turned away to gather supplies from their would-be murderers' camp.

24

"Your lips are like wine and I want to get drunk."

— WILLIAM SHAKESPEARE

They walked the horses off the path and into the woods as the sky lightened and the birds began to sing. When they made it far enough from the road for the trees and distance to shield them from travellers, they found a patch of dense moss to make camp. A sweet summer wind rolled through the branches and caressed Cora's skin as she tied up the horses. Ronin set out the bedrolls and made a small fire.

They had more food after raiding the hunters'

supplies and Cora looked forward to a hot meal and sleeping on a proper bedroll.

She turned to find Ronin studying her, lips quirked up and weight shifted slightly forward as if he prepared to pounce.

"What's wrong with you?" she asked.

His grin grew. "I was just thinking about yesterday."

Heat spread across her cheeks. She'd thought about the kiss too, but every time the memories scorched her mind, she pushed the thoughts and feelings away. Now was not the time. It would never be their time.

"I think we should push the bedrolls together," Ronin said.

"Why?" Maybe if she continued to play dumb, he'd get so tired of explaining things to her he'd forget his original plan.

"You know why."

"I really don't."

He crossed his arms in front of his chest. "We have a kiss to finish."

"Oh, that?" She shrugged and forced her face to remain neutral. "It was okay, I guess. Not feeling any urge to continue, if I'm being completely honest."

"Okay?"

"Yeah, just okay. About the same quality as your attempt at seduction right now." She tossed the saddle bags by one of the mats. She turned away from Ronin and bit her lip. "Nothing worth repeating."

"Oh, I don't know about that." Ronin practically purred. "Seemed like you enjoyed yourself."

"I was trying to get you to stop."

"By grinding against me?"

She clamped her mouth shut and whirled around to find Ronin's knowing gaze raking her body.

"Congratulations," she said. "You successfully seduced the sole woman trapped in a cave with you, your only option. I'm pretty sure I would've climaxed if I rubbed on the rocks the right way."

His grin grew.

Argh. "You're so full of yourself."

He shook his head. "I want you to be full of myself."

She groaned. "I think I preferred you arrogant."

He frowned. Right, he was being arrogant right now.

"As opposed to arrogant *and* horny," she clarified.

"There's a simple solution to that."

"Yeah, I'll hold down the fort. You can get reacquainted with your hand."

Ronin dipped his head back and laughed. He actually clutched his stomach. "That's not what I had in mind, unless you wanted to give me a hand."

She folded her arms across her chest. That was not happening. She didn't need to tell Ronin that. She needed to tell her own over-eager brain because her mind was clearly not getting the message and sent her all sorts of steamy thoughts instead.

"How about we push the mats together and cut the tension between us?" Ronin tried again. He'd probably never put much effort into seduction, and it showed. With his looks, lazy smiles, and status in sapavian society, he had women throwing themselves at him all the time. He didn't have to ask what they wanted because it was painfully obvious to everyone. And ask twice? Never.

Though this effort with her was more matter of fact than smooth, it called to every bone in her body. He continued to seduce without effort, and she wasn't immune to his charm. His unspoken words said: *Come sleep with me. You'll enjoy it. I'll make you see the stars and turn your legs to jelly.*

And that was the problem. She would enjoy every second of it. She would melt into the heat of his body, get lost in the rhythm of his hips, and drown in the depths of his smouldering gaze.

And she'd never recuperate.

She wouldn't come up for air or find her way back.

If they survived this mission, he would return to his position as the crown prince, surrounded by swooning courtiers, bickering politicians, and loaded expectations. He had no time or place for a cormorant messenger in his life. At best, she would be a pleasant memory for him to recall when he was lonely, at worst she would be a shameful mistake.

"Sex won't help. You would only get more insufferable."

His gaze darkened and he stepped forward, his large body casting a long shadow over her. "You're right. A single night of hot sex wouldn't be enough. I've only had a taste and I already want more. If you gave me a night, I'd become insatiable."

She sucked in a breath and looked away. Be strong. Stay strong. "No, Ronin."

"That's the sexiest, breathless 'no' I've ever heard."

Hah! That's funny. Like he'd ever heard that word before. She scowled at him and promised herself that if he tried anything now, no matter how much she wanted it, she'd throw something at him. Like a knife.

"How's the wing?" she asked. Good. Neutral ground.

"It could use some more healing." His gaze continued to melt her on the spot.

Nope. Not touching that one. "Did the men have any first aid supplies in their packs?"

He shook his head and fanned his wings out. "It does feel nice to stretch."

She finally agreed with him on something. She followed suit, stretching her wings out wide. The middle of her wing pinched where the javelin arrow had broken the ulna. The bone still knitted together, frantically trying to mend the damage. The pierced patagium of her other wing had mostly healed, the occasional pain and throb annoying her. And the oldest and trivial of her recent wounds, the nicked shoulder, had completely healed, leaving a thin red line where a scar would eventually appear.

Father had told her aches and pains let her know she was still alive. Not sure she appreciated the life lesson all that much, but right now, even with the complaints of her injuries, the stretching felt great.

The gentle breeze through the trees played with her feathers. The cave hadn't allowed for a full wing stretch and leaving their wings out while climbing to the waterfall with only the metal bars for support and balance increased the danger of the wind picking them off.

Ronin watched her stretch, the hunger in his gaze lingering. He shuttered his expression and cleared his throat. "What's the plan?"

25

"Fate has a strange way of making plans."

— DAVID LEVITHAN

The plan was simple—get in, release Ava, and get out. Preferably without raising any alarms or losing a limb or life. Ronin listened to Cora's plan as they retraced their steps to Alara on the horses. At least Cora didn't have a martyr complex or grandiose plans of bringing the human with them.

Outside of town and out of sight from the main road, they rested before slathering mud over Ronin's wings. The mud muted the white of most of his feathers, but as far as camouflaging went, the attempt was rather futile. He kept his mouth shut, though. If Cora wanted to rub him down, he wouldn't complain. It had been a heroic effort on his part not to grab her, throw her down in the mud and find an even more enjoyable way to get dirty.

Currently, Cora crouched by his side behind a dense hedge, peering over the edge to watch the town through the trees. Ronin would rather watch Cora, but she'd probably slap him and tell him to focus.

"I just don't know where she'll go if her whole village has allowed her captivity and torture." Cora flicked a small rock with her finger.

"Not with us." He stretched out his wings, enjoying the freedom of movement without the splint. The swelling around the break had disappeared, leaving only a dull throb in the middle section of his wing if he overused it, or a pinch of pain if he moved the wrong way. Right now, "overuse" involved too much extending and flapping while standing. He wouldn't risk flying with it yet. If he rebroke the bone now, they'd never get back to the Eyrie.

The minx rolled her eyes. "Yes, Your Majesty. I've already agreed with you the other eight million times you mentioned it."

"First of all, stop calling me that. The proper way to address me is 'Your Highness' or 'Oh My God.' Second, you're exaggerating. We've discussed Ava maybe five times, tops." He liked it when she got all sassy and spoke back to him like this. No one else in the Eyrie dared, except his sister and father. "I don't particularly care where she goes. I just want to find out what she knows."

Cora blinked at him.

"What?"

"Just wondering when you were going to mention the bard training."

Goes and knows. He'd rhymed unintentionally. "Cute."

She dipped her chin. "If you wanted to get more information, maybe you should've let one of the hunters live long enough to question."

He scowled. The thought had occurred to him, too, but the idea struck him as he hurtled the second man over the cliff's edge. A little too late to recover that one. He'd been so focused on securing Cora's safety he hadn't thought two to three moves ahead. His father would've been so disappointed in him.

A gentle breeze teased Cora's black hair, whipping the part that had a streak of white across his face. The little slaps of hair reminded him to focus, but before they arrived at the outskirts of the fishing village, his mind kept drifting back to that kiss and how good Cora felt in his arms.

Cora glanced at him, her dark eyes unreadable in the night. "I could go alone."

"One of us is trained for close combat and it's not you."

"And one of us is also the heir of the Eyrie who has

bright white wings that stand out like a nudist at court."

"You slathered dirt over them."

"Not enough. You still don't blend in well."

He leaned in, savouring the fresh sea scent lingering on her skin that reminded him of clear blue waters. "You sound worried."

"Of course, I'm worried," she hissed.

Ronin sighed. Of course, she was. She'd be a fool not to be. And Cora was never the fool. If anything happened to him, she would be dead on arrival and her father as well. He loved his own father, but the king didn't pause to think all the time. He was methodical and calculating, but if his family was threatened, he reacted. If no one was present to advise or temper his reaction, his knee jerk response tended to err on the side of pain.

Ronin hadn't set out to remind Cora of the consequences of failure. He sighed again.

"Anymore heavy breathing over there and I'm going to have to insist I go in your place," Cora said.

"That's not happening."

She pursed her lips.

"I've got this," he said.

She dropped her shoulders. "Try not to kill her."

He winked and stepped out from behind the bush. With light steps, he maneuvered from the tree line to the rear of the cabin that backed onto the forest. They'd watched the village all day. Cora identified this house as Ava's—she'd always known where the woman lived—and someone came by three times a day with a small food basket and left with it empty.

Ronin waited in the shadows. Firelight flickered down the street. Raucous laughter travelled from one of the buildings on the other end of town. The bellows echoed around the buildings and down the street. The pub. No footsteps though, so the drunks remained there for now.

He unsheathed his knife, opened the door to Ava's house and slipped inside.

Ava sat in a wooden chair in the middle of the room. Her hands were bound to the armrests and her ankles to the chair legs. A pool of urine drenched the floorboards under the seat and blood spatter decorated her clothing. Otherwise, the inside of the cabin was exactly as he'd expected from the outside—wood slatted walls, a ladder to reach a loft with a bedroom and the underlining smell of pine. Small, and with the internal doors already open, easy to determine they were alone without having to move from his spot.

Ava's head swayed back and forth. She didn't look up or register someone had entered her home, but he saw enough of her face to know the men he killed deserved their deaths all over again.

Her face was swollen, her eyes and her jaw were bruised, and someone had tied a cloth around her head to gag her.

"Time hasn't treated you well," he said.

Her head snapped up and her eyes widened.

He stepped farther into the room, closing the distance so they could speak in quieter tones. He knelt by the chair, careful to avoid the pool at the base.

"If I take the gag out, will you scream?"

She stared at him.

"I don't plan on hurting you. I have some questions, but I also came to free you. For obvious reasons, I'd prefer not to alert your fellow humans."

She blinked at him.

"Can I trust you not to cry out if I remove the gag and promise not to hurt you?"

She hesitated, shifting in her wet seat. Her gaze scanned the room, looking side to side. She nodded.

Of course, she could lie and scream the moment he removed the gag, but she'd die before any help reached her.

Ronin tugged the gag from her mouth. The cloth fell around her shoulders like a soggy necklace.

Ava licked her cracked lips and swallowed. "Why?"

He rested his arm on his bent knee, still crouching in front of her so they were close to eye level. "You can thank Cora for this. She likes you."

Ava's pained expression softened briefly. "I don't deserve it."

Ronin agreed, but freeing Ava wasn't his goal for this rescue mission. "We know you told the men about us and our injuries."

"I didn't tell those *men* anything." She winced. "At least not right away. I told my dad. I didn't even mean to, it just slipped out that Jacoby was dead. He asked how I knew."

"Who's Jacoby?"

"My fiancé."

"How'd you know he was dead? When we spoke, his party was still missing."

"Cora had his dagger."

So, she had spotted it. He'd hoped the lighting too poor for her to identify the weapon. Dread shimmied along his spine. If Ava knew Cora killed her fiancé, this could be another set-up.

"I didn't want to marry that leather-skinned dolt. I may not be besties with Cora, but I knew her well enough and Jacoby even more to know she killed him because she had no choice. He deserved it." Ava bit her lip. "This wasn't the news my family wanted, but Cora did me a favour."

"But then your father had some questions."

She nodded and flinched. Her head must hurt even worse than it looked.

He got up and found a cup and water pitcher. After he filled the cup with water, he walked back to Ava. Wedging his dagger between the straps and the armrest, he cut through the bindings.

"Thank you." Ava took the glass of water with her free hand. "Yes. My father had a lot of questions and then those men came to town and started asking more questions, offering money for answers. And then they were in here asking even more. My father sold me out for five gold coins."

He nodded, a sinking feeling tugging at his gut. "Where's your father?"

Her face jerked and her mouth turned down as if she tried not to puke and swallowed it back. He didn't need her to answer. Her father had outed his own daughter for money, thinking no harm would come from it. When he saw how they treated Ava, he tried to stop them, or maybe he just criticized their method. Whatever he did, they eliminated him swiftly.

"I'm sorry," he said.

She bit her lip and nodded, gaze turning glassy.

He reached forward and cut the binding on her other arm. "What did you tell them?"

"I told them about the dagger and your injuries."

He nodded.

"They already knew about you. They described you down to the feathers."

"Were they King Aeneas' men?"

She shook her head.

Ronin rocked back on his heels. "Who are they?"

"They're a group of jackasses who formed a resistance of sorts. They call themselves MAS. It's an acronym for 'Men Against Sapavians,' but it stands for a whole lot more. The king has hinted at peeling back some of the forgetting, using non-electrical technology to benefit our society and relieve some of our daily stresses. So now, in addition to wanting a war against the Eyrie, they wish to depose the king as well. They spent most of the time here bragging about how they sabotaged your meeting with him."

Ronin's mouth grew dry. The water in the pitcher suddenly looked very inviting. He didn't know what to say or ask next, so he cut her legs free from the chair.

"Take me with you." She spoke into the glass of water she cradled in both hands.

"No." He stood up and sheathed his dagger.

"I can't stay here. They think I'm a spy. All those years of receiving anonymous tips about the salmon runs and this is how they thank me. They will not be gentle. Or kind. If you leave me here, you may as well slit my throat now."

"No." He turned and walked toward the door.

"I'll do whatever you want."

Ronin froze and glanced over his shoulder.

Ava staggered to her feet and lifted her chin. "I'll make you happy."

Ronin gaped at her. What could she possibly mean by that? "Doing what?"

"Whatever you want." Her hand drifted down her torn shirt to trace the line of her breast. "I know I don't look too great right now, but I clean up well. I will devote myself to you. I can be your mistress."

Ronin sighed and grabbed the shawl. Ava wasn't

the first woman or man to make that offer, but she was the first to do it under duress. It was all kinds of wrong and made his skin itch. He wanted to recoil or yell at her to stop, but he did neither. He took two steps to reach her.

Her lip trembled, but she held her head high.

"I scare the crap out of you." He wrapped the shawl around her shoulders. "Why would you offer such a thing?"

"You might scare me a little." Her swollen lip twitched. "But you're also...you're also very fascinating."

Unbelievable.

"You're going to leave here," he said. "Slip away in the night with whatever you can take with you. Make up a believable story and find a new place to live."

She shook her head.

"The answer is no, Ava." He looked away so he didn't have to see her expression.

"You can protect me."

He barked out a laugh. "I can barely protect myself right now."

"Or Cora?"

"Or Cora. We're on the run and eventually we'll leave. We can't take you with us. Why would you think I have the power to protect you?"

"You're the king of the Eyrie."

Ronin sighed. "No, I'm the prince. You're thinking

of my father, but he'd never risk the kingdom by coming here himself."

She shook her head. Dark brown hair falling across her face. "I know who your father was. With him dead, though, doesn't that make you the king?"

And just like that, his world tumbled down.

26

"Bad news isn't wine. It doesn't improve with age."

— COLIN POWELL

R onin's vision wavered and his grip on the dagger loosened. Ava said something else and a blurry image of her grew closer. Time slowed and his heart thudded. The room swayed.

Dad was dead?

Someone gripped his arm and shoved him to the side. Tripping over his feet, he staggered a few steps.

Time sped up to reality. His vision cleared.

A few feet away, Cora held Ava. Her dagger hilt stuck out from Ava's abdomen.

Ava dropped a knife. The weapon clattered against the wood floor. When had she grabbed that?

"S...s...s...sorry," Ava said. "Hoped...he'd go for first option."

Cora held Ava, iron grip on her arms and helped her walk back to the chair. Setting her down, Cora took a few steps back and knelt to speak to her. "They tied you up and told you they'd let you go if you killed us?"

Ava jerked her head up and down once. Colour drained from her cheeks.

"Did they know we were coming?"

"No...They hoped."

Cora nodded. "Is everything you told Ronin the truth, or did you lie to get free?"

"T...truth." Ava closed her eyes and took a deep shaking breath. "More."

Cora waited.

"Members of MAS betrayed King Aeneas."

That wasn't more, she'd already told him as much earlier. Ronin stepped closer. What trickery was she up to now?

Ava's gaze flicked to Ronin. Her body trembled. "Just like you...were...betrayed."

She sucked in a breath and held it.

Cora straightened from her crouched position. She hesitated and glanced at Ronin. "Do you know who betrayed the king of the Eyrie?"

She must've heard Ava's news. His stomach sunk. Someone killed his father. Just like that he was gone.

His last words to Ronin were, "Don't let me down." And he had. Did Father know he'd failed his mission before he died?

"N...no," Ava answered Cora's question. She didn't know who betrayed Father.

Ronin's mind scrambled. They could have been separate incidences, but logic said the two betrayals had to be linked. His gut churned again. Only a few people knew of his plans to leave the Eyrie to meet the king of Iom. He refused to believe his family or Cora's double crossed him. There had to be a mole in the castle. What else had they discovered? What other secrets had they uncovered?

Cora's expression looked pained, like her mind had run through the same sequence. She studied the woman in front of them. "If I leave the dagger in, you might have a chance of living if the blade didn't hit anything vital. Wait until we're gone, get help, staunch the blood flow and stitch the wound, avoid infection and you could live." Cora paused. "Or I can take the dagger out now. Stomach wounds are a terrible way to go. You'll hopefully bleed out before organ failure or sepsis kicks in."

Ava's lips twitched and she rolled her head back up to look at Cora. "I'm dead either way. Leave me to make my own decision." Her gaze dropped to the dagger sticking out of her stomach. She was panting now. Her time was running out. "Fitting that my fiancé's dagger...be the one to...kill me. Seems I was... destined for it."

Cora forced her face to relax, stepped forward to cradle Ava's head in her hands and pressed her lips to her forehead. "Go easy into the night wind, Ava."

A tear streaked down Ava's cheek. "In a different world...we'd be friends."

"Great friends." Cora jerked away from Ava, turned on her heel and walked out of the wooden cabin without looking back.

Ronin paused before following.

Ava slumped in the chair, her breathing coming short and shallow. He hadn't wanted things to end this way. Cora had been optimistic in her assessment. Without a medical mage or the village doctor to treat her immediately, Ava faced a painful death.

As if hearing his thoughts, Ava lifted her heavy head again. Her gaze flashed with defiance. "I would've made a fucking great mistress."

Right up until she tried to stab him. Why did she think he was interested? He'd never want someone who stayed with him out of obligation or servitude. No, thank you. But he didn't have the heart to tell off a dying woman.

"Yes, you would have," he said.

Her gaze flickered with resignation and she nodded. "If you hurt her, I'll fucking haunt you."

Memories of this moment would haunt him anyway.

With a deep breath, Ronin stepped from the cabin and into the cool night air. He made his way along the rocky path to the woods where Cora waited. Without a word, she turned from the village and the bellow of drunk patrons echoing down the streets and followed the path of grass to where they'd tied up the horses.

"How did you know?" he asked.

Cora's smile was grim as she untied the horses' reins from the thick tree branch. "It doesn't take that long to untie someone and ask questions."

"So, you assumed she detained me with her expert ninja skills?" Though he used light-hearted words, the news of Father's death pushed down on him like an invisible weight. Dead? Gone?

Cora gripped the saddle and sighed, resting her forehead against the hard leather. "I assumed she'd try to seduce you. Either to get you to take her with us or to lure you closer to kill."

"That's one hell of an assessment."

She thumped her head against the saddle. "Okay, it was just taking too long, and I was worried."

Ronin swung up into the saddle. The black horse huffed and shifted her weight side to side. The wild beast didn't seem to appreciate his wings and made a point of letting him know. "You have great intuition."

Cora laughed as she mounted the horse but sounded bitter. As if tainted by poison, the happy sound spoiled the moment she released it, and the laugh ended in a choked sob.

They were both acting to hide the pain.

They didn't have time for Ronin to figure out how to make it better for either of them. No time for consolation. She'd just lost a friend and she'd been the one to plunge the dagger into her stomach. Nothing he said or did right now would take away the grief and guilt that most likely consumed her. Just like nothing she said or did right now would take away the pain of losing his father.

"Come on." Cora nudged the cow horse and turned the mare to the path south. Once again, Cora was right. They needed to move before Ava was discovered.

"I didn't fall for it, you know," he spoke to her back, trying to claw his way out of the grief. "The seduction."

Cora straightened in her saddle. "Of course not. You're impervious to the charms of a common woman."

"What in the bird-loving hell does that mean?"

The outline of her body, barely visible under the night sky and the dimming firelight from the village, tensed. "You're always surrounded by women fawning over you. I assumed you'd become impervious or at least desensitized to seduction."

Ronin snorted but remained quiet. He knew a loaded comment when he heard one and Cora was looking for a fight. Part of him wanted to give her one.

They had a long trip ahead and only each other for company, she was bound to get her wish eventually. "I'm sorry about your friend."

"I'm sorry about your father," she whispered.

Was she though? She hated his father. Her words were more for his benefit and to make him feel better than they were to express her own feelings. "Thank you."

27

"You don't cross my mind. You live in it."

— UNKNOWN

Cora let the cool freshwater from the river glide from her hands and run down her body, caressing her skin like icy fingertips on a hot day. As if she could wash away the guilt of killing Ava, she let the water rush by her, cleansing, rejuvenating, bone-numbing. If only it could take away the grief plaguing Ronin from his father's death, too. He was gradually working his way through it, but his pain still lurked in the shadows of his gaze and hardness around the mouth.

Under the new moon, they'd fled Alara with the

limited light from the stars. For the last four days, they'd travelled on the roads at night, banking on the humans' fear of the dark and the unknown to keep them relatively safe.

Frankly, Cora was amazed they hadn't run into anything.

The only benefit to travelling in almost near darkness was if anyone did spot them, they were unlikely to make out their wings as long as they kept Ronin's dirty.

After nights of hard travel and days of restless, broken sleep, filled with tense fear of discovery, they'd found a little bathing nook off one of the feeding rivers. With no signs of recent visitors, they decided to make camp for the day to rest at the private location.

In case they had to leave quickly, they made camp on the southern side of the bridge so they could flee in the direction of their destination without having to cross the river.

Cora ran more cool water over her neck and shoulders and rolled her head back and forth. If only she could sneak off into the ocean and let the salt water heal her. She couldn't let Ronin discover her secret though. One of many, he'd start asking questions and she had no answers.

Instead, content to enjoy the freshwater, she stretched her muscles to the point where it felt good, but almost painful. She moaned softly as she worked the tension from her shoulders.

"If you moan any louder, I'm going to have to ask

you what you're doing over there." Ronin growled from the campsite. He'd left to collect wood for a fire but returned remarkably fast.

Cora dropped down, covering herself with the water so only her head bobbed above the surface.

Ronin stalked into the campsite with an armful of dry branches and driftwood. He scowled at her hasty attempt at setting up the bedrolls. She'd wanted to bathe in private.

Ronin dropped the wood, turned his back to the water and started to set up the campsite.

Cora eyed her clothing resting on a rock near the shore. She wasn't a shy woman. Days filled with flying and nights spent abroad meant her body was a lean, mean flying machine. Even if she did have soft jiggly parts, she had nothing to be ashamed of. Something about being naked in front of Ronin, though, set her teeth on edge. It wasn't embarrassment or vulnerability. Oh no. And she certainly wasn't scared. Ronin was many things, but abusive or manipulative wasn't on the list of faults.

Nope. She didn't want to be naked around Ronin because she didn't trust herself. One heated look from him and she'd try to slap her body onto his. It had been too long without the companionship of a man. If Ronin showed any interest, any inclination he planned or wanted to seduce her, and she'd forget how much she hated him. She'd forget his arrogance and pig-headedness. She'd forget the painful past. All those things would get shoved out of the way so she could feel his body on hers, his hands stroking her skin, his tongue tasting her mouth, his—

"Cora?" Ronin called out from the shore. "Are you okay?"

"Yeah." She splashed some water around and scrubbed her already clean arm with a cloth. "Why do you ask?"

"Your face went red. Very red. Are you sure you're feeling all right? Did your injury get infected? I could take a look."

"Of course, I'm all right." She turned away. Why did he pick now to grow attentive and concerned? Why couldn't he mind his own business and let a girl fantasize in the bath?

"It's just..."

She stopped scrubbing and turned to Ronin. He'd moved to the edge of the water and considered the river as if he contemplated diving in. "You've been in there for a while."

"I was really dirty."

"Your skin or your mind?"

Said mind chose that moment to go blank and forget words. She sputtered.

"Because it looks to me like your daydreaming turned naughty." He removed his belt and reached behind him to unbutton the back of his shirt before pulling it off.

Oh, no. Why was he undressing?

"I think you're the one lost in a fantasy," she said.

He raised his eyebrow and pulled off his pants. The muscles in his arms and chest contracted and relaxed. "Did I mention in addition to your red face, you were caressing your breast and breathing hard?"

Her mouth suddenly became dry. "Lies," she croaked.

Ronin stepped into the water. He still wore his underwear, but it did little to hide his growing erection. "Do you want to know what I think?"

"Not particularly."

"I think you've been reminiscing about that kiss." He waded into the water, sucking in a breath when the cold river hit groin level. "I know I have."

Her face heated more but she refused to look away from his stormy gaze. The grief was gone. For the first time since leaving Alara, he saw only her, and the potency of his look shook every bone in her body.

Ronin was mesmerizing in predator mode. Devastating. He'd zeroed in on his prey and had sensed her weakness. She waded to the section of the river beside a massive boulder that jutted out of the water. Ronin changed his path to intercept her.

"I've been thinking about how good you felt in my arms." He stopped a foot away, the river rushing between them. "And now I can't help but wonder what other things would feel like."

"It's probably a good thing, then, that you chose to come into the cold water. You need to cool off." She crossed her arms over her bare chest. This close, Ronin could see below the surface of the clear water.

"It's not exactly what I would choose to *come into.*" His lip quirked.

She bit the inside of her mouth and tried not to laugh.

From the dance in Ronin's gaze, she failed to hide her amusement.

She lifted her chin. "I don't particularly care where you come."

"You kinky minx."

She squeezed her eyes shut. That's not what she meant, and he knew it. Her face grew warmer. Why did she have to blush so easily? She was a badass messenger spy. This was ridiculous. "Behave."

"Make me." He shot forward in the water, gripped her face in his hands and crushed his mouth against hers. None of the tender tease from earlier existed. This wasn't a gentle kiss. It was a demand, an admission of want and longing, a line drawn in the sand. It was bone-melting perfection.

He snaked one hand behind her neck to grip her hair at the back of her head and raised his other hand to squeeze her hip and pull her into the heat of his body. In the cold rushing river, his body was an inferno of need.

The numbness in her skin disappeared and she grew warm, very warm. Ronin's kiss travelled from her mouth to taste her skin. She wanted more. She wanted all of him.

She ran her hands along the hard planes of his back and grabbed his tight ass. She ground against his hard erection, wanting, begging. The thin layer of clothing doing nothing to dull the sensation of his member rubbing her most sensitive skin. God, she could ride him like this and come.

Ronin growled into her shoulder and nipped the skin. His erection strained against his underwear. She reached down, snaked her hands inside the thin material and gripped the hard shaft. She stroked him, up and down, and he growled again.

With quick, fluid movement, he grabbed her arms and pulled her up on the rock. She had to let go of his shaft but his mouth sucking on her nipple took away any complaints. His hot mouth on her cold skin stoked the fire inside. She burned with need. Need for him to be inside her. Now. She wrapped her legs around him and tried to pull him closer, to grind along that hard shaft again.

He smiled, lips twitching on her breast, and nipped her nipple. Instead of ending her torment, he pulled her farther out of the water and splayed her over the rocks. Water dripped down her body in rivulets. The wind playing on the surface of the river rushed by her exposed breasts. The ache between her legs intensified. She was so wet and ready. She needed him. Wanted him. And instead of giving her what she wanted, he slowly kissed his way down her body.

Her breasts grew heavy with desire. Her skin, hyper-aware tingled with anticipation. The ache between her legs became an almost painful throb.

He glanced up at her before lowering himself in the water to place his mouth on her. His hot tongue stroked her from the inside. He sucked on the sensitive nub. He devoured her passion and still she wanted more.

"You taste like perfection." Ronin continued to lick and suck.

She gripped his head, tangling her fingers in his silky hair and held him to her as he growled and consumed. The pressure inside built and built, threatening to explode. "Yes," she gasped, not sure what she was saying or responding to. All she knew is that if he stopped now, she would die.

"Did you hear that?" A man's voice cut through Cora's daze.

Ronin moved swiftly, pulling back and yanking Cora into the water. The freezing cold water extinguished the burning lust. Ronin pressed her into the large boulder he'd splayed her over moments ago.

"Probably some randy ducks. It's mating season," another man said, voice not as deep as his companion's.

Cora dropped her head back on the rock and squeezed her eyes shut. Though he made no sound,

Ronin's chest rumbled against hers with supressed laughter.

"I see smoke," the first man said.

Water splashed. Damn it. They spotted the campfire.

Ronin released her and eased away, stepping to the side, while still using the giant boulder for cover. He flicked his hands in the air.

She leaned forward and squinted. Was that supposed to mean something?

Ronin's expression grew pained.

"Do you see anyone?" one of the men hissed.

"It could be them."

Cora held her breath and inched her way to the edge of the rock.

"Probably some locals, sneaking away from their parents."

"This far from Cladding and Zircaloy? Doubtful," Guy One said. "We should check it out anyway."

"Fuck that. I'm not getting our gear wet. It's getting dark. Our stuff will never dry in time." With one of those ambiguous tones, Guy Two could actually be a woman with a low voice. Hard to tell.

"No, you nimrod. We'll take the bridge."

The nimrod groaned, probably realizing there'd be a delay in getting his or her dinner. Guy One said something else, but it was too faint for Cora to catch. Boots scuffed the river rock and a horse nickered. Were they actually going? Or was this a trap?

"Come on," Ronin whispered, suddenly standing beside her. "We need to move."

"Are they gone?" It would only take one arrow shot from the tree cover.

A horse snorted farther away, answering her question.

Thanks, horse.

Ronin peeked around the boulder. The tension eased from his shoulders. "They're gone."

Without another word, they bolted for the shore. Water splashed and sprayed. The drag slowed her down. They had to get to shore, get dressed and get away. Right now, they were naked and defenceless.

The trail around the river via the bridge would take the men at least ten minutes to complete. That wasn't a lot of time.

Cora scrambled up the rocky shore and pulled her pants on. The leather stuck to her dewy skin. With a curse, she hopped up and down, shoving her legs farther through the clothing. Some skin went along with the pants, but she got them on and quickly slapped on her flying vest. Normally she wore her shirt under the vest, but she'd worry about that later. Since the vest clasped together to accommodate her wings, it was easier to put on in a hurry. She clutched her shirt in one hand and turned to the horses, shaking out her wings in the process.

Already dressed and appearing unfazed, Ronin threw her bedroll at her. She snatched the bedroll from the air, grabbed her boots and ran for the cow horse.

The demon spawn raised her head from munching grass and eyed her approach.

"Come on, beast. Look lively." She strapped her gear to the horse and untied the reins. The horse's ears pricked forward. Laying the long boots and shirt over the back of the cow horse's neck, she gripped the saddle horn and swung up into the seat. The instant her ass hit the seat, her inner thighs and butt muscles complained.

She ignored the dull ache, tucked her boots and shirt under one of her arms and squeezed her legs.

The horse sighed and swayed side to side. Definitely not forward.

"Stop pissing around." Ronin hissed over his shoulder, his horse already on the move. Of course, he was a natural at this crap.

She clicked her tongue. The horse's ears pinged back, and she swished her tail.

Cora leaned forward, squeezed her legs again and gave the horse's belly a little nudge with her heels.

The horse shot forward. The quick, unexpected motion flung Cora back and almost out of the saddle. She flailed her free arm and wings. With her heart in her throat, she grabbed the pommel and held on for life, raced past Ronin and hurtled through the forest. The horse cleared a log and abruptly slid to a stop.

Cora flew forward, straight over the horse's head.

She instinctively flung out her wings. Pain lanced through the injured bone. Her wing faltered. She threw her hands out and braced her fall as she face-planted in dense moss. She skidded to a halt a foot away from two sets of hooves. Her boots thumped on the ground beside her.

"I'd give that dismount a nine," someone said.

"Most impressive tactical maneuver. I'd give her a perfect ten," another man said with a much deeper voice.

Their voices didn't sound familiar, but their accents did. The men from the river.

"Cora," Ronin hissed. "Get up."

She groaned and scrambled to her feet. Dirt and strings of dry moss coated her mouth and she spat out a leaf. She tucked her wet wings in tightly against her back and ignored the scream of pain reminding her of her injuries. When the pain eased to a dull throb, she straightened and lifted her chin.

Two hunters, a man and a woman, sat in their saddles on almost identical horses. Brown horses. Big stalky horses. Horses that looked like they listened to their riders. Guess that made the "nimrod" from the river a woman. They wore leather armour made for moving quickly and blending in with the forest...and not to hunt pheasants. The swords strapped against their backs spoke of a different prey.

As Cora continued to study them from the wrong end of a notched arrow, she had an inkling of what they hunted. Their scarred faces showed exposure to the elements and the creases around their eyes spoke of times when they weren't so serious. But they weren't old, probably only a few years older than Cora or Ronin. They were experienced hunters.

The man on the left made eye contact with her and cursed. The arrowhead aimed at her chest dipped a fraction before he corrected it.

His partner looked over at him and raised a dark bushy eyebrow. "You okay, Phil?"

Phil narrowed his eyes and scanned Cora's body, head to toe and back again. "Do all female sapavians look like you?"

She stiffened. What the hell as that supposed to mean?

Phil turned to his companion. "We've been missing out."

The woman snorted but kept her aim trained on Ronin.

The crown prince was somewhere behind her, probably firmly mounted on his horse without a white hair out of place. She didn't need to see Ronin to know he'd be scowling.

Cora leaned forward. She needed to focus on more pressing things, like what other weapons did these hunters carry?

"That's close enough," the woman aiming the arrow at Ronin grumbled.

Phil sighed. "Ease up, Karla. We have a message."

Karla looked at the sky as if divine intervention would save her from this situation.

Cora waited. They all waited. Nothing happened.

Cora carefully took a step back. Then another. And another. She made it to where her stupid cow horse sniffed the moss, looking for food.

Ronin pulled up beside her on his black mare, concern flashing in his gaze briefly before he turned to the hunters. "Are you King Aeneas' hunters?"

They nodded.

Somehow, the news didn't reassure Cora.

"If you're here to finish the job, why haven't you released the arrows yet?" Ronin asked.

Karla sighed, long and dramatic. "We're not here to kill you. We're here to deliver a message."

"Your notched arrows are doing a mighty fine job doing the delivery for you."

Karla and Phil exchanged a glance and lowered their bows and arrows together.

"Your surprise attack startled us," Phil nodded at Cora. "I've never seen a woman used as a sapavian missile before."

Cora ignored him and grabbed her boots to stuff her feet into them. Once booted, she shoved her foot in the stirrup and hefted her aching body into the saddle. Everything complained. Even her vagina throbbed, but for completely different reasons.

The cow horse snorted. The vicious beast probably

already planned her next attempt at murder. These last four days hadn't been filled with joyful riding.

"What's your message?" Ronin drew himself straighter in the saddle.

Karla spoke this time. "He'd like to meet with you in Giga."

A bark of laughter erupted from Ronin. "His men drugged and abducted me the last time we were to meet. They planned to torture me before slitting my throat. They spoke of how they'd do it, too. Right in front of me. How they'd make a spectacle out of my long, drawn-out, humiliating demise." Ronin's jaw tensed and anger flashed in his gaze. His free hand rested on the pommel of the sword and during his speech, he'd wrapped his fingers around the grip.

Though Ava had provided a different narrative for the abductors' actions, they still couldn't trust she told the truth. Cora knew Ronin a little too well, it seemed. He'd lay the blame at the human king's feet until someone else corroborated Ava's information.

Karla shook her head. "That's the second part of our message."

"Maybe you should've led with the second part," Phil muttered.

Karla waved her partner off, keeping her focus on Ronin. "The king had no part in that. He was betrayed by a rebel group known as MAS."

28

"Each betrayal begins with trust."

— MARTIN LUTHER

Cora perched on the back of her horse and stared at the rear ends in front of her. Horse butts and hunter butts. They were all a bunch of buttheads as far as she was concerned. Honestly, they needed to work on their communication skills.

She waited for Phil and Karla to pull ahead a little before turning to Ronin. The heir of the Eyrie wore a stern expression. No, not the heir, anymore. The king.

She sucked in a breath. She couldn't use "Majesty" for Ronin anymore. They hadn't spoken about his father's death, not since Alara. Ronin would talk when and if he wanted to. Until then, she took her cue from him, and kept her thoughts to herself.

Cora's mind reeled and tried to keep up. Though she hoped for Ronin's sake, Ava received incorrect information or lied about King Edgar's death, with everything else going on, things didn't look good.

Regardless of Ronin's current title, she'd seen this particular look often enough during his formal court appearances when she caught glimpses of him through the crowd. With his eyebrows bunched, forehead creased, and jaw clenched, he gripped the reins tightly and sat stiffly. These things could be explained away with his inexperience with riding, but when paired with all his other tells, Cora knew how he felt.

Ronin was worried.

Good. So was she.

"Why are you doing this?" she hissed, keeping her gaze trained on the hunters. "They can't be trusted. They've already betrayed our people. They betrayed you." And these particular humans made fun of her, which was completely irrelevant and insignificant in the face of a peace pact between their two nations.

Ronin drew in long even breaths in a visible effort to calm himself. "They could've shot us down outside the campsite."

"Actually," Karla bellowed over her shoulder. "We could've shot you *in* the campsite, but we thought it best to let you finish dressing."

"Figured you'd be more receptive to the message." Phil nodded. "Plus, we were completely mesmerized by Cora's intricate dressing routine that we needed a moment to recover."

Heat spread across her face and neck. She clutched the reins and imagined punching them both in the face.

"I have to admit, it mesmerized me, too," Ronin grumbled. He didn't sound pleased, though.

"Screw all of you," she said.

Karla twisted in her saddle. "Is that some kind of sapavian offer?"

"If so, I'm down," Phil called out.

She glared at both of them. Karla winked before turning back around.

"They had an opportunity to kill us and didn't need an elaborate ruse to do so," Ronin said. "I believe their story. It matches what Ava told us."

"Your previous abductors also had ample opportunity to kill you," she pointed out. "Instead, they drugged, chained and dragged you through Iom."

Ronin's jawline bunched as he clenched his teeth.

"Has it not occurred to you these guys have the same motives, they're just going about it in a nice way?"

"Of course, it's crossed my mind." He glared at the path ahead of them. "Did it cross yours that we don't really have a choice here? These two are not amateur hunters."

No, they weren't. They were trained killers. Their movement and posture gave away their skill more than any words could express. If they somehow missed or only injured them with arrows, they were armed with daggers and swords. Cora was good with her weapon but not that good. Ronin excelled with a sword, but how much fight could he put up, two against one with an arrow lodged in his chest? He might manage to cut them both down, but not before she was taken out and not before he sustained a lot of additional injuries. Then he'd probably bleed out.

She sighed and nodded, acknowledging his point.

"We may as well take the time to discuss something else," Ronin said, stony expression fading away.

Oh no. That didn't sound like a conversation she wanted to have. "And what's that?"

"Your grip."

Her grip? What the hell was he talking about? She hadn't gripped—Oh.

Oh.

Instead of sputtering, she took a deep breath, relaxed her face, and turned to Ronin. His knee was within kicking distance. She'd strike there first. "Excuse me?"

His gaze twinkled with mischief. "How you hold the shaft is very important."

Her mouth dropped open. She promptly shut it and glared. He hadn't been complaining about how she held his shaft less than an hour ago. Instead, he'd thrown her up against the boulder to demonstrate just how pleasing he found her grip.

Her body pulsed with an unresolved aching need.

So not happening right now.

He chuckled and held his hands up in mock surrender. "Okay, shaft was the wrong word. Worth it. I love seeing fiery murder flash in your eyes. I meant your dagger hilt. I noticed you prefer the RGEO."

"The RGEO." Seriously? He wanted to discuss dagger grips?

"Yeah, it stands for reverse grip, edge out. It's when the dagger is held—"

"I know what it is." She stopped glaring at him and turned back to watching the king's hunters leading their little procession. Straightening her spine in the saddle, she readjusted her wings. Her back muscles screamed, begging for a long stretch.

"And yes," she said. "I use a reverse grip. So what? It ensures the cutting edge is always facing the enemy and reduces the chances of accidentally cutting myself. I'm not from the Eagle Clan, or the Hawks. My dagger is primarily for defence."

Ronin nodded. "But it also gives you limited reach and if your attacker is directly in front of you, it limits your range of motion. You can't make any...deep thrusting moves."

Did he seriously go there? The ache between her legs screeched that yes, yes he did. She smothered a groan. "And deep thrusting is important?"

"It is to me." His grin grew. "Especially for a frontal assault. I could demonstrate, if you want."

She widened her eyes. "I don't think I could handle a frontal assault from you."

"I think we've already established you can *handle* me just fine."

Dear bird lord, this innuendo was going to kill her. The memory of holding him in her hand flared up and made her throat dry. His mouth on her skin. His wicked tongue...

"Are we still talking about daggers?"

"Of course," he said, completely unaware of the heat he stirred inside her. "I agree with your reasons for using the RGEO, but I think you would benefit from practicing the hammer grip."

She squeezed her eyes shut briefly. The hammer grip was the most predominant dagger hold as well as the most instinctual. If she asked a random peasant from the Eyrie without any combat training to pick up a knife and come at her, nine out of ten times, the person would use the hammer grip, holding it like, well, a hammer.

Used more for offensive tactics, the forward grip allowed for greater reach and finesse. It also provided no subterfuge as it made the dagger and, therefore, the wielder's intent, more visible. The other downside was an opponent could trap the arm easier since it extended past the body more.

Cora had quickly switched to the RGEO technique as it fit better with her needs. Ronin wasn't wrong in his assessment though. Practicing dagger combat defence tactics with a hammer grip and switching grips would be beneficial and increase her ability to protect herself. Sometimes, the best defence was a great offence.

Of course, none of this came immediately to her mind when Ronin mentioned the hammer grip.

Nope. A different kind of hammer flooded her dirty mind and now her body pulsed harder with need.

Ronin drew his horse in closer. "I can still taste you."

She stiffened.

"And I want more."

Ronin waited, his amused expression had faded to something else. As if he read her thoughts and sensed her reaction to his words, his gaze now smouldered. Ripping away some sort of internal security screen, he let her see his real emotions, the ones simmering, barely contained beneath his mask. He wanted her. He was thinking of her naked. Of how she tasted and turned to putty in his arms.

Ronin leaned toward her in his saddle, lust and naughty promises clouding his expression.

"You two need to stop that," Karla barked out from ahead. "I can't handle this kind of blatant sexuality."

"Prude." Phil snorted and then twisted around on his saddle to look at Cora. "If the two of you want to go at it, don't let our presence stop you."

Cora flipped him off.

Thunder streaked across Ronin's face. He was now contemplating murder.

Phil turned to Ronin, ignored the promised rage in his expression and asked, "How exactly do sapavians do it?"

Was that a trick question? Did he think their anatomy was that different from humans? They shared a common ancestor. Some historians argued sapavians hadn't diverged enough evolutionarily speaking and were still only a sub species of *Homo sapiens*. They theorized humans and sapavians could therefore inter-breed and produce viable offspring.

Cora shuddered.

"I imagine the wings get in the way. Probably uncomfortable to lie down on them," Karla said with surprising insight. "They probably do a lot of stuff from behind."

Phil nodded but didn't turn back around. Instead, he stayed twisted in his saddle and moved his gaze between Ronin and Cora. "So do you call it doggy style, too, or is it called birdy style?"

Cora smacked her face with her palm. Seriously. These were the professional killers the king of Iom sent after them?

Karla snorted and then proceeded to choke on her laughter.

Ronin shook his head but refused to answer.

Like hell she'd say anything.

Phil grinned like he said the wittiest thing known to humankind.

Boys.

Arriving at their destination—which may or may not result in their painful demise—couldn't come soon enough.

29

"The best way to find out if you can trust somebody is to trust them."

— ERNEST HEMINGWAY

The fireplace crackled and snapped as the others gathered their supplies and set up around the camp. Ronin stood in the shadows and surveyed the site. It wasn't the best location to defend, but not the worst, either.

Phil considered the current layout of the campsite and hesitated. When he threw his bedroll down beside Cora's, Ronin chuckled.

Like Cora would put up with that.

Phil stepped over the soon-to-be-removed mat and

approached Ronin. What did this hunter want? Instead of talking right away, Phil turned to stand by Ronin's side to watch the campsite with him.

"I think we should have two on and two off tonight," Phil said.

"Of course, you do."

Though Ronin wanted a chance to speak with Cora privately, he'd take the opportunity to ensure her safety first.

Cora stomped around camp, saw Phil's offensive bedroll and without missing a beat, moved hers to the other side of the fire.

Phil shook his head, a smile tugging at his lips. "Do all female sapavians look like her?"

Look like her? Is that all the hunter saw? Irritation stirred in Ronin. Of course, she was beautiful. Of course, others would notice. And of course, they wouldn't pause to see how much more Cora offered than a striking face. "There's no one quite like Cora."

"Does she know?"

Ronin shifted his weight on his feet and crossed his arms. "Knowing Cora, no. And if you told her, she'd spend the next half an hour explaining how much of a turkey you were for even thinking it."

That wasn't entirely true. Cora was intelligent. She'd know she was attractive, but she wasn't the stereotypical beauty and would write off any attention her looks garnered. She wasn't the type to use her beauty as a weapon, nor would she drown in an inflated sense of entitlement. No. Not Coraline Cormorant. She'd clinically note her positive attributes and log them in her brain along with her flight times and boot size.

"A turkey?" Phil frowned. "Is that an insult to sapavians?"

"Would you like to be called a strutting bird with a small brain?"

Phil chuckled and shook his head. "Feisty thing. I like that."

Ronin bit back a curse and clamped his mouth shut.

Phil studied him out of the corner of his eye, not because he attempted subtlety, more likely so he could keep his eyes on the campsite and Cora. "Don't worry. I'm no competition to you."

Ronin turned to him and glared. "I don't know what you're talking about."

Phil rocked back on his heels. "Sure you do. You have a thing for your bodyguard. Or is she a colleague? Some sort of princess? I'm not entirely sure what her role is in all this."

"Her role is none of your business." He had a thing for Cora. A large thing. A thing that got bigger every time he thought about her.

Phil's knowing grin spread and he raised his eyebrows. Kingsman or not, if he kept flashing Ronin that smug expression, Ronin planned to punch him, and keep punching him until the look disappeared.

As if sensing Ronin had reached his limit for his bullshit, Phil shifted his attention back to the campground. The amusement fled from his expression and he straightened.

Cora stood a few feet away, hands on her hips and a scowl on her face.

Ah, didn't hear her approaching, did you?

"There's something I don't understand," she said.

Phil sighed and held his hands out to his side. "I know, but it's true. I'm still single."

The way Cora narrowed her eyes at Phil made Ronin smile. She wasn't amused. And she certainly wasn't falling for the other man's charm.

Not that he was worried, or anything.

Maybe they'd have to flip a coin to see who got to punch him first.

"I don't get how you made it around the river so fast," Cora said.

Phil frowned. "What do you mean?"

Ronin's brain scrambled to pick up what she was referring to as well. Where was she going with this? They were in the river when they heard Phil and Karla. As soon as the hunters left, they ran for shore, got dressed and made a run for it. They knew it was going to be close.

"It would've taken you at least ten minutes to get up to the bridge, cross it and make your way to our campsite," Cora explained. "Yet you saw me shove my pants on and commented on my improvised dressing technique. Those pants were the first thing I threw on when I made it to shore and I know it didn't take me ten minutes to get out of the river. How'd you make it around so fast?"

Phil still frowned. "We didn't."

Cora stilled. Her hand drifted to the hilt of her dagger. Though the sun had dipped below the treeline and encased their world in shadows, enough light streaked through the trees to illuminate the flash of understanding in her steely gaze.

There were two people unaccounted for, most likely two men, and they probably picked up their trail and followed, after they found Cora and Ronin's empty campsite. They'd be less than ten minutes behind if they set off right away. The presence of the hunters would've held them back for a bit, but now they just had to wait for an opportunity.

He gripped his sword hilt. "We made camp about fifteen minutes ago," he answered her unspoken question in a whisper.

Phil, for all his silly banter, wasn't a simpleton. He must've figured out what Cora's observations meant. He fluidly switched from easy going to serious, moving to a ready position, gaze alert.

Meanwhile, Karla, oblivious to their conversation, whistled and puttered around the campsite like a content fisherman's wife waiting for the daily catch to come in.

A branch snapped. The three of them crouched

and tensed scanning the trees. Without a word, Phil slipped away and disappeared into the shadows.

Ronin looked back at the campsite. Karla had disappeared as well.

Fuck. They were good.

He pulled his dagger and jerked his chin toward the trees. Though they stood near the treeline, they were still too exposed, and Cora had been shot with two too many arrows already. They needed more cover.

Cora didn't argue. He appreciated that about her. She'd dig her heels in, bicker and argue, but she'd also choose her times. Now was not the time to disagree. She knew he had experience and training for this sort of situation, and she followed his lead.

Cora unsheathed her dagger and seamlessly flipped it into a reverse grip. The harpy winked at him when she passed, her wings smacking his face.

Little love taps.

She totally wanted him.

And he wanted nothing more than to grab her and give her a love tap of his own, but the timing was off. Way off. He needed to give his own head a shake.

He followed Cora into the darkening forest. She nodded at a deer trail to the right while she stepped onto another one leading to the left.

He didn't want to leave her. He should be at her side to protect her. And if he ever voiced such foolishness to the accomplished messenger who faced sea monsters and thunderbirds, she'd stab him out of annoyance.

He nodded and took the other path. They moved slow and low, scanning the foliage and treeline, listening to the sounds of the forest, waiting for the men who must've followed them from the river to give themselves away.

Another branch snapped to his left.

And another.

Dirt crunched, branches swayed.

A man grunted.

Instead of running to the sounds and exposing his position, Ronin waited. He edged closer toward another trail that intersected with the one he was on. The forest was riddled with these little paths.

Quietly, he crouched by a large bush filled with waxy leaves and giant fragrant flowers.

More sounds of a skirmish echoed through the forest, bouncing off the trees.

Ronin gripped his dagger and resisted the urge to call out to Cora. She was fine.

Footsteps crunched on the intersecting trail.

Ronin tensed, crouched lower, ready to spring.

A dark shadow passed the bush. The air rippled behind the man in an invisible wake. He smelled of smoke and meat.

While his heart thudded and Ronin fought to keep his breathing steady and controlled, he waited instead of lunging. *Take another deep breath. Calm down. Control.*

He waited another second. And another.

When the shadow man had moved down the path toward the sounds of the scuffle, Ronin emerged from the bushes. He stepped on the path behind the man and stayed low, ready, and silent. The sun had long disappeared, leaving them in the dregs of light until the moon and stars showed up.

Ronin's injured wing snagged a branch.

He froze.

The branch, ensnared in his feathers, pulled in the gentle breeze. He moved back, lifting his wings. The branch swung free.

Ronin breathed out slowly. With a step forward, he focused on the dark shadow stalking ahead. A twig snapped under Ronin's foot.

The shadow spun around.

Fuck.

Ronin drew his other dagger and crouched. He couldn't hide and an ambush attack was out now. Faded light struck the shadow's face. Deep creases and a scar running down his face emphasized his animal-like snarl. His dark gaze carried no emotion, only death.

The shadow lunged. Ronin spun with the man. Flipping his dagger into a reverse hold, Ronin thrust his fist out, slicing the other man's arm.

No howl of pain.

The shadow kept moving, pivoting to renew his attack, like some sort of unfeeling machine. They met in a clash of daggers. Their knives flashed under the night sky as they thrust, blocked, and sliced.

Ronin let his instincts and training take over, slipping into that zone reserved for fighting where he turned off all his other worries, focusing instead on stimulus and tells.

Ronin's training partner called him chaos in motion.

At first, Ronin had been insulted, because it implied sloppy skills, but soon he realized his partner referred to the unpredictable nature of how he fought.

No one was immune to knives, though, and this guy was good.

Shadowman was smooth and smooth was fast.

Ronin ducked and narrowly missed getting kicked in the head. He lashed out in a slashing combination.

Shadowman stepped off the centre line at an angle and eluded Ronin's attacks. Ronin cursed again. Shadowman was hard to read and didn't fight like anyone from training. If Ronin was chaos in motion, this guy was a storm of ambiguity.

Everything was angles.

But Ronin practiced patience. He'd outlast his opponent. Keeping his range of motion conserved, tight and controlled, he'd bleed this guy out if he had to. The weapons master always referred to a fighting box formed by the width of his shoulders from the neck to the waist. Ronin kept his attacks within this box, preventing himself from overextending and getting his arm trapped. He also preferred to move off-centre, stepping out at forty-five-degree angles. If anyone watched this fight, they'd think the two warriors were dancing with each other instead of fighting.

And it was a dance of sorts. A dance of death.

Ronin's opponent broke form and jabbed down. With no warning and no chance of evading, he raised his arm to block. The man's dagger missed the vambrace and sank into the meaty flesh of Ronin's arm. He bit back a howl and kicked the guy away. Shadowman flailed backward, taking his dagger with him. The weapon made a sick wet sound as it ripped free from his arm. Blood ran down the inside of his sleeve and pooled inside his vambrace.

Before the would-be assassin had a chance to reset, Ronin rushed him. He covered the man's face with his hand and with a lightning fast swipe, slashed his neck. Blood sprayed against his hand and face.

Shadowman's eyes widened and he raised the hand holding his weapon only to have it flop back to his side.

Ronin caught the man's body and lowered him to the ground as the attacker's life drained from his body. They'd only heard two men's voices by the river, but there could be more.

Ronin straightened over the body and cleaned his knife.

"About time," Cora said.

Ronin whirled around to find Cora, Phil and Karla standing a few feet away with their arms crossed.

"Honestly," Cora continued. "I wasn't sure if the two of you were fighting or about to make out." Cora's expression was full of sass, as usual.

But the hunters' held something else—wariness. They'd witnessed him fight and now they knew the level of training he'd received. If it ever came down to a fight between them, they wouldn't make the mistake of underestimating the prince.

Ronin cursed.

He'd just lost an advantage.

"Courage is knowing what not to fear."

— PLATO

When they stopped their horses outside the small fishing village of Giga, Cora finally gave in to the unease brewing inside her and turned to Ronin. "Are you sure about this?"

The wind flowing off the nearby ocean tussled his hair. His stormy gaze focused on her, swirls of emotion like angry waves crashing against a rocky shore. "No."

He'd been brooding since the attack by the camp-site last night. With the sun now dipping below the horizon, he'd spent almost a whole day stuck in his head and she was done with it.

"But you're going anyway?" she asked.

"Of course." His tone brooked no argument.

Fine then. She'd go with him—no point in staying safe when her only assurance of survival was hell-bent on destruction.

What was his deal? They'd taken out the two men who'd followed them from the river. She'd tended his stab wound. Phil had taken out the other man swiftly before he made it to Cora. She was never in any danger, not with Phil and Karla around.

Oh.

Was Ronin jealous?

She glanced over at him again—brow furrowed, mouth turned down, eyes squinting.

Did he wish to be her saviour? Or was he upset that he was the only one injured? Though deep, the cut wasn't serious as long as he kept it clean.

"We discussed this already," he said. "I don't have a choice."

Phil and Karla rode ahead to the village, probably giving them space to have this conversation, even though they all knew the outcome. The distance was a false sense of freedom. The king's hunters could catch up to them if they tried to run.

"There's always a choice," she said, glancing over her shoulder at the empty road behind them.

"We wouldn't make it."

"Probably not." She glanced at him sideways and bit the inside of her cheek. She shouldn't say this. Bad idea. "I mean, they're too good."

Poke.

Ronin scowled.

"So fast and silent." Poke. Poke. "Lethal." Poke.

His brow furrowed more.

"Two of the most talented fighters I've ever seen." Okay, she was pushing it now.

He squeezed the reins and his hands turned white from the pressure.

"You should've seen Phil take down that other guy. He made it look so effortless. And he did it so much faster than—"

"You've made your point," Ronin snapped.

She twisted in her saddle to face him. "Are you out of your funk now?"

"That was your objective?" His eyebrows almost reached his hairline. "Because I've got to say, you went about it in a spectacularly wrong way."

"Well, at least you're stringing together more than one sentence. So, success, I guess."

"Why do you even care?"

The horses sidled close together and his knee brushed against hers. "I care because I'm probably walking to my death in that town." She jabbed her pointer finger in the air toward the fishing town just in case he was unsure to what she referred to.

"You're not going in," he growled.

"Yes, I am."

"No, you're not. You're staying outside."

"Outside is not safer for me than inside whatever shell-shucking shack they've decided to squat in. At least inside I have a chance to help. You need someone to watch your back and I'm the only option." Her heart hammered to the point of pain. They weren't even facing the king yet. She needed to tone it down. She took a breath to calm her nerves. When that didn't work, she took another one. "Need I remind you, if you die, I do, too?"

Ronin's glare did little to move her.

"And if I'm going to die, I don't want my last memory of you to be that pissy face you've worn all day."

Ronin's face jerked and he straightened in his saddle. No longer filled with indifference, his gaze flashed with something else. Something more calculating. "Is that so?"

She faced forward in the saddle again. "Yeah."

Whatever she said worked because the scowl was gone, and his normal arrogant smirk returned.

Maybe she should've kept her mouth shut.

He nudged his horse forward and after a couple of extra prods, Cora's horse followed suit. They remained silent as they rejoined the other two and entered the town.

The ocean crashed nearby, and pressure built inside of Cora. The Sea Beast was near, his presence tingling her senses as if ringing a bell to say, "Hello." She swallowed her fear and pressed her cow horse forward.

The sun had already lowered past the horizon, but the air still held the lingering heat of the day and the last rays of sunshine lit the skies in a palette of pinks and yellows.

The town of Giga sat at the southern end of Carrion Bay. The access to the ocean and fishing grounds, plus its close proximity to Zircaloy's large market meant better profits and more stable incomes. Though the streets weren't cobbled, they were hard packed with smooth river rocks and dirt. The group of four made their way down the empty main street.

The lanterns outside the buildings had been lit and though the smell of fish lingered in the air, it wasn't rancid. Not like the town of Alara. Instead, Cora breathed in savoury scents of nicely cooked salmon with herbs. Her mouth watered. Her stomach growled.

Ronin turned to her, eyes wide. "Was that your stomach?"

She scowled at him and turned back to studying the town as they moved toward the large building with the glow of a roaring fireplace and laughter bursting from the windows.

A pub.

The location for their meeting with King Aeneas. No big deal.

Hopefully, the pub still served food.

A curtain fell back into place from the upstairs window of the house to the right. The hinges creaked as a door clicked shut on the house to the left.

A lock slid into place.

Though the majority of the townsfolk appeared to have turned in for the night, Cora and Ronin's presence had not gone unnoticed.

Her skin prickled and she turned to Ronin. He nodded. Yeah. He'd seen it, too. If this meeting didn't end well, they were unlikely to make it out of the pub alive, much less the town. Maybe they huddled inside their homes sharpening pitchforks.

More laughter filtered down the street. The lingering sunlight faded away, drenching the streets in darkness. Streetlamps created glowing pockets of warmth in the night, and the air quickly lost its heat.

With a blazing fireplace so bright the light cascaded down the street, and smells of savoury food so tantalizing her mouth watered, the pub at the end of the road became more appealing with each step of her cow horse.

Maybe they could spend the night in a real bed.

On cue, her sore aching muscles screamed in protest. Logging long flights, injuries, poor sleeping conditions, an unruly mount and a nutrient poor diet had taken their toll. They'd have to add conditioning training to their agenda if they ever hoped to make the flight back to the Eyrie in the next decade.

Without a word, they dismounted outside the pub

and tied their horses to the hitching post. Ronin redid hers, changing it to a slipknot.

Ava had told them MAS betrayed the king, but was she telling the truth, or was it one last attempt to betray them—her lies carefully laid to lead them into another trap? And Phil and Karla were in on it?

Cora sighed and patted the cow horse's neck. The animal turned to her and snorted. Well, that was something. At least the beast didn't snap at her.

"Have you changed your mind?" Ronin asked.

Lifting her chin, she spoke with more confidence than she felt. "I'm coming."

Maybe her life wouldn't be forfeit if she returned without Ronin. If they believed the words from Ava's silver tongue, Ronin was the king now, not his father. That meant Edgar couldn't carry out his vengeance if she failed.

Sasha's cruel smile popped into Cora's mind.

If Ronin perished now, his sister would become queen, and nobody wanted that. Not even Sasha. Where the previous king would quickly and effectively eliminate Cora and her father, Sasha would exact revenge with pain. Public torture seemed likely. Sasha loved her brother and would tear her grief out of Cora's skin in strips.

Cora shuddered.

Gaze intense with emotion, Ronin stepped close and stared down at her.

"What?" She straightened. If he planned to give

her tips on dagger grips or warn her about the seriousness of this meeting, she was going to—

Ronin reached out, lightning quick and gripped her face in both hands. Before she could screech obscenities, he leaned down and kissed her. Warmth spread through her body along with potent need. The unresolved tension from their last encounter rose and clenched her muscles. Ronin angled his mouth on hers and deepened the kiss, stirring her need with his naughty tongue.

She moaned into his mouth and pressed her body into his, slathering herself along his armour as if he were the cake and she the icing.

Ronin pulled back, gaze smouldering.

"Wha...what was that?" Damn it. Her voice was breathier than she would like. He didn't need to know how much his kiss affected her. He'd never make it through the pub door if she inflated his ego further.

"You said you didn't want your last memory to be of me sulking." He turned away from her and walked into the pub.

Phil waited a few feet away by the door and held out a rag.

"What the fuck is that for?" she asked.

"The drool."

She walked past him and ignored his offer, wiping her mouth on her sleeve instead. Just in case.

Phil chuckled behind her, but the heat of the room

smacked her face and stole her attention. She stopped just inside the room to avoid running into Ronin.

The once lively room full of boisterous laughter, booming chatter and clinking glasses fell silent. Only the crackling of the fire in the grand hearth in the middle of the room continued as if two foreign sapavians with giant wings hadn't just stepped into the pub.

Cora shifted to the side where she could see past Ronin's broad shoulders and wings without standing on her tiptoes and hopping up and down like a bratty little kid.

On the far side of the room, at the centre of a long table, a man sat with his back to the wall. His dark skin still held the smoothness of youth, yet wrinkles creased the corners of his mouth and eyes, ever so softly, making his age hard to determine—not young, not old, anywhere in between. His black hair was cut close to the scalp, but it held no gray. His brown eyes studied them with intelligence and a spark of recognition. He didn't wear a crown, but he didn't need to.

The men in full armour with the Court of Iom colours stood to each side of the man. The way the townspeople in the pub kept glancing nervously between them and the man told Cora all she needed to know. King Aeneas had shown up for the meeting.

And so far, they weren't dead.

Finally, some good news, even if it was short-lived.

King Aeneas commanded attention and obedience. His handsome face probably got him in all sorts of trouble when he was younger. Cora glanced at Ronin. Then again, if the king of Iom was anything like her comrade, his good looks probably got him out of a lot of trouble, too.

"Leave us." The man's voice was deep and growly. It reminded Cora of a bear.

The townspeople deserted their ale and bread and scurried from the pub. Cora and Ronin stepped farther into the room to avoid getting trampled. While patrons streamed past them, Cora eyed the abandoned food and swallowed.

Phil and Karla also moved out of the way as the crowd left, pressing against the walls. Though the warriors had acted honourably during their travels, and gave Cora no reason to distrust them, her body shook with unease. The two highly trained killers now blocked the only exit. With Phil and Karla behind them, and the king and his men in front, Cora and Ronin stood in the middle of a room, trapped by humans.

Ronin's expression reduced to something more akin to stone.

Yeah, he didn't like their situation, either.

"Please." The king waved at the bench seat across from him. "Join me."

Ronin walked across the room. He didn't hesitate. He sat down on the bench and folded his hands on the table as if he had no concerns about his precarious position.

A smile tugged at the king's lips. "I'm sorry about the bench. They didn't have any sapavian seats available and we didn't have the time to make them."

Just as sapavians designed shirts with buttons, snaps, or ties at the back to accommodate their wings, they built specialized furniture. Sapavian seats had a single piece of wood up the centre as the backrest. The slender piece fit nicely between the wings without squashing them and made sitting back in a chair a lot more comfortable. The wider backrests of human chairs required sapavians to spread their wings out to the side and crushed the wing bones with bodyweight. The king had made a point to think of Ronin's comfort for this meeting. Maybe this wouldn't go terribly wrong.

Ronin dipped his chin. "The bench is fine, thank you."

King Aeneas nodded. His dark gaze shifted to study her. She remained still, refusing to fidget or reach for her dagger.

"Your companion may join us as well," he said.

Sit down with two kings? No, thank you. Hard pass.

Her gaze drifted to the abandoned food on the neighbouring table again. Would it be too trashy to eat the food while the royals discussed politics? The humans had left it, after all.

Cora's stomach growled again.

Ronin glanced at her and amusement tugged at his

lips. He lifted his eyebrows, daring her to speak for herself. Asshole. He was the king of the Eyrie. He needed to act like it.

"I'll stand," she said, turning her body so she had Ronin, the human king, and his men to her right and the exit and the killers to her left. She wasn't trained as a bodyguard or guardian, but she'd watch Ronin's back.

"As you wish." The human king turned back to Ronin. "I'm glad my men found you. We heard reports of your capture. Our messages had been intercepted and replaced with different information."

"It was not the welcome I expected or hoped for," Ronin said stiffly.

"Nor the one I intended. One must wonder how the wrong date and time made it to you."

Ronin stoically didn't look at her. "Are you suggesting I have a traitor in my kingdom?"

The king's grin wasn't friendly, and anger flashed in his gaze. Though he was a big man, with wide shoulders and strong looking hands, he'd given off a "gentle giant" image until this moment. Now, he'd slipped, revealing his true self—the king was a very dangerous man.

Cora settled her hand on her dagger's hilt.

The king laced his fingers together and leaned over the table. "I'm saying we both do."

Cora shuddered. The king's evaluation was correct. If the duplicity was one-sided, the correspondence would've uncovered it. An unhappy thought poked at Cora's brain.

Correspondence.

Cora had crossed the channel a lot lately and a royal visit quickly followed her delivery of a message to Iom. Had she been the one responsible for carrying out the traitors' communications?

Was Father involved? Doctoring them before delivering them to the recipients? Or did he know and instead of alerting the king, he sat back and watched? Cora doubted either of those theories. If Father had known, he would never have allowed Cora to escort Ronin to the meeting.

Not only had Father mentioned his contacts growing quiet, he swore to never read the royal communications after they returned to the Eyrie. He didn't want to know, and he didn't want to get involved. He'd already been burned by the king and labelled a traitor.

Would Ronin know that or would he suspect Cormorant Clan's involvement?

Cold seeped through her veins.

Ronin shifted slightly to look over his shoulder, a question in his gaze. Had she'd carried the messages? She hadn't knowingly helped anyone. No professional messenger broke the seals.

She shook her head.

Ronin's expression hardened and he focused on the

human king again. "If there is a traitor on the Eyrie, I'll find them."

Her exchange with Ronin hadn't gone unnoticed and now the king's attention travelled to her again. "Are you going to introduce me to your lovely companion?"

"No."

The king's grin grew, this time not nearly so lethal in appearance. "There were reports of a stunning sapavian messenger. A female with black wings and hair spotted near the Cap. And another report of a similar sapavian having contact with a spy in a nearby fishing village. Might your companion be this messenger I've heard so much about?"

"She's mine and that's all you need to know," Ronin said, his deep voice bordering on a growl.

The king finally looked away from Cora. She almost breathed a sigh of relief. Almost. She kept her posture relaxed and her breathing regular, but the weight of the human's attention unnerved her. It took every ounce of self-control not to react. Not to draw her dagger or bolt from the room.

Ronin's words still whispered through her mind. He'd claimed her as his. But the silly fluttering in her belly was misguided. He didn't mean it like that. Not how she wished he'd mean it. He couldn't. As king, he needed to make alliances, not dally with a lowly messenger spy. Heck, this meeting might be to arrange a marriage for all she knew.

"Let's focus on the truce," Ronin said.

The king nodded. "The hatred and mistrust between our people are misplaced and unfounded. We will agree to cease shooting sapavians on sight and cede a portion of our land to house a sapavian settlement."

That sounded good. That's what the Eyrie so desperately needed.

"In return, sapavians will also cease any unprovoked attacks on humans. You will house and welcome an ambassador and selected guardsmen on the Eyrie. You will share all information on salmon runs and aid our boats in a sapavian-human fishing collective."

That sounded doable. A nice win-win.

Ronin nodded. "As discussed in our correspondence, we agree to those terms."

The king straightened. "There's just one more thing I'd like to add."

Ronin waited.

Cora held her breath.

"We'd like you to kill the monster in the bay."

Cora's whole body jerked. Her breath hitched. Which monster? The land, sea and air were rife with them. He couldn't possibly mean—

"We want sapavians to kill the Sea Beast."

Cora's stomach twisted and before she could consider the ramifications, she stepped forward. "No!"

31

"The possession of anything begins in the mind."

— BRUCE LEE

After her outburst, Ronin pulled Cora outside the pub. With his hand still wrapped around her upper arm, he turned to her. "What the hell, Cora?"

"It just...seems wrong." She scratched the back of her neck. "I don't think we should agree to that."

Waves crashed against the nearby shore and the ocean called to her.

Mine... A deep voice vibrated in her head.

She recoiled, but Ronin's grip on her arms kept her in place.

Ronin studied her, dark brows furrowed. "Wrong? That thing almost ate us on the way over."

She didn't have an explanation. No reason percolated to explain her overwhelming tangible, gut-wrenching response to the human king's request.

Time to insert logic.

"We've tried to kill the Sea Beast before," she said. Obviously, neither of them had personally, but history books filled the Eyrie's library, books packed with details of disastrous attempts to rid the surrounding ocean of the biggest known sciper. "It never ended well."

"I'm aware, Cora." Ronin's mouth tightened. He let go of her arms and she suddenly wanted him to hold her again.

"You can't agree. We'll fail to hold up our obligations and this whole agreement will fall through," she said.

"I know," he said. The glow of firelight through the window danced along his serious expression. "Had you given me the chance you would've heard me explaining that exact concern."

She swallowed.

"You undermined my authority. Now, if I go back in there, they'll assume the response came from you, not the king of the Eyrie."

She ducked her head.

Ronin sighed. "Why do I get the feeling this very

logical and understandable reason is not why you emotionally objected to the king's new terms?"

She rubbed her arms, now cold. "I can't explain it. Something in my gut is telling me this is wrong. It will be a mistake to agree to that term."

He continued to study her in the flickering lamplight for another long minute. Maybe for an eternity. It was hard to track time under the heat of his gaze. Without words, he nodded and walked back into the pub, leaving her to face the heavy wooden door.

Well, guess she had to follow after him like a good little subordinate. She yanked the door open, paused to enjoy the rush of heat and followed Ronin back to the table.

The king and his men waited, expressions neutral.

"We can't agree to the additional request."

Cora forced every muscle in her body to remain relaxed. *Do not react.*

The king's eyebrows shot up. "May I ask why you're willing to throw away months of planning and a mutually beneficial alliance for a monster that reaps as much destruction and chaos on your people as it does on mine?"

"We've tried to kill it. Multiple times. And failed. To have the fate of our agreement rely on something with a low probability of success is unacceptable." Ronin leaned forward. "Either way, the alliance is in danger. It's almost as if you want this to fail before it even starts."

The king's head jerked back. "You need us."

"You need us as well or we wouldn't be here." Ronin straightened and lifted his chin. "I came here in good faith. My presence in Iom is evidence enough of our commitment to this alliance. Either agree to the original terms, or I walk."

Right, like he could simply walk past all the armed guards. His confidence and courage were remarkable.

The king stood up, pushing back his chair in the process. The legs dragged against the floor and the wooden planks creaked. The surrounding guards tensed, shifting into a ready position with their weight on the balls of their feet.

"We have a deal." King Aeneas reached his hand across the table.

32

"Good company in a journey makes the way seem shorter."

— IZAAK WALTON

R onin sat straight in the saddle on his mighty black mare and kept his expression controlled. He couldn't let anyone see how his mind reeled from the recent events.

Stay strong.

Stay solid.

Stay in control.

Turned out, Aeneas agreed with him. They needed each other too much to squabble over a have-to-kill monster.

Now, Phil and Karla escorted them from town toward Hadren's Keep. They were to stay at the remote location long enough to heal before returning home safely. Ronin had hoped the alliance meant no more running. Certainly, he and Cora could stay with the king in Giga until they recovered and returned to the Eyrie. Or at the very least go back to the Cap.

King Aeneas disagreed.

For the first time since they sat down at the table, real emotion clouded the human king's gaze. Though he'd ferreted out the traitors in his court, he hadn't caught them all. The abductors from the forest were still at large. Now that the king had cut the head off the snake, he had to wait to see if it would grow another one or die a swift death.

Aeneas didn't trust anyone outside those who surrounded him in the pub. He didn't want to risk bringing Cora and Ronin into his camp—both for their sake and his own.

So instead of a nice warm, proper bed, they were off again, placing as much distance between them and the king. At least they were permitted to remain in the king's presence long enough to eat. If they had to stay quiet and hidden, they needed to keep Cora's stomach content.

King Aeneas also sent Phil and Karla with them. Extra hands and weapons would help for the trip ahead, but did he have another motive? The hunters might be friendly, but they didn't report to Ronin. He needed to be careful with what he said in front of them and not grow complacent. Sure, they signed an alliance, but things changed, and Ronin needed to prepare for all possibilities.

Including their current one.

Despite every effort to avoid this outcome, they headed to the Outpost Access Point. The site of Cora's mother's murder. Hadren's Keep.

Cora kept glancing at him, expression creased with worry. He wanted to hold her, gather her in his arms, bury his face in her neck and just breathe.

She'd probably knee him in the junk.

Totally worth it.

He'd only need a few minutes with her in his arms to quell the nerves and racing thoughts.

"You're awfully quiet over there," she whispered.

The king's hunters had drifted far enough ahead that they wouldn't overhear the conversation.

"Trying to work out if Aeneas had an ulterior motive for kicking us up the road instead of letting us stay with him to ensure our safety," Ronin said.

She nodded. "I've been thinking on that, too, but if he wanted us dead, he had ample opportunity."

"Not a comfortable thought, but accurate."

"I think his motives were to protect us. He's still not sure if more traitors lurk in the shadows and he knows human reception of sapavians is not favourable. It will take time, patience and constant communication from his court to tackle that mountain."

"I came to a similar conclusion," Ronin said.

"There's another possibility."

"Oh?"

"He had six warriors with him. Eight if you count, Phil and Karla." She paused dramatically.

"If I'm supposed to see the point, I don't. Please continue."

"That pub had four, maybe five rooms, tops. He didn't want to share his room."

Ronin snorted. "Are you on about beds, again?"

"Of course, I am. I had a tree root digging into my side last night."

An image of Cora tangled in his sheets on his bed at home surfaced. Blood rushed to his cock. He cursed and looked away.

Cora tensed and scanned the forest. "What?"

"It's nothing," he rushed to say. "I think it's time to set up camp. I'm going to fall off this horse soon."

"You're going to fall off that horse anyway. You may have taken to this whole riding thing better than me, but you still look sketchy anytime we pick up the pace."

"Are you...insulting my horsemanship?"

She raised her eyebrows. "Are you getting defensive?"

"I have many skills."

"But riding a glorified cow is not one of them."

"Says the woman whose horse looks like a cow."

Ronin snarled and leaned over. He stabbed the air with his finger. "And who actually fell off her horse."

"I prematurely slipped from the saddle." She lifted her chin and refused to make eye contact.

He smirked. "I've never had any issues with slipping off, or out, prematurely."

Cora groaned. The glare she sent his way lost its impact though because her lips twitched from supressing a smile. "You're incorrigible."

He maneuvered the mare closer so he could whisper. "And you like it."

He kicked the horse and the mare bolted forward, leaving Cora to sputter behind him.

"Rat bastard!" she called out when she found words.

He chuckled and pulled up beside the other half of their troop. Phil grinned and pulled on the reins, so he could drop back beside Cora and join her. Jerk.

"If you keep poking the bear..." Karla warned.

"I like poking her."

Karla snorted. "If you keep at it, she's going to bite back."

He thought about it and smiled. "I think I'd like that, too."

Karla laughed and shook her head. "We need to make camp. I think we should only have one person up on watch instead of two. We all need to rest."

He nodded. The thought had already crossed his

mind. At a certain point, they'd have to trust one another.

His hands tightened on the reins. They needed to survive and return to the Eyrie. Only then could he face the reality of his father's death, somehow manage a kingdom and ease sapavians out of generations of hate and into a time of acceptance to honour the new alliance with the humans.

Pressure squeezed his gut.

Could he do it?

He wasn't ready. He wasn't supposed to be king so soon.

Sasha would help him, and Cora...

He took a deep breath and tried to ease some of the tension clamping his shoulders. Cora would help him, too. She might have plans to return to her role as a messenger, but he'd find a way to make her see how vital she was to the kingdom in a different role.

By his side.

33

"It is strange, but true, that the most important turning-points of life often come at the most unexpected times and in the most unexpected ways."

— NAPOLEON HILL

Cora nestled into Ronin's warm chest. His arm tightened around her waist. Sleep still lingered and she wanted to drift back to her dreams. But the rock digging into her stomach, the pressure of her bladder and the weak rays of light teasing her face said it was time to get up.

Too bad.

She pulled free from Ronin. His arm tensed but his hand released her. When she stood up, his arm flopped back to the ground. He was out. He would've just finished his shift, so hopefully he'd get a bit more sleep before they broke camp. She hadn't noticed him coming to bed or holding her like he had when they hid in the safety cave. Not that she was complaining. She certainly wouldn't object. The added warmth was a welcome reprieve from the cold nights, and she felt safer in his embrace.

She stretched her arms in the air and leaned to each side, stretching her back.

Phil looked over from where he perched on a boulder as a lookout. "Good morning, Highness."

She stiffened. "Don't call me that."

Phil shrugged, still scanning the forest. "Why not? He's the king and it's obvious you two have a thing."

Heat spread through her body, quickly doused with the ice of reality. "A thing that will never happen."

Phil frowned. "Why not?"

"He's the king." Why was Phil acting so dense? "Kings don't have relationships with messengers."

"That's what I said. He's the king, he can make the rules."

She shook her head. "I will never be more than a messenger."

Phil turned to her, his dark gaze flashing. "I didn't peg you as a liar."

"I'm not lying." She pulled her shoulders back. "I'm from Cormorant Clan. I'll never be seen as more than a servant to the Eyrie, to him and to myself. Once we're home, he'll quickly remember our roles and he'll distance himself from me and the memory of our time together here."

He shook his head again and looked away.

Whatever. She needed to pee. Slipping away from the camp in the opposite direction, she found a nice dense bush to hide behind. She had no wish for the others to hear her pee, but she needed to stay close.

It didn't take long to finish her morning routine. She headed back to camp when a melancholy song wove through the trees and reached her. Whispering through the leaves, the song clutched her gut and twisted.

She whirled around and scanned the forest. Dappled light played off the morning dew and a soft breeze teased the leaves. Birds sang to each other and a steady buzz of insects hummed in the air. She unfurled her wings, stretching them out and arched her back. Something popped. Relief spread through her limbs.

Ahh. That's the spot.

A sense of unease stabbed at her brain, urging her to turn. She flung up her arm and twisted. A large fuzzy thing barrelled into her. Breath stolen, she gasped for air.

Sharp teeth punctured her arm. Pain exploded.

She flew through the air with the beast attached to her arm and hit the ground hard. The monster released her, backed up and crouched to attack again.

A bearcat.

Dread slammed through Cora and choked off the scream stuck in her throat. Instant recognition of the animal from cautionary tales and horror stories from her youth paralyzed her.

A cross between a black bear and a mountain lion, the obsidian coloured bearcat showcased the truly twisted ideas of the pre-cascade scientists. With a bear's speed, size and strength, and the large cat's agility, stealth and prey drive, the bearcat was an apex predator originally created as a weapon. Like all things of the wild, though, the bearcat never took to the training process. The "Bearcat Project" had been slated for termination when the nuclear apocalypse struck. The monsters that survived the intense radiation emerged as something far more fearsome than the scientists had hoped for.

The bearcat snarled and launched.

Still sprawled on the ground, she scrambled to avoid the beast. Claws ripped at her flying leathers. She rolled and flung out her free arm. The other was trapped under her body.

The furry beast struck again and latched onto her forearm. Sharp teeth sunk in. Drool dripped from its mouth and splattered Cora's face. Pain stabbed her shoulder.

She was going to die here.

Mauled by a bearcat two feet from a pool of piss.

Ignoring the pain, she wrenched her trapped arm

from under her body. Something popped. Blood ran down her other arm as it lost feeling. With numb fingers, she clutched her dagger hilt and drew it.

The bearcat swatted at her. Claws shredded her flying leathers and the skin beneath. The beast swung again, higher. Cora ducked, catching the heavy paws with her arms and shoulders. More blood flowed from her skin.

Breathing hurt. Her heartbeat hurt. Everything thudded in her ears.

The bearcat gripped her arm in a bone-crushing hold with its teeth and shook its head back and forth.

Cora flung the dagger up, stabbing the beast in the neck.

Too weak. The blade didn't sink in past the tough fur-covered skin. Some history books claimed the fur was more akin to little hairs of metallic armour than the fur of a bear or mountain lion.

Her arm wasn't responding correctly. She screamed and drove the weapon in with as much force as she could gather. The dagger pushed through the fur.

The bearcat's eyes widened and its grip on her arm loosened.

She brought her legs up between them and pushed the animal off her. Covered with blood, the dagger slipped from her grip, still stuck in the bearcat. The animal flew backward.

She scrambled to her feet, slipping in a pool of blood.

The bearcat crouched again, ambivalent to the dagger sticking out of its neck. She must've missed the carotid. Damn it. How was that thing still standing?

An arrow whistled through the air and ripped through the animal's skull.

With eyes rolling up, the bearcat flopped to the side and twitched.

What? How?

She stumbled and turned in the direction the arrow had come from. Ronin stood twenty feet away. He sunk another two arrows into the beast.

"Cora!" He threw the bow down and ran to her.

Cora staggered, blood coursing down her arms and side. Her vision wavered.

Ronin caught her in his arms before she hit the ground.

"No, no, no, no," he kept saying.

That couldn't be good. She must be in bad shape.

He lay her on the ground and patted her body down, pressing a cloth against the wound on her side. He gripped her head, clutching the back of her neck and a bit of her hair. It should've hurt, but everything was going numb.

"You can't die, Cora. You hear me?"

She tried to smile and tell him off. How arrogant. He thought his words powerful enough to defy death. Her mouth didn't move quite right. "That...an order?'

"Damn right, it's an order." He looked away and barked at someone to help.

Her mind drifted and her vision closed around her.

Ronin held her close, his iron and pine scent curling around her. The heat of his body provided warmth where everything else was getting so cold.

"You will always be more than a messenger to me, Cora."

His words accompanied her into the darkness.

34

"So much of who we are is where we have been."

— WILLIAM LANGEWIESCHE

"A fucking bearcat," someone cursed.

Cora blinked against the dense fog in her mind. A warm glow of firelight danced against her face and the right side of her body.

"I've never seen one before," someone else said.

"Of course not. No one survives seeing one," the first guy said. Phil. His name was Phil. The other one was Karla. Memories came rushing back.

Where was Ronin?

She shifted her head and groaned. Oh. That didn't feel good.

"Try not to move," Ronin said. He crouched down near her side opposite of the fire, his wings fanned out to block the wind from reaching her.

Phil and Karla sat near the fire and cast wary glances at her. "How did you survive?"

Had she survived? It certainly didn't feel like it. "Luck." Her voice cracked and her dry throat screamed for water.

Phil shook his head. "No one hears a bearcat attack."

"How do you know if no one's seen or heard them?" Ronin asked.

"I've been on guard duty and heard the victim's screams," Phil said. "No warning. No sighting of the animal, just the...remains."

Karla nodded. "They're silent. It should've killed Cora right away. No one's reflexes are that fast."

She closed her eyes. She hadn't heard the bearcat, but she had sensed its presence as it launched through the air and she'd heard a song through the trees. In that split second, before impact, she'd managed to adjust her position enough to get her arm in the way of her neck.

"Cora's good at surviving," Ronin said over her, his deep breath rumbling. He didn't sound altogether pleased with his statement.

Her brain stumbled to make some sense of that. Why would he be angry?

Karla grunted. "I'll say. She's healing well, too. I

didn't know sapavians were gifted with accelerated healing."

"We're not." Ronin's voice came out short and clipped.

"So Cora's special?" Phil chucked another log onto the fire. It crackled and popped, and a wave of heat and smoke hit her face.

"Cora's always been special." Ronin moved a strand of hair from her face.

They grew silent.

Cora stared up at the night sky and waited for her brain to finish waking up and push past the numbness.

The smell of meat lingered in the air.

Karla squatted near the fire, using her knife to cut away at something furry. The kingswoman caught her gaze and held up the severed bearcat paw. "I thought I'd make us all claw necklaces for souvenirs. If you survive, I'll let you have first pick."

Phil glared at Karla and Ronin growled.

"What?" Karla stopped her work, shrugging with her knife in one hand and the paw in the other. "I was going for inspirational."

The distant waves of Carrion Bay called to her, urging her to draw closer. Like a magnet brought too close to its polar opposite, the marine water pulled at every cell inside her. Cora's chest hurt and emptiness spread through her body, not from Karla's words or the sight of the bloody paw, but from her injuries. She'd lost too much blood.

"Ocean," she whispered.

Ronin continued to brush strands of her hair to the side with his fingers. "The ocean?"

"I need to go to it." She made no sense, even to herself.

"We'll make Karla shut up," Ronin said.

"Not that. Ocean." The tugging increased.

Ronin shook his head. "We're too far away. I'm worried about moving you."

The sea called to her. She needed to go to it. Her body ached with need. A life-threatening need akin to breathing. Like her empty lungs needed air, her dry throat needed water and her belly needed food.

"Ocean," she repeated.

"I'm not taking you there to die, Cora." His gaze darkened and he balled his hand into a fist. "I ordered you to live. Remember?"

"I don't want to go to the ocean to die." She reached out and rested her hand on his chorded forearm. "I want to go to live."

He grumbled.

"Please?"

The others stood by the fire and started gathering their stuff.

"What are you doing?" Ronin growled.

"Getting ready to leave," Phil said.

"Oh?" Ronin's voice grew dangerously low. "Where to?"

"The ocean," Karla answered, dropping the paw by the fire and slinging her bag over her shoulder.

"Is that so?"

"You heard the lady." Phil strapped his bedroll to his horse. "She even said please."

"Don't pretend like you're capable of denying her anything," Karla said.

Ronin snarled and rose to his feet. "You're finally right about something."

Cora relaxed into the makeshift bed and smiled. The emptiness stopped spreading, filled with hope and an odd understanding that the ocean would make everything better.

35

"The advance of genetic engineering makes it quite conceivable that we will begin to design our own evolutionary progress."

— ISAAC ASIMOV, *THE BEGINNING AND THE END*

Ronin swung his leg over the back of the horse to dismount first. Despite Cora's protests and colourful language, he insisted she ride with him and not on that stubborn horse that looked like a cow. He'd held her the entire ride. Instead of fighting him and sitting rigid in the saddle, she'd slumped against him, resting her head on his shoulder with her forehead pressed into his jaw.

Not good. She never would've shown such vulnerability under normal circumstances.

She'd lost too much blood.

The ride should've taken twenty minutes or so, but they took double the time. Phil had stitched Cora's wounds together and Karla had dressed them, but too much jostling could open them again.

He tightened his hold on her.

Too much blood.

An image of her in a bloody heap at that beast's feet flashed through his mind and twisted his gut. How could she survive that? One look and he thought he'd lost her. The others had to pry him off to tend to her wounds.

To sit in front of him with her back pressed to his chest, Cora had to span her wings out and back, essentially bordering him between two walls of black feathers. It couldn't be comfortable but having the feathers brush against him eased the tension gnawing at his muscles.

She was here. She was okay. She was going to be all right.

Another memory of lifting her shredded, limp body in his arms rose. He swallowed the rising stomach acid and patted the black mare's rump.

Cora still sat in the saddle, face pale, expression drawn, and lips pressed tightly together.

He held both his arms out. She really was feeling awful. Instead of arguing or fighting, she slowly swung her leg over, reached out and held onto his shoulders, letting him pull her from the saddle. She clung to him, with what had to be the last of her strength, breathing heavy. She pressed her forehead to his chest as if her head weighed a hundred tons.

He didn't let go.

He'd never let her go again.

"We're almost there," he whispered into her hair. "You can do this."

She trembled and leaned into him more. "I...I don't know if I can."

He held her up, taking on more of her weight to prevent her from falling. "I'll carry you, then."

She nodded.

He reached down, hooked his arm under her knees and hoisted her into his arms. She coiled her wings tight to her body. Hopefully, he wouldn't trip on them. He'd spent their trip here wondering what the hell they were doing. He'd wanted to yell, to rail against the absurdity of a trip to the beach. But he didn't. He sucked back all the criticism and questions, choosing to make Cora as comfortable as possible instead.

Over Cora's head, he caught Phil's gaze. Neither of the king's hunters had dismounted.

"Will you two give us some privacy?" he asked.

Without a word, Phil nodded and nudged his horse away from the shore.

Karla stopped her horse in front of them. "We'll

secure the perimeter." She spurred her horse to follow her comrade.

Ronin held Cora to him and turned to the ocean. It wasn't as angry today. This section of the bay had a protective inlet surrounded by trees.

Ronin stepped away from the forest and onto the sand. "The ocean is right here, Cora. You made it."

She clutched the neck piece of his armour. "I need to go in."

He shook his head. "We don't have enough field dressings to replace the ones you have on. They need to last until we make it to the outpost."

She looked up at him, eyes wide, lashes long. "I need to go in. I can't explain why. I just do."

He sighed. "You will not die on me."

Her lips twitched. "Promise."

"Clothes on or off?"

They both looked down at her damaged flying leathers. They were ruined. While they waited by her bedside to see if she'd live, Phil had stitched the gear into something workable. They'd never function as proper protection against the elements again.

"Off."

He nodded and set her down. Normally, he'd relish peeling off her clothing one piece at a time, but not now. Not this time. He concentrated on removing the clothing without catching the stitches or tugging the bandages free. She stood naked in his arms and all he wanted to do was wrap her back up in a blanket and make her pain go away.

He was now the king of the Eyrie. He commanded an entire island of sapavians. He had warriors, guards, and spies. He could snap his fingers, bark an order and someone would see it done.

And he'd never felt so helpless in his life.

Cora reached up with her hand and rested her palm on his face. "It will be okay"

He closed his eyes and released her. She stepped from his arms and turned to walk into the ocean.

The gentle waves slapped against her shaking legs. She wobbled, but kept going, walking slowly until she was submerged to her neck.

She spun in the ocean and faced him. For the first time since the attack, her expression was no longer pinched. She looked at ease. Relaxed.

She took a deep breath, closed her eyes, and dropped back into the water, falling beneath the water's surface.

Ronin froze. He squashed the urge to race into the water after her. Instead, he squeezed his hands into fists and curled his toes inside his boots. He began to count.

Tiny bubbles surfaced from where she went under. The ocean lightened and the swells grew stronger.

What in the bloody bird hell?

Thirty seconds.

Come on, Cora.

A ball of light glowed from beneath the surface. An inhuman, non-birdlike groan vibrated through the air, so low, the waves lapping at the shore almost drowned it out. It sounded as if the ocean had opened its mouth and sung the lowest note possible.

Fifty seconds.

How long could she hold her breath?

He'd been holding his the entire time and already grew light-headed.

Cora's head popped out of the water. She took a long breath and whispered something too quiet to hear.

Her gaze locked on his and she walked out of the ocean. The water trailed down her body, caressing her breasts, and trickled down her legs before returning to the ocean.

His mouth grew dry. He swallowed. If only he could reach out and follow the path of the water with his fingers. Or tongue.

Her body, lean and strong from flying was something he dreamed about and continued to dream about. Strong legs, soft around the hips, flat stomach, full breasts.

He licked his lips. He yearned to touch her and show her exactly how much he appreciated her physical beauty. But that's not what drew him to her most. It was never about possessing her body.

Her dark gaze bore into his, challenging, defiant and intelligent. There it was. Her spirit. That's what he loved about her most. She embodied strength and perseverance.

The woman who chose him would need plenty of both.

He frowned and studied her body again.

Wait a minute.

Wait a damn second.

The bandages had fallen away, lost in the tide. The skin underneath still showed the teeth and claw marks, but instead of raw, weeping wounds recently stitched together, newly healed scars sat in their place. The stitches remained, but they were no longer needed to hold anything together.

His mouth dropped open. "How?"

She shrugged.

"Oh no, princess. You're going to tell me everything."

Gloriously naked and defiant to the core, she stopped and placed a hand on a cocked hip. The ocean hit her calves, but she appeared unaffected by the frigid water.

She shrugged again. "The ocean heals me."

His brain misfired. "How?"

"I don't know."

"Has it always healed you?"

She hugged herself. "I'm not sure. I didn't really go for lots of dips in the ocean with serious wounds. It's been calling to me ever since I sustained injuries from our crossing, but I haven't had a chance to go in until now."

"When did you notice?"

She frowned.

"When did you notice or suspect the ocean healed you?"

Pain flashed across her gaze like lightning. He knew the answer before she spoke. Only one thing in her entire history made her look like that—as if she were about to faint, puke and wage a war at the same time.

One of her hands drifted up to the scar on her cheek. "Since the attack that killed my mother. I should've died in the ocean, but I didn't."

"Did the ocean carry you home, too?" That would be incredibly convenient right now.

She shook her head. "I don't think so, but I also don't remember everything about that time. I get flashbacks and moments, but I've never been able to put the pieces together."

The pain and loss on her face and in her voice stabbed at his heart. That was the most she'd ever shared with him about that time.

Guilt sucker-punched him. He hadn't made an effort to find out what happened after she returned all those years ago. Instead, he'd avoided her, unsure of what to say or do. Unsure of whether her father truly was a traitor as his father suggested. And worse, his sister followed his lead, hurting Cora even more, though neither of them truly realized the extent of their actions.

Fuck. He was an asshole.

"I'm sorry I abandoned you all those years ago."

She sniffed and looked away. Her arms tightened around her body.

He stepped into the ocean. When she didn't say anything or move, he closed the distance, ignoring the bone-numbing water splashing against his boots and pants. He ran his hands down her arms, smoothing the tiny hairs that stood up from the chill.

"I won't make that mistake again," he said.

What the hell was coming over him? His father drilled him throughout his youth not to make promises, especially ones that would be hard or impossible to keep. As a king, his word meant his life and he had to weigh his words carefully, scrutinize his promises.

Never promise something you can't deliver. Never make open or vague declarations. Keep your obligations minimal to maximize your options. His father's teachings rang through his mind.

Ronin meant every word he spoke to Cora. Despite his father's advice and a lifetime of programming, he spoke the words from his heart and didn't regret a damn thing.

Cora snapped her head up, her gaze studying him. Her hard expression softened, replaced with understanding, and need—a desire so strong, it burned from the inside and nearly knocked him on his ass.

He cupped her face and kissed her. He let his lips and tongue tell her how much he wanted her. How much he needed her.

She moaned and melted to fit him. He loved how she did that. How she seemed to need every inch of her body in contact with his.

She tasted of surprise and desire. He gripped the back of her neck, snagged some of her wet hair and kept her trapped in his kiss—not that she tried to escape.

Cora responded with another moan and wicked flicks of her tongue.

He explored her body with his free hand, trailing the path of the water as he'd wanted to earlier. Cupping her full breast, he gently squeezed.

God, he wanted her.

He could spin her around, lay her down on the sand and be inside her, buried deep in less than a minute. He could bend her over the large dry log that had washed up on shore and take her from behind.

Cora pressed into his body, grinding herself against his erection. All thoughts and planning flew from his mind.

He nipped her bottom lip, trailed kisses along her jawline. He was ready to explode and he hadn't explored nearly as much of her as he wanted.

She needed to pant and scream his name first. He wanted to give her more. Hell, he'd give her everything.

She could ask for the entire kingdom right now and he'd say, "Yes." Anything to keep her in his arms.

He'd already given her his heart. He just hadn't realized it until now. Until the bearcat almost took everything away.

Ronin dragged his teeth along her shoulders. She responded by arching her back, exposing her chest to wordlessly ask for more. He trailed his hands from her waist to her back and leaned down.

A man cleared his throat.

Cora straightened. At the same time, he snapped his wings around her, hiding her naked body and protecting her at the same time, even though he already stood between her and the shore.

He growled over his shoulders. "What?"

"MAS trackers," Phil said. "We took their scout out, but we need to move."

"Give us a little warning next time instead of sneaking up."

"And alert them of our location?" Phil scoffed. "Sure."

"Do we have time for Cora to get dressed?" he asked.

"Yes. They haven't picked up the trail or discovered the missing scout, yet." He hesitated.

Why wasn't he gone? "What?"

"We all saw how Cora dressed herself last time. Maybe you could help her?"

Cora cursed into his chest.

He ran his fingers up and down her back, caressing, but he couldn't help the chuckle rumbling through his chest. He often replayed the memory of her trying to hop into her tight leather pants with wet legs and how her bare breasts had bounced.

A smile tugged at his lips. His erection pulsed, as if trying to remind him of what he was supposed to be doing. *Thanks, cock. Like I could forget.*

Cora giggled.

Giggled.

"Are you okay?"

Her gaze laughed up at him. "Just fine."

"Go away so we can get ready," he hissed over his shoulder.

Phil grunted and walked back into the forest.

Once Ronin was satisfied the other man was far enough away, he turned and headed for shore, making sure to keep his wings spread to provide a privacy screen for Cora.

"How's your wing?" he asked.

"Healed."

"So you could've dipped in the ocean and healed it at any time?"

"I think so. I never had the opportunity, though. The cave was too high up to risk diving in. and I was distracted from venturing into the ocean from the river bathing spot."

And she didn't trust him with the truth. Not then. But now?

They reached the shore and he held out her clothing. Fully healed, she didn't need his help, so he stood and shielded her from the wind while she clambered into her clothes. "We need to take the stitches out."

"I'll take care of it." She stepped out from behind his wings and faced him, straightened, her once open expression now closed off.

"This isn't over, Cora," he said.

She rocked back as if his proclamation surprised her and she didn't believe him. Her scowl sent warmth spreading through his chest. He grinned, already forming a plan.

36

"Being brave isn't the absence of fear. Being brave is having that fear but finding a way through it."

— BEAR GRYLLS

Cora took a deep breath as the horses emerged from the forest and trotted into a field of tall wildflowers that bordered the entrance to the outpost. Once a majestic fort, Hadren's Keep now stood in disrepair on the edge of the Outpost Access Point.

Stories from Cora's childhood created a shroud of mystery around the keep with conflicting myths of its creation, numerous violent events, and gut-wrenching tales. Erected on the orders of King Hadren of Iom as a symbol of his authority and grandness, the keep later became his tomb. Hadren fled Calandria after a failed assassination attempt and his brother assumed the Iom throne in his absence. Unwilling to relinquish control without a fight, Hadren took out his anger on the nearby city of Zircaloy. Instead of commiserating or rallying behind him, the people turned against their once beloved king, stormed the keep and executed him.

Now, Cora and the king of the Eyrie were fleeing to Hadren's Keep and the irony or at least the parallels between them and the keep's past wasn't lost on Cora.

They'd managed to evade the trackers and spent the last week completing the journey to the outpost. Ronin's wing was almost healed, and he would only take another week or so to regain his strength.

Currently, Ronin's furrowed brow said more than his silence. He was worried. If he didn't make it home, his sister would have to take up the throne, if she hadn't already done so. Maybe she held out hope he still lived, but they'd been away for so long. Instead, Sasha would assume the humans betrayed them and declare war. She was probably already planning an attack. Ronin's cold and calculating sister at the helm of the Eyrie spelled disaster for everyone.

Cora shivered and studied the old stone keep that perched on the edge of a cliff. When Ronin's father exiled her family here, they decided to look at it as a new beginning and make Hadren's Keep their new home. Cora had been heartbroken, but she'd toured the grounds with a sense of adventure and romantic optimism.

The bees had buzzed around the thick bushes lining the base of the tower, drunk on honey, and covered in pollen dust. Waves had crashed against the exposed rocks at the keep's base and the warm summer air had rustled the sweet leaves of the forest trees, bathing them in soft fragrance.

Their new home had carried fear and anxiety for the unknown, but excitement had also danced in young Cora's belly—the butterflies of new adventures. At least at first.

She had played in these fields, running her hands through the flowers, and daydreaming about the day the handsome prince would realize his life was empty without her. She'd looked to the skies, longing to see him, longing to see anyone, but no one visited. They were outcasts and alone.

Instead of new adventures, death came for Cora's family. Death and pain.

Run! Her mom's final cry screeched through Cora's memory.

She flinched.

"Are you okay?" Ronin asked.

He'd insisted on holding her every night since the bearcat attack and she'd become used to his touch, his strength. Dependent on it, even. Like a drug, she wanted his arms around her now—something, anything to chase away the resurfacing memories.

God, she was so pathetic and didn't want to change a thing.

She squeezed her eyes shut and clutched the bearcat claw necklace Karla made for her. They'd had to ditch the remaining portion of Bearcat meat, paws included, to avoid the scouts, but Karla had salvaged one of the claws. Strung on a thin strap of leather, the hunter had chucked the necklace on Cora's lap one night when they sat around the fire.

"This is yours," was all Karla had said.

Cora squeezed the three-inch long claw, feeling the bite of the tip in her palm. If she could survive a bearcat attack, she could do this.

"I'll be fine," she said.

"We can camp near the base," he said. "We don't need to go in. Phil and Karla can check it out and make it ready in case we need to go inside for protection."

She shook her head. "I'm a little over sleeping on the ground, aren't you?"

His gaze smouldered. "Oh, I don't know. I enjoyed some aspects of it."

She didn't know what to say to that, so she looked away.

Seagulls squawked like sky rodents and circled the turrets lining the top of the tower. She used to love going up there—the view was amazing, and the wind would blast her hair from her face. Seagulls would circle, hoping for scraps, the birds in the forest chirped and sang with each sunrise and sunset, but it was the ocean below that mesmerized her. The churning, dark blue depths called to something deep in her chest, beckoning her to dive into the icy unknown.

Ever since she could remember, she'd felt the pull of the sea. When she'd asked her dad about it, he'd laughed it off as childish whimsy, then teenage daydreaming and finally adult delusion.

"All cormorants love the ocean, but it doesn't call to us, Cora," he'd say, usually right before patting her on the head and telling her to run along.

It was Mom's face that gave it away—whatever *it* was. Mom would get that pinched look. When Cora first went to her, Mom appeared alarmed, then worried, then concerned...

Cora sighed.

And then she was gone. With Dad looking at her as if her brain got addled, and no one else to ask, she'd let the matter drop.

Here, though. Here, the ocean didn't whisper or beckon or call. It demanded.

She gripped the reins and squeezed. "Let's go. We need to secure the keep before nightfall."

Ronin wisely shut his mouth and followed, his giant presence reassuring.

Phil and Karla watched the entire exchange with interest but didn't comment or question. She liked that about them. They knew when to shut up. Usually.

They tethered the horses outside the keep. The others dismounted and unsheathed their weapons. She swung her leg over the saddle and Ronin whipped his head in her direction to snarl at her.

"I'm coming," she said.

"No, you're not."

Cora swung her leg back over and sat on her stupid cow horse, who wasn't nearly so stupid and most assuredly was not a cow. Phil told her the mare was a paint horse. What an absurd name. This mare had a botched paint job and needed an attitude adjustment. Karla had promised to take the horses back to Calandria with them and find them a good home. She patted the creature's neck. She'd actually miss this stubborn beast.

She should've joined the others to secure the keep. Injuries no longer plagued her. The set of Ronin's jaw told her arguing would be futile, though. After the bearcat attack, he was in full protector mode and a part of her loved it.

Gah!

That was so messed up.

The other part of her, the part that still had a brain capable of logic, knew Ronin was at the end of his rope. He cared for her and he'd watched her almost bleed out from extensive wounds. Fully assuming her request to visit the ocean was a dying request, he took her anyway. Instead of watching her die, he watched the ocean heal her. Instead of hammering her with questions, he'd accepted what she could offer at the moment. He was trying to be patient. So, as annoying as his overprotectiveness was, she stayed in the saddle. Not for herself, but for him.

She couldn't have the king of the Eyrie collapsing in a panic or having a heart attack.

A chorus of birds singing drew her attention away from the keep. She turned in the saddle to survey the forest. The woods waited and watched a couple hundred feet away, the trees creaking from the wind flowing off the ocean, the grass and tall wildflowers swaying, the leaves rustling. The birds chirped at ease, completely ambivalent to the war of her emotions.

She closed her eyes and breathed in the sea foam and forest scents. The smell of sun-ripened berries and something floral clung to the air. There used to be blue lilacs that grew on the cliff side of the outpost. Maybe they were still there.

A heavy warm hand rested on her thigh.

"Ready?" Ronin asked.

She jumped in the saddle. If Ronin hadn't held her leg down, she probably would've catapulted off the horse altogether.

His eyes narrowed.

"As ready as I'll ever be," she answered.

She swung her leg over the horse and dismounted. If she stayed outside, she'd have another night on the cold hard ground.

No, thank you.

Time to face her past.

She took a deep breath and stepped into Hadren's

Keep, no more than a rectangular building with a large tower jutting out of its centre. They said Hadren's daughter jumped from the roof to her death when she realized her lover never intended to marry her.

Cora breathed in the stale air. The stone walls kept the atmosphere cool, even in the summer. There used to be a hint of wildflowers from the ones Mom used to bring in. That smell was gone, replaced with dirt.

She stepped farther into the room. The large fireplace was exactly how she remembered it. The patterned stonework surrounded the fire and travelled up the wall to each floor, carrying the heat and smoke within until it reached the chimney on the roof. In the winter, Dad would build a giant fire and the heat would move in scorching waves, almost blistering her skin when she walked past.

A layer of dust coated the floor, disrupted only in the paths the others took to clear the building. The base of the wooden staircase that curled up the tower still stood. The third step used to creak so badly, it sounded like someone groaned in pain. They probably all creaked now.

She headed over to find out.

Ronin grabbed her shoulder "Do you think it wise?"

She shrugged off his loose grip. "I think it's inevitable."

"Well, I think it's downright confusing," Karla said.

"Will someone please fill us in? What's up with Cora and this building?"

Apparently, the time to shut up had passed.

"What happened?" Phil asked, his tone surprisingly soft.

"My mother died here."

37

"You're my favourite place to go when my mind searches for peace."

— UNKNOWN

Cora hadn't ventured upstairs. The echoes of painful memories whispered from the stones and beckoned her forward, while the ocean outside called to her. And she yearned to reach over and touch the man sitting across from the fire.

She was losing her fucking mind.

The heat of the fire bathed her skin and she cradled the cup of water in both palms.

Karla had caught a rabbit and the food warmed her

belly. The sun had set long ago and now they had to settle into the waiting game. Would Ronin's wing take longer than a week to heal? Would the other humans discover their presence before then?

Cora could leave Ronin and return on her own, but she didn't trust Sasha's reaction. Her former friend wouldn't believe a word out of her mouth or trust a letter penned, signed, and sealed by her own brother.

Cora would end up on the executioner's block for a most-likely painful death and Ronin wouldn't arrive in time to exonerate her.

Hard pass on that plan.

Besides, she didn't want to leave Ronin on his own. She couldn't provide much assistance in the way of physical defence. If Karla and Phil decided to betray them, she'd just be another body. It was the trip home that caused her to hesitate. The path to the Eyrie from this location was even more challenging than the channel crossing. Only two people alive successfully made the trip—Cora and her father. She hadn't attempted the crossing from here since...

She shivered.

The memories of the last crossing came in broken fragments and waves of intense emotion. She still couldn't piece them together or recall her journey home when she fled for her life.

"I'm off to bed," Phil announced. "Wake me for my watch." He slapped Karla on the back and disappeared from the firelight. The steps creaked and groaned as he made his way up the winding staircase.

"I don't know why we need a watch," Ronin grumbled. "Those stairs will act as a better alarm system than any of us."

Karla stood and stretched. "I'm off to my perch." She had drawn first watch and would sit out on the balcony from her fourth-story room. "You two should turn in soon and get some rest. Proper rest. None of that hanky-panky crap."

Not waiting for a response, she followed her comrade from the room—leaving Cora and Ronin to their silence.

Karla was right. She needed rest. But—

"Building up the courage to go upstairs?" Ronin asked, watching the fire instead of her.

"I don't think I can do it." The admission hurt like a dagger to the gut. Asking for help had never been a strength of hers.

"You need to sleep, we all do." He turned to her, the fire's light flickering in his dark gaze. "It's just wood and stone."

"It's the memories."

He moved from his seat—smooth as to not frighten her, and slow as to give her time to bolt. When she didn't flee, he knelt in front of her, gathering her hands in his. "What exactly happened? Maybe talking through it will help."

She sighed but didn't brush his hands away. "The humans found out we were here."

"The place was watched?"

She shook her head. "My father scouted the surrounding area when we first arrived. There was no sign of anyone camping out or coming anywhere near the keep. There are so many rumours of ghosts, most people avoided this place. He thinks someone from the Eyrie tipped them off." She let the silence fill in the blank.

"You suspect my father."

She shrugged again. "Getting the humans to take care of us would eliminate his need to get his own hands dirty. Your parents were the only people aware of our destination. It's possible others guessed. After all these years, my father still hasn't figured out the source."

"Is that one of the reasons why he agreed to come back?"

"It's the only reason he came back."

Ronin's smile was sad. "I don't know about that. I think he came back for you, as well." His mouth twisted down as if a sudden thought made him want to puke and he looked away. "What happened then?"

"They attacked when my father was out fishing. We were caught off-guard and trapped inside."

The sound of the men breathing heavily as they chased after them. The thunder of their boots hitting the stone flooring, the scrape of their weapons against the walls.

"We tried to make it upstairs to launch out the window. I made it." She pulled one of her hands free from Ronin's grip and touched the scar running down her right cheek. "My mom didn't."

"She held them off so you had time to get out the window and escape," Ronin guessed.

She nodded. "They were so much faster than us. We were unprepared." They'd grown complacent to their surroundings when they should've maintained constant vigilance. Sapavians did not move as fast or as easily on the ground as humans. They relied too much on the ability to fly away from danger. When they couldn't escape to the sky, their wings got in the way. They should've anticipated an attack that put them at a disadvantage.

Ronin squeezed her hand. "You escaped out the second-floor window. The one in the room Phil took?"

She nodded. "I made the mistake of looking back." She forced her hand down from her face. Metal flashed through the memory rushing forward, hot and gut-wrenching. She'd leaned back and twisted, just in time to catch the tip of the blade instead of getting her neck severed. She'd fallen out of the window, her last image of the room was the man's snarling face and her mom lying in a pool of her own blood at his feet.

With not enough time to right herself and gain the

updraft, she'd hit the rocky cliff face. Rushing toward the gray stone was her last coherent memory. She didn't know what happened next, but she must've bounced off the cliff and into the water.

"And then what happened?" Ronin reached out to hold her free hand.

The warmth of his touch spreading through her body quickly turned to ice as more memories resurfaced: frigid water, the churning depths of the ocean, lungs so full they wanted to burst, panic, a cave surrounded with cold air and bone-numbing wind, an air duct with sun overhead, and a hauntingly familiar voice.

She shivered. "I don't exactly know. I hit my head from the fall out the window but made it home somehow."

"Barely."

She bit her lip. "Physically, I was fine." Even her face wound had healed by the time she washed up on the Eyrie's shore.

Ronin sighed. "But starving and incoherent. Your ocean healing doesn't fill your body or fix your mind."

"No. Time did that."

He smiled softly and let go of one hand to stroke her face. "You're a survivor. I admire that about you."

She sucked in a breath. He was so close. His breath brushed her skin and the heat of his body continued to caress her. It would take so little to close the distance, to press her lips against his and let him take her body and mind somewhere else.

"What is it you want?" she asked.

"That's a loaded question."

"I just spilled my heart out," she said. "Answer it."

"I want a truce between the humans and sapavians. I want a solution for our space issues. I want to ensure my sister's happiness. I want to make my father proud, even though it looks more and more like he's no longer with us."

All admirable things.

"But that's not what you're asking, is it?"

She shook her head.

"I want you, Cora."

The words should've comforted her more than they did, but she'd always been one to let her brain rule her actions, not her heart. "We may as well have this conversation now. You're the king of the Eyrie, Ronin. You need to marry for connections, position, finances, or any combination of the three. I don't offer any of those things, only a temporary respite from responsibility and boredom."

His brow furrowed and his body tensed. "There would be nothing temporary about us."

The truth in his words stabbed at her chest. She needed to steel her heart from the warmth of hope and the subsequent heartbreak. "But you would never be mine. Not truly."

"I'm the king now," he growled. "I'll do what I

want. I have enough connections, position and finances for the both of us."

She shook her head again, her hair falling in front of her face. He might think that now, but once they returned and those snotty advisors surrounded him with propriety, rules and expectations, things would change, and her heart would get crushed.

It was already breaking.

"Come. Let's go to bed." He straightened and pulled her up with him. "You have last watch and need to get some sleep."

She nodded and let him guide her to the stairs. The weakness that had temporarily taken over her limbs faded away, and with a deep breath, she climbed the stairs. Each step brought forth a memory.

Run! Mom's desperate cry.

Cora's rasping breath as she raced up the stairs.

The pressure of Mom's hand on her back pushing her forward.

Their feet smacking the wooden steps.

The groan and creak of wood.

Cora shook her head again and continued to place one foot in front of the other, walking through the memories and the ghosts of her past until she made it to the third floor. Maybe this place truly was haunted, but with memories instead of ghosts.

She stopped in front of the bedroom door. It wasn't her old room or her parents', nor was it the room where Mom...She squeezed her eyes shut and banished the flood of memories and emotions. It wasn't the room she'd escaped from. They'd used this space for storage, and it was one of the few places in the entire keep that held little emotional value or impact.

Ronin stopped behind her instead of continuing to his room.

She turned to face him, her hands balling into fists. "Can you—"

"Yes," he cut her off, his tone solemn.

"You don't even know what I was going to ask."

"I'll stay with you."

Okay, maybe he did. Maybe she was predictable, or easy to read. "Just to sleep though." He might be sticking his head in the sand, but she couldn't lose sight of reality. They could never have a true relationship.

"Cora, relax." He reached out and ran his hands down her tense arms to hold her clenched fists. "I'm not going to ravage you."

She raised her eyebrows.

His answering grin was wicked. "Unless you want me to."

Ravaging certainly had its appeal. Sex with Ronin would take her mind off other things. If only she could let it be just that, but her heart was already too invested.

Ronin didn't wait expectantly for a response. Instead, he let her go and reached past her to turn the handle. The heavy wood door swung open and stale air crashed over them.

Cora turned and walked into the dark room. A double bed had been pushed against the far wall. A small window let the moonlight bathe the bed and surrounding floor in a silvery, ethereal glow. When the others had scouted the rooms earlier, they'd dusted off the beds and found extra sheets, but Cora didn't pick up a cozy vibe. The window was too small to squeeze through if there was an emergency. She'd be trapped in this room.

The walls closed in.

Ronin cleared his throat and pulled his belt free from his pants. He rested the sword in its sheath against the wall beside the bed and started removing the rest of his weapons. In the cave, he slept beside her in almost nothing, preferring to sleep only in his underwear. His armour would be next.

Cora peeled off her leather flying gear careful not to rip it anymore. She'd tried to salvage parts of it, but the leather was ruined.

She folded the clothing carefully and placed it on the old wooden chair. When she turned around, Ronin stood a few feet away. Though he hadn't moved and didn't intentionally crowd her, his large presence filled the room. His dark gaze reflected the flickering candlelight.

"You promised," she whispered. "No ravaging."

"Something I'm already intensely regretting." He pulled her into his arms, but instead of said ravaging, he held her and dropped his face into the crook of her neck. She leaned into him, resting her forehead on his shoulder. Eventually, they moved to the bed and she curled up into his warm body and drifted to sleep in the comfort of his arms. The memories would continue to plague her but for now, Ronin's presence dulled their pain and chased them away.

38

"It's what you practice in private that you will be rewarded for in public."

— ANTHONY ROBBINS

"Cora, you're not holding it right," Ronin growled. The joke wasn't just old, it was beaten to death and buried under six feet of dirt. He couldn't help himself.

Cora scowled and adjusted her grip on the dagger. "I still say the hammer grip isn't practical for me. The RGEO is better for defence."

"And I'm still telling you, sometimes the best defence is a good offense."

"For a couple who spend their nights together, the

two of you still have a lot of tension to work through," Phil quipped from a few feet away where he ran through drills with Karla. "If you aren't getting those kinks rubbed out, Cora, I'd be happy to step in and help you out."

"And I'd be happy to punch you in the face, but we're not getting everything on our wish lists right now, are we?" Ronin snapped.

Phil cackled, only to leave himself open for a vicious jab from Karla.

Hah! Karma.

Cora's face reddened. She clamped her mouth shut and launched into the air. If they didn't have witnesses, he'd join her and kiss her, right here, right now. The tension was slowly killing him. He held her every night, soothing her back to sleep when the nightmares woke her. Not expecting anything in return, he held her because he wanted to. He wanted her to feel safe, and he wanted to be there for her like he should've been all those years ago.

He also wanted to taste every inch of her body, but now was not the time. Ronin always excelled at compartmentalizing.

What unsettled him most, though, was how much his wants and needs had shifted from when this trip started.

Cora swooped down from the air, wings wide, legs drawn up and blade out.

He brought his own weapon up in time to block

her attack, but it wasn't enough. Her body slammed into his and they crashed to the ground.

"Fuck, Cora," he growled in her ear. "This is practice."

"Not my fault you're distracted." She panted as she blocked his strike. "Where's that constant vigilance you're always bragging about?"

He grinned and using her own limb as leverage, disarmed her. The dagger went flying, sunlight glinting from the blade.

Instead of using his own to get her to yield, he chucked his dagger to the side, far enough away from where they sparred to worry about it later.

"Careful." She lifted both her eyebrows. "You're still mending. You don't want to pull something."

He locked her arms, shifted his weight, and rolled them, pinning Cora to the ground with her wings trapped beneath her. It was the most vulnerable position for sapavians...and the ultimate submissive pose.

And his thoughts went from fighting to something else entirely. "It's you who should be careful."

"Oh?"

He nodded solemnly. "You're the one at risk of tearing something."

"Your heart? Please."

"Your outfit. You only recently managed to string it back together. Sort off." His gaze drifted to her chest. "Though I think I prefer the new plunging neckline."

Her gaze flashed and she attempted to roll again.

He blocked her legs and smiled.

Cora huffed, her chest rising and falling with each breath. She was sucking in air and trying to control her breathing. She did that a lot.

"Your father taught you well," he said.

She laughed. "That's what you're thinking about right now? My father?"

"I don't think you can handle what I'm actually thinking about right now."

"None of us can!" Karla snapped. "Just get on with it or get off her. We're trying to practice over here."

"Speak for yourself," Phil grumbled.

Ronin hopped to his feet and offered Cora his hand. She took it and he helped her stand.

"Like you'd focus on your technique if we actually went for it in front of you two perverts," Cora said.

Phil dropped his sword arm to his side. "What do you suggest we focus on then?"

Ronin sheathed his dagger and walked over to clap Phil on the back. "My technique. You might learn something."

Cora giggled.

Her eyes widened and she slapped her hand on her mouth and shook her head.

He met her gaze and she shook her head again.

Right, like she could deny that happened. Her giggle, a sound almost as rare as a unicorn sighting, was the most adorable sound ever.

. C. MCKENZIE

And adorable wasn't a word he'd ever use to describe Cora.

He held his hand out toward her. "Come on."

She looked down at his open hand.

He flapped it in the air. "The sun is going to set. Let's get a flight in."

Her gaze sparkled and her whole demeanor changed. From guarded and unsure, she morphed into ecstatic excitement and anticipation.

She slapped her hand in his and let him lead her away from the others.

39

"The best and most beautiful things in this world cannot be seen or even heard, but must be felt with the heart."

— HELEN KELLER

Something about this flight was different. Instead of flying quietly side by side as they travelled in loops around the tower, Ronin took off, swopping in and out, up and down. Playfully tugging on her wings or blasting past her.

He wanted to play.

Cora wanted something else entirely, but she went along with it, enjoying the dance in the wind and the air flows rushing by her wings.

Ronin swooped down and caught her in his arms. They started to fall toward the cliffs.

"Ronin!"

He grinned, his teeth flashing white in the moonlight. Instead of letting her go, he pulled her closer and kissed her.

What?

She pushed back and he let go. They spread their wings, caught the updraft, and rose once again to the clouds.

"Have you lost your mind?" she shrieked.

Instead of answering, he swooped in again, gathering her in his arms. His gaze, cast in shadows, met hers, emotion flashing like a thunderstorm. His hold tightened, one hand travelling up her back while the other drifted down to grip her butt. "Definitely."

He kissed her again, hard and full of need. Her belly flipped as the air whooshed by and they plummeted toward the land. She pushed against his chest again and he released her. She flapped her wings, regained altitude, and gaped at him.

The eagle's plunge. Cartwheeling.

"What are you doing?"

He barred his teeth and growled "You know exactly what I'm doing, what this is."

He shot forward to grab her again, but she backed up.

"No!" she gasped.

"No?" He looked incredulous. "Why the hell not?"

"You're the heir...you're the king."

"Exactly. I'll do as I want, and I want you."

"And that will last two hours once we're back at the Eyrie."

"Do you think that little of me? That I would abandon you and what we have? Would I be cart-wheeling with a fling?"

"No. I don't think that little of you, but I think a lot of the system of entrenched bias and expectations. It made your father turn his back on his best friend. Instead of exonerating my father, he banished him and probably patted himself on the back because he avoided having to execute his best fucking friend. My father did everything for yours. He was loyal to a fault. And look what that got him. Look at how well your father got to do what he wanted."

Ronin scowled. "This isn't about our fathers. It's about us."

"There can't be an 'us.' Even if you don't leave me, you'll end up resenting me. I can't do it. I can't..."

Ronin barked out a laugh. "I won't resent you."

"How can you be so sure?"

"I love you."

She continued to flap her wings to maintain her position. Ronin did the same. He raised an eyebrow, mocking, daring her to argue.

Her heart fluttered like a wild thunderbird.

Why shouldn't she be with him? Why shouldn't she take a chance and trust her heart? Because he'd break it? Wasn't her heart already breaking?

She'd been broken before and learned how to put herself back together again. She could do this. She deserved this.

"Fine," she said.

"Fine?" He folded his arms, hovering in the air. "That's how you're going to respond to my declaration of love?"

"Take it or leave it."

Mischief flashed in his gaze. He unfolded his arms and leaned forward.

Uh-oh.

He licked his lips and smiled again. "I'm definitely going to take."

"Typical."

He laughed, a deep rumble from his chest this time. She couldn't take her eyes off him. Anticipation clenched her stomach and squeezed the air from her lungs.

"I'm more of a giver than a taker," Ronin purred. "But I'll make an exception if that's what you need."

She needed him inside her. Heat drenched her body. Yet, she hovered a few feet away, remaining distant, deciding how to respond. Instead of running, instead of squealing and making him give chase like they were teenagers all over again, instead of using an excuse to diffuse the emotionally charged moment,

Cora beat her wings once and drifted into Ronin's open arms. She pulled her wings in, letting him hold her aloft. The wind played with her hair and bursts of air brushed her skin with each pump of Ronin's wings. She tilted her head up. The tension around Ronin's eyes eased away. Mischief still sparkled in his gaze—surprise, too—but this tenderness he showed her stole her breath away.

"I need to hear you say it," he said.

"Why?"

"Please?"

"Ronin, I've loved you since the day you punched Jerome in the sack for calling me ugly."

He sighed and pulled her into his body. "Ready?"

"Try not to hurt yourself."

THE CARTWHEELING DIDN'T last long.

Cora followed Ronin around the cliff face while Hadren's Keep loomed over them from the ledge. They'd found a few caves and alcoves during their daily explorations, some she remembered from her past, some new. Which one was Ronin leading her to now? Did he even know?

Instead of a cave or a bedroom, Ronin took her to a private nook farther from the point. Still at the edge of the cliff and sheltered by the trees, the flat clearing was covered with dense moss.

When had Ronin found this place?

The moment her feet touched down in front of Ronin, he took her chin in his hand and lifted. Gaze searching hers, he studied her, letting the stillness fall over them like the moonlight from overhead.

She had so many questions, so many things to say, to doubt, but none of those things mattered. Not anymore.

Ronin leaned down, bringing his lips to hers. They'd kissed before—passionate kisses, tender kisses, kisses filled with need.

This kiss, though.

This kiss had everything rolled into one, with love woven in. As easy and simple as breathing, this kiss stole her will to breathe, to care about anything other than the feel and taste of Ronin. He was her drug and she was getting her fix.

More, please.

He might break her heart, they might die on the journey home, his sister might execute her...none of those things mattered. Not right now.

He lifted her and she wrapped her legs around his torso, latching onto him like a limpet.

Hers.

The king of the Eyrie was hers.

They tumbled to the ground, the thick moss cushioning their fall. Cora landed on top of Ronin. When he winced, she pulled away. "Your wing?"

"It's fine."

"But—"

"If you stop right now, I'll die." He claimed her mouth again.

She laughed against his lips. If he wasn't hurt, she had other things to worry about—mainly how to get him out of those clothes. She pulled at his vest, unlatching the buckles, and pulling down the zipper. Once open, she slid her hands along his smooth skin.

More. She needed more.

She kissed his jaw and tugged at his belt. When it pulled free from the loopholes, she chucked it away. The leather belt flopped into the moss.

Ronin lifted his hips, pressing his erection into her. She ground against him, still wanting more, delighting in the sound of Ronin's growl.

Without warning, Ronin rolled them to their sides. He wrenched her bodice, ripping it apart. Her breasts spilled out, free, heavy and in need of his touch.

"My shirt!"

"It was ruined anyway," he murmured against her breast before taking her nipple into his mouth.

Goddammit.

His hands explored her body, rough, almost harsh, his patience shattered. He roamed her skin with his hot mouth and Cora drowned in a torrent of sensations. A few more touches, a stroke, a lick, and she'd come undone. She was so close.

"Please," she said. *More.*

Still on his side, Ronin looked up from between her

thighs. He'd moved there seamlessly, hooking one of her legs around his shoulders to continue his assault, to make her writhe with need, to make her beg.

He licked his lips. "Should I stop?"

"Don't you dare." Her whole body ached. Why was he tormenting her?

He licked the inside of her thigh and moved his wicked mouth back up her body. She nearly screamed in frustration.

When he claimed her mouth again, she held on and rolled them, pulling Ronin on top of her, pinning her wings beneath her body, offering herself to him.

Ronin's gaze went wild.

He pressed the head of his shaft into her, slowly, letting her feel every inch of him until she was full, too full, until no space existed between them. There was no Cora or Ronin. Just them. Joined. Connected.

Part of Cora ached to flip him over and torture him with slow undulating movement, teasing and frustrating him as he had done to her before, riding him into oblivion. But she didn't. Couldn't. She needed him now and she was done with flirting and teasing.

Ronin growled into her neck. He pulled in and out, most likely planning to torment her more, but something snapped.

Probably the same thing that snapped inside her.

"Yes," she whispered. "More. Harder."

Ronin growled again, gaze wild. He took her fast and hard, thrusting deep and driving her into the moss and to the point of delirious madness. He gripped her shoulders and slammed into her, again and again, the pace brutal, the sensations exquisite. Cora loved every second of it. He pumped into her until they both roared from the intense release and came undone.

40

"There's nothing more beautiful than the way the ocean refuses to stop kissing the shoreline, no matter how many times it's sent away."

— SARAH KAY

Ronin let the wind wash over him. Even at this altitude, the air held a little sea spray from the waves crashing against the rocky shore below

Cora stood beside him, pensive, tense. She'd rather stay in the place her mother died than return home. She didn't need to speak the words, but he knew she was worried things would change when they touched down in the Eyrie. She'd never say it, of course. Not now. Not after what they shared. He knew her logic well. In Cora's mind, she'd already explained her concerns and continuing to voice those concerns held no added value. But she wore her emotions on her face and after spending the last two weeks savouring every inch of her body and studying every nuance of her expression, he read her like a book.

He didn't want to leave, either. Not because he was worried about what he or she would do once they returned, but because he knew duty would call and he'd have to spend some of his day doing work. So would Cora. And the idea of sharing her with trips across the channel without him created a hollow feeling in his gut—like someone had reached in, grabbed everything, and pulled it out.

He tightened his grip on her hand. They'd been gone for over a month. His sister probably thought he was dead. He needed to return.

She squeezed back.

"Ready?" he asked.

"No."

He grinned. Cora had healed since her little splish-splash in the ocean, but he knew what she meant. "Me, neither."

"Maybe we should stay? I think I'm going to miss that cow horse."

"No, you won't."

"You're right. I won't. But maybe we should stay anyway."

"That would be irresponsible." The Eyrie had impending problems that wouldn't solve themselves.

"But a lot more satisfying."

He looked down at her. If he had his way, he'd pick her up, stomp back to the keep, rip off her makeshift flying gear and show her just how satisfying it could be.

"Oh, would you two just leave?" Karla barked from a few feet away. "I want to go home."

"And you have fucked enough these last couple of weeks. You can wait a couple of days until you get home," Phil added.

"Debatable," Ronin grumbled.

Cora snorted and dove off the cliff. Before hitting the water, she spread her wings, caught the wind, and rose into the skies.

Phil whistled.

"See you soon," Ronin said.

"Hope not," Phil said. "Send Cora on her own next time, eh?"

Ronin flipped him off and followed Cora. The wind streamed by, pressing his face, pushing on the humerus bones of his wings. The mended one still felt weaker than the other—not quite one hundred percent, but it held. The last two weeks had been training, fucking and fighting.

Best. Time. Ever.

"I'll actually miss those two." Cora hovered above, waiting. She waved to the two king's hunters watching from the cliff's edge. When he drew closer, she let her hand fall and turned to him.

"Ready?" she repeated his earlier question.

"No."

She smirked and turned northward, setting an easy pace.

"So what abominations do I have to look forward to on this trip?"

"The Sea Beast."

"And?"

"Just the Sea Beast."

That sounded ominous. When he was in court, reports constantly came back from the cormorant and albatross patrols on the eastern opening of the channel with sightings of the sciper. They theorized it had a lair in the northern area of the bay.

What a nice pleasant thought for a morning flight.

"It will take us all day to get to Outpost Island," Cora called out over her shoulder.

They'd already spoken about this. Why was she bringing it up now?

"The Sea Beast doesn't usually patrol this far south. Tomorrow's trip is when we'll have to be more cautious."

"You don't sound worried."

"What?"

He repeated his question, yelling over the wind.

She looked over her shoulder, tendrils of hair

already escaping her braid to slap her face. "I can sense him."

What? "What?"

"I sense him."

"Right now?" Though warm from flying, a chill spread through his body. He scanned the water below. Where was the fucker?

"He's north of here and distant. When he gets closer, I'll feel it."

First the ocean healing, now this? All sapavians retained some birdlike behavioural ticks from the DNA used to genetically enhance and alter their ancestors. Eagles tended to be monogamists, the urge to cartwheel with their chosen mate strong and instinctual. He'd never felt the drive to free fall to his possible death while making out until he kissed Cora.

Seagulls craved to buy, trade and endlessly searched for better deals and more profits. Most Seagull Clan members found themselves in merchant trades, market vendors and store owners.

Pigeons excelled at short distance communication. Often acting as messengers within the kingdom's walls. Technically, they delivered messages to Iom as well, travelling the route through the waystations, but anyone with money and means went through Kane.

Hawks were driven to protect and gravitated to enforcement roles, making up the bulk of the police force and the royal guard.

And cormorants? Officially known for ocean scouting and fishing, their clan had an unofficial reputation as spies and long-distance cross-water messengers.

What other traits did the Cormorant Clan retain from their avian DNA?

"Is that a cormorant thing?"

She shook her head. "Neither is the ocean healing. It's a Cora thing. Something...Something's different with me."

He drew up beside her and they hovered in the air, aided by a strong wind. "Do you think something happened to you after you escaped the outpost? You don't really remember that time."

She bit her lip and looked away.

No, that wasn't it. Had she always sensed sea monsters? Was that how she evaded the beast? Is that why she didn't want it to be killed? What exactly was the connection between her and the monster?

"Something definitely happened during the time I can't remember." She paused and took a deep breath. "But I think I've always sensed the sea monster. I've always had this...awareness. This tingling at the base of my neck that would intensify and fade like the ebb and flow of the tide. The first time I really sensed the sea monster was when my family made the trip to Hadren's Keep and then it stayed. No longer a faint feeling, a strong awareness remained in my head as if the Sea Beast stalked the shores of the Oap waiting for me." She shivered and ran her hands over her arms. "Hell, maybe he did."

"You keep saying he."

She nodded.

"What aren't you telling me?"

A gust of wind pushed them up, bringing with it salt and little puffs of sea foam.

They both looked up at the sky, the clouds more gray than white closing in.

"Rain," Cora said.

He nodded. "We need to move."

Without speaking, they turned north and flew. This time Cora set a harder pace. Fast, but steady, aiming for Outpost Island. The odd rock formation that reached up from the ocean might provide them with safety from the elements, the approaching storm and allow them to rest for the night, but Cora wouldn't be safe from his questions. With each wingbeat, he added another to his list.

41

"Be alone with the sea for it is there you will find answers to questions you didn't realize exist."

— KHANG KIJARRO NGUYEN

In the middle of Carrion Bay, a jagged rock jutted from the ocean. The ruins of an ancient outpost perched on a ledge above the crashing waves. The water was always turbulent here. Strong currents from Carrion Channel, the bay and the Eyrie Ocean seemed to collide in this one despondent spot. As she didn't carry a death wish, Cora never ventured beneath the surface of the angry ocean at this particular location. There didn't appear to be a ledge under the water.

No shoreline. The slice of mountain rose straight from the deep depths of the bay.

Cora led Ronin to the shelter within the ruins. It wasn't much. A hastily erected roof constructed from the building's remains and extra survival material stashed away, safe from the elements. Messengers travelled light and rarely travelled this route.

She paused.

Never travelled this route.

She sorted through the old supplies and set up the bedding while Ronin made a fire. Everything smelled of mould.

"You're quiet," she said.

"I have a lot of questions. I'm trying to sort out which ones I should ask first."

She nodded, waiting for regret or disgust to flash across his expression. Instead, he sat down and patted the spot on his right. He splayed his wings behind him and leaned back on his arms.

She sat down and spread her wings to block the wind. "Hit me with them."

His eyebrows shot up.

She shrugged. "I may not have all the answers, but I don't intend to hide anything from you." She'd decided on the last leg of today's travel that she wouldn't lie or evade. If Ronin truly wanted to be with her, she needed him to know who she was.

His smile was slow and lazy. "What aren't you telling me about the Sea Beast?"

She sucked in a breath. Straight to the point. "He talks to me."

His eyes widened. "Out loud? All I heard was a creepy moan."

"No," She tapped her head. "In here."

"And do you...talk back?"

She nodded.

"Of course, you do." He paused, scrunching his mouth as he probably mulled over his words. "How do you talk to him? In your head as well?"

She nodded again. She'd never told anyone about her connection to the Sea Beast before. Not even Father.

"What does he say?"

"Not much. The speaking is actually new. Before, I just sensed him and his great hunger. Then it was a word. Then a few."

"What does he say?"

She sighed and poked the fire with a stick. "He says I'm his."

"You're his?"

She nodded, wishing she wouldn't regress into a bobbing head when faced with these questions. Sometimes, it was just easier to nod than voice the truth with words.

"Well, he's wrong." Ronin leaned over. "Because you're mine."

Her chest grew warm despite the cold wind. "I don't think he means it romantically. I think he means

I'm his to eat."

Ronin's gaze sparkled as he silently laughed at her.

She reached out and shoved his shoulder. "Shut up. Not like that."

Ronin chuckled and picked up another stick to poke the fire. "Is this connection the reason why you objected to King Aeneas' amendment?"

"Partly. The main reason is the one I gave you. It was a bad deal to take. Even with my connection, which I'm not willing to share with others, we'd fail at killing the Sea Beast."

Ronin nodded. "I'm glad you led with that reason. If you'd claimed you had a telepathic link to a murderous sea beast who wanted you on his dinner plate, I would've been more inclined to agree to the king's new terms."

Cora laughed.

"Now, come here. I have just enough energy to perform some dirty sex acts."

"You really know how to charm a lady." She crossed her arms. "Didn't you learn anything at court? Don't they give you lessons on how to be noble?"

"This is for generating heat and saving our lives." He winked. "A noble cause."

She narrowed her eyes at him.

"And I want to hold you. Feeling your body pressed to mine makes me feel like I'm finally home."

Well, how could she deny him with sweet words like that? She opened her arms and he gathered her up and proceeded to show her just how much energy he had left.

42

"I started making plans thinking we would get that far."

— DANIEL HANDLER

The bone-numbing wind howled past Ronin's face. Salt spray splattered his clothes as the sea raged below. The day had started with clear skies and no hint of bad weather on the horizon. He'd wrongly looked forward to a smooth second leg of their trip home to the Eyrie.

Cora soared beside him, her face drawn, brows furrowed, and her hands balled into fists. He didn't need her to say anything to know they were in trouble.

The swells grew larger. White caps lined the crests

and created veins along the ridges. Sea spray licked off the surface and spread through the air.

After spotting a thunderbird flock that according to Cora shouldn't have been hunting in this area, they'd stuck closer to sea level, aiming to hide in the peaks and valleys of the large ocean swells.

None of the feral birds had dropped out of the gray sky to attack them so the camouflage must've worked.

Cora turned to him and shouted. The wind and waves drowned her out. She flung her hands around, waving them to the side.

He flapped his wings to draw closer. They needed to work on their hand signals. They spoke two completely different languages.

She squinted at him, mouth pursed and then something changed.

Her whole body tensed. Her eyes widened. Without warning, she abruptly changed direction and dove toward him. She tucked her wings in and barrelled into him, knocking him off course.

At the same time, a large monster shot from the ocean below, gaping maw open.

Ronin spun around in the stormy wind, righted himself and turned in time to see the monster's mouth close around Cora.

No!

He drew his sword and screamed.

A large eye on the side of the Sea Beast's gigantic head rotated around and stared at him.

Ronin pointed his sword at the bug-like protruding eye and dove.

Too late. The Sea Beast sank into the water, the waves crashing around his scaly body, covering his retreat.

Ronin shot past the area where the beast had hovered, driving his sword through the empty air. Too late.

The water splashed and sprayed, a frothy marker of where the sciper had disappeared with Cora.

The wind jostled him back and forth. The rain beat at him. Emptiness expanded in his soul as if his heart formed a fist and punched him from the inside repeatedly until nothing else remained except a hollow dull ache.

Ronin bellowed at the ocean, but no one answered.

He hovered there, for a few minutes, hours, days—he didn't know. He hung suspended over the ocean, hounded with disbelief, and stared at the water as if Cora would somehow resurface. As if the Sea Beast would regurgitate her back into being. If only he could rewind time, take back this last moment and correct it. He should be in the empty belly of the beast. Cora should be the one to make it home.

If only he could rewind time.

If only she'd displaced him farther and the sea beast missed.

If only.

If only.

If only.

Ronin hung his head and turned toward the Eyrie. He needed to go home, if at the very least to let Cora's father know what a champion his daughter was. To let the kingdom know his hero's name.

The next few hours were a blur. He coasted, jostled this way and that, until he crashed out of the angry sky onto the rocky shore of the Eyrie. Ronin turned to face the ocean and sank to his knees.

43

"Let the waves carry you where the light cannot."

— MOHIT KAUSHIK

T he mouth closed around Cora. The long fangs snapped shut and sealed her in a toothy cage, casting her in darkness with a pocket of air.

Cora held onto something—a slimy molar—while caught between a wet, spongy tongue and the moist gums of the Sea Beast.

She gripped the slick tooth with one hand and reached for her dagger. The beast turned. Her whole body flung to the side. She screeched, abandoned her dagger, and held on for her life.

What in the bird-loving hell was she thinking? Even if she managed to stab the beast in the cheek from the inside, all that accomplished was pissing him off. He only had to open his mouth to drown her or swat her with his tongue to incapacitate her. Survival meant keeping a calm head and trying to figure a way out of this without angering the beast.

"You ate me!" she screeched out loud and in her head.

I'm holding you in my mouth, the deep voice rattled inside her head.

"I fail to see the difference!"

Do you really? He responded. *If I actually ate you, you would be dead, skin corroded by the acid of my stomach. You are very much alive.*

Not sure she appreciated this new coherent speech. Each instance she'd communicated with him, his words sounded more and more like normal conversation. Either he'd improved his ability to speak in her mind or she was losing her grip on reality.

She was in the mouth of the largest known sciper and mulling over his speech patterns. Clearly, she was losing her mind.

"For how long? Until you get a little peckish and feel like a snack?"

Everything shook.

Her grip slipped and she scrambled to regain her hold on the boulder sized tooth. Saliva dripped from her drenched wings. Her feet slid in the beast's spit.

I don't plan to eat you, birdy. You're mine.

She shuddered. Did he plan to wear her like a trinket?

Pressure built in her head and she ground her teeth together. "Arghhhh."

Why do you scream?

"My head hurts. Did you dive?" The pain was similar to when she dove too deep in the ocean or descended from a high altitude too fast.

Yes. Almost there.

"Can hardly wait." She bit her tongue and kept the rest of her snarky responses to herself. Best not to irritate the beast. He held her life in his hands.

Mouth.

Whatever.

The pain from the pressure eased.

Her feet hit the beast's tongue—he must've leveled out.

And then he changed direction again.

Cora dangled from his tooth and stared down at the back of his mouth. At least that's what she assumed was down there. With no light, it was impossible to see.

Again, without warning, the beast changed direction and abruptly stopped, flinging Cora forward. Her grip on the tooth slipped and she flew through the air. She hit the beast's tongue hard, smacking the lumpy taste buds with a splat. Her stomach rolled.

The mouth opened. Air hit her face. She pulled up from the rough surface and peered out of the beast's large mouth, past the saliva-dripping fangs longer than her own body and into what looked like a dimly lit cavern.

Make it quick, birdy. I'm not keeping my mouth open all day.

She stumbled out of his mouth, tripping on the last row of teeth and flailing onto a smooth slab of rock. She threw her hands up and her wings out to break her fall. Her knees slammed into the wet rock, then her hands. Her momentum stopped with the top of her nose an inch from impact.

She studied the cavern. Rock walls rose up around her, high and narrow, making the cavern look like it rested at the bottom of a naturally formed well, too narrow for her to fly up. Light snuck in from various cracks along the sides and from higher up, but the light-emitting crevices within climbing distance were too small for her to squeeze through. Rain trickled down the wall of obsidian rock and sprinkled from above.

The ocean roared against the walls lower down. She must be standing below sea level, with the tower extending beyond the surface.

There was only one structure within the entire Carrion Channel that jutted up like this.

Outpost Island.

The Sea Beast had brought her to a secret cave inside the mountain on which the outpost sat. Ronin and she had slept in the ruins at the top of this tunnel last night. Had the Sea Beast waited below? Had he listened to their conversation? Their love making?

Did it even matter? No one knew the rock of Outpost Island was hollow.

Oh god.

No one would ever find her.

Cora's stomach sunk.

The floor of the cavern was a giant slab of smooth rock that sloped into the ocean lapping at her feet. There must be an access point to this place beneath the surface of the water. How low though? Could she hold her breath long enough to get down and back up the other side?

And not die from hypothermia?

Given the pressure in her ears earlier, escape using the ocean route seemed unlikely.

A low keening echoed in the room. She turned to where the Sea Beast had beached himself.

She froze.

The Sea Beast shrunk in on himself—condensing. Sea water gushed out of the leathery hide as the body of the Sea Beast reformed into a man.

A giant man.

At least seven feet of hard packed muscle, a naked man stood where the Sea Beast lay moments ago. Gray streaked his dark hair and his skin had a grayish-blue tinge. No one would look at this man and think "human." He radiated power. His sea-green eyes shone with an otherness that sent chills racing along her spine.

Cora unsheathed her long dagger and held it in front of her. The hammer grip would make Ronin proud.

The man glanced at her weapon. The corner of his mouth turned down. "Do you intend to poke me with that?"

"I'll poke you with whatever I want." Wait. That didn't come out right. She winced.

He raised a dark brow. "You can try. You'll find my skin difficult to penetrate with your puny weapon." He patted his flat abs. "All that condensed tissue brings a whole new meaning to thick skinned."

She scowled but didn't sheath her dagger. If he attacked her, she'd go for the eyes. She glanced down his body. Or the dangly bits.

A thought stabbed her mind. "You called me yours. Why? What do you intend to do to me?"

Ice flowed through her veins. No matter how good-looking the monster was, no matter how well-endowed, she'd never be willing. Her heart and body belonged to Ronin.

The man's face paled and he stilled. "Not that!"

Some of the tension released from her shoulders. "Then what? And does it involve you putting clothes on?"

He sighed and walked over to a large boulder she hadn't noticed before—there was a lot going on

—and picked up faded pants. They had rips along the legs and the cuffs were frayed. They also ended mid-calf when he pulled them on. The shirt he threw on after the pants was in no better shape.

Like she could judge. She now wore a hodgepodge of flying leathers and old armour hastily sewn together by herself and a human.

"I don't take this form often," he said. His deep voice remained the same as the one in her head, a little quieter, but it held the same gravelly quality.

"Did your mother ever tell you the story of a man she rescued over twenty-five years ago?"

Cora tightened her grip on the dagger handle. Why was he talking about her mother? Why did he claim Cora as his?

She stiffened. "You're not my father."

He couldn't be. Her mother was faithful, loving and Cora was too much like her father to not be his.

He smiled weakly, flashing rows of jagged teeth, and sat on the edge of the boulder. "I'm not your biological father. Your mom was already pregnant with you when she saved me. She could've killed me, or turned me in, but instead, she showed mercy and compassion."

That sounded about right.

"In return, I blessed her unborn child, you, with my essence."

Cora froze.

"So while you are your mother and father's child, you are also mine."

What the fuck.

"Did you ever wonder why the ocean heals you? Why it beckons to you? Why you safely make the trip across the channel and no other monsters bother you?"

She scowled in unison with the man.

"Except those stupid thunderbirds, of course," he said. "How they're not extinct yet is beyond me."

"You've been protecting me?" He'd eaten one flock of thunderbirds for her, had he consumed others?

He nodded.

"All this time?"

"The Cetus essence running through your veins also acts as a natural deterrent. Scipers like myself recognize the scent."

The memory of the unicorn's face and the recognition in its gaze flared up. All the signs had been there, but how could she have possibly guessed?

"But sapavians..."

"Are too much like humans for their own good. They cannot detect sciper essence unless it practically smacks them in the face. Some might feel different around you, like you command fear or respect, but they probably wouldn't be able to say why." He shrugged.

"Why didn't you say something sooner?"

He looked away and wrung his hands together. "It's hard to focus on coherent thoughts when I'm in beast form."

"You formed words just fine."

"I've gotten better with practice, but sometimes all I can get out is 'mine.'" He paused. "But I thought you already knew."

"Why would you think that?" Was Mom supposed to have told her?

"This isn't the first time I've brought you here."

Another memory of pain, blood and the ocean tumbled through her mind. "After the attack."

He nodded, expression drawn. "I couldn't save your mother, but I could save you."

The rest of the tension in her shoulders eased away as Cora's flittering memories of that awful day returned. She'd fallen into the ocean. While the water healed her head wound, leaving her with the scar she wore today, she'd been knocked unconscious. Or close enough not to recall anything between hitting the cliff and a fuzzy awareness at the bottom of the ocean floor, filled with sand, confusion, and painful lungs.

"I would've drowned," she said.

"I couldn't let you heal on Iom near the humans who killed your mother. I couldn't risk your safety, so I brought you here, told you of your heritage and then returned you to the shores of the Eyrie. Your concussion was bad, though, and the events at the keep traumatizing. I didn't realize you'd supressed your memories until recently."

A pain stabbed at her chest. She owed this sciper so much, and she'd had all these awful thoughts about him. And he deserved so much better than what she'd given. "So all this time you thought I was rejecting you?"

He shrugged. "Or processing."

She rocked back on her heels.

"You took the news the first time fairly hard. I was willing to wait. I'm the last of my kind. There are no more cetodes roaming the oceans. The dreaded Sea Beast will die with me. But my essence will live on."

"How..." She swallowed and looked away. Maybe this wasn't something she should ask. "How did you bless me your essence?"

He smiled sadly. "I placed my hand on your mother's swollen belly and willed it to be so."

"Willed it?"

"I wasn't sure it would work, but I felt the energy radiating from my hand the moment it happened." He shrugged. "And when you were born, I felt the waves of my own energy roll out across the ocean like another nuclear cascade."

Oh. My. God. "Are you...radioactive?"

"I don't think so." He looked at his hands. "But I think I have something like it—the ability to manipulate matter."

That explained the shape-shifting.

"What I do know is your line will carry my gift without any of the negative aspects of my nature. I don't think your mother understood the true extent of my gift when I bestowed it on you, but I hope you will.

I hope..." He cut off again and looked down at his hands. "Maybe it's foolish of me, but I hope the memory of me will live on with you. Maybe my image won't be hated and entangled with fear. I haven't eaten a sapavian since the day your mother saved me. I've terrorized human ships taking more than their share of the ocean spoils, but I've protected the Eyrie."

"We just didn't realize it," she whispered.

He nodded. "It's easier to fear the unknown than to pause and try to understand. If any other sapavians had found me that day, I would've died. It wouldn't have mattered that the injuries I sustained were from thwarting an attack."

Cora straightened. "The humans had launched an attack?"

"A joint attack. Sometimes, I float near the surface and listen to the sailors talking. This particular attack was orchestrated by a sect of humans and the queen's lover."

Queens's lover?

Ronin's mother had a lover?

A sheet of ice flowed through her veins as a dark twisted realization bloomed in her head. She patted her vest and pulled the last message from Ava from the pocket. A diligent messenger, she hadn't opened it, even after all this time. She'd pushed it from her mind, instead.

Stored in one of the few surviving waterproof pockets of her flying leathers, the message remained undamaged. It had no official address, only a number that would undoubtedly match a post office box. She tore the seal open and read the message: "Eagle down, but not out. In pursuit. We'll hold up our end of the agreement. Make sure you do the same."

Nausea clutched her gut.

She looked up at the man, whose name she didn't even know. She hadn't thought to ask. "I need to go home."

44

"Beware the person who stabs you and tells the world they're the one who's bleeding."

— JILL BLAKEWAY

Ronin heaved in deep breaths of salt air. The tears never fell. The pain in his chest was too strong for anything other than a wracking ache with each breath.

Cora was gone.

It didn't seem real. Last night, he'd held her in his arms as they stretched out and watched the night sky. The moonlight had played with the angles of her face, he'd traced her scar with his finger. She fell asleep like that, her head resting on his chest, arms and legs tangled up, white and black hair had fanned over his armour. With every breath, he'd take in her scent and all the anger, grief, and uncertainty broiling within would ease away, replaced with just her.

And now she was gone.

His chest constricted and he wheezed again, nausea twisting his gut again.

Rocks crunched behind him. "My liege?"

Oh good. At least he didn't have to tramp through the town like a half-drowned rat until he found someone from court.

He staggered to his feet, pulled his shoulders and wings back and turned toward the guard.

A large fist flew at his face. It was the last thing he saw before everything went black.

THE ACHE POUNDING inside Ronin's head woke him up. He lay sprawled on expensive tiles, his hands bound behind him.

He knew these tiles.

He knew the rose-laden smell in the air and the gentle whisper of the silk drapes along the floor.

Someone had brought him to the private chambers of the king.

He scrambled to his knees and struggled to straighten. His vision wavered. The pounding in his head intensified.

The clack of a woman's boots echoed in the room.

He looked over his shoulder from his kneeling position.

Sasha walked around him. Nestled in complicated knots and braids of her tawny hair, she wore their mother's crown. Instead of one of those fluffy dresses the courtiers favoured, she wore black leather pants, a white silk blouse and boots with heels. Wicked heels. Like the kind that could be used for walking or stabbing.

"Sasha?" He straightened some more and pulled his shoulders back. "What's going on? Release me."

She tsked, clicking her tongue at him and crouched in front of him, weight on her toes. "Oh no, dear brother. That just won't do. We can't let the traitor of the Eyrie loose."

"What?"

Her mouth quirked up. "Of course, I was devastated to learn my own brother was responsible for poisoning our father. Too greedy to wait any longer for the throne. Such a shame."

A chill spread through his body with a sickening realisation. "It was you. You betrayed us." He swallowed, but his stomach continued to churn as if a giant had delivered a debilitating body shot. He'd had time to grieve on Iom, but part of him still held onto a tiny bit of hope that Ava had lied. Even when the other pieces of information she'd given turned out to be true, he'd clung to that hope. Desperately.

Now faced with not only the reality of his father's death, but the cause and the perpetrator, air fled his lungs and his stomach twisted into a knot.

"Why?" He forced the words out, the dry air shredding along the inside of his throat.

Sasha's smile turned into a scowl and she stood abruptly. "You wouldn't understand."

"Try me."

"You were the golden one. The heir of the Eyrie. Placed on a pedestal and bathed with love and affection."

He jerked back. "That doesn't make any sense. Father loved you, too. He paid for tutors and trainers. You've had everything you wanted."

"He tolerated me." Her hands balled into fists. "And he did it for you. He might've thrown baubles and training at me, but only for appearances, only for you. Never for me."

"Why would he do that?"

"If anyone found out I was the illegitimate bastard of the queen and her lover, it would throw your own legitimacy as the heir into question. Your father needed everyone to believe I was a true daughter of the Eagle Clan."

"Her lover..." Ronin whispered, mind reeling.

"Lord Gable."

Ronin flinched. He knew the name. Everyone on the Eyrie did. The man had been publicly executed about nine years ago, a few months after Father banished Cora's family to the outpost.

No.

The secret?

Was this the secret Kane Cormorant discovered that led to his family's banishment?

No.

It couldn't be true.

He glared at Sasha. "You're lying."

"I'm not. Mother loved my father, not yours. The affair spanned many years. They had a plan and an alliance with a group of humans to take over the Eyrie. They tried twenty-six years ago, when mother first discovered she was with child with me, but the Sea Beast attacked the human ships and they had to regroup. If Mother hadn't kept a diary and if I hadn't found it along with her contacts, I might've never known the truth. But I did and I do, and now I'll finish what should've been done years ago."

Ronin froze, still kneeling on the hard tiles, too shocked to speak.

"Kane Cormorant discovered the affair and brought it to the attention of King Edgar and ruined any future chances for my mother and true father to overthrow him." She lifted her chin. "They wanted me to be queen and now I've made it happen all on my own. I avenged my parents in the process."

"Father didn't kill our mother. She died from the bone sickness." He ignored the pain in his chest pinched every time he thought of Mom's last moment —her pale face, bleary eyes and the lump on her leg that kept growing despite all the concoctions the doctors kept throwing down her throat.

"He may as well have." She looked away, the muscles of her jawline bunching. "He executed Lord Gable. My father. Edgar's actions took Mother's life better than any knife in the back."

Ronin disagreed. Mother's own choices led to her downfall, but clearly, he wasn't in a place to argue. Father had discovered the affair, the identity of Sasha's biological father and plans to overthrow him. To protect the kingdom and Ronin's claim to the throne, he continued to act as if Sasha was his and executed Lord Gable for treason. "And that's why he sent away Cora's family."

Sasha shook her head. "Edgar didn't send anyone away. Cora's dad offered to leave. Your father couldn't bring himself to kill his best friend to protect the secret. He couldn't eradicate all traces of Mother's deceit."

"Including you," he said. "He could've just killed you, made it look like an accident. But he didn't. He raised you as his own for sixteen years."

"And then things changed. He learned the truth and couldn't stand to see me as the reminder of his wife's infidelity. My face. My wings. All slaps to the face."

"He loved you."

She hesitated. Instead of lashing out, she narrowed

her eyes and took a deep breath. "I will finish what he started and eradicate all evidence of the affair for him, save myself. How convenient he got Cora to escort you to Iom. Now, I only have her father to eliminate after you."

"I'm surprised you haven't already." She wouldn't have left Kane Cormorant to chance. Sasha was brutal and efficient. She always had been, and he'd admired her practical ruthlessness. Until now, of course.

She pursed her lips together. "He thwarted my earlier attempts and went into hiding, but I'll ferret him out like the pest he is and finish this once and for all. Those turkey-headed twins have disappeared, too. They'll be the weak link."

"Why?"

"Because the two combined don't have one full working brain." She frowned and looked at him like he had the turkey head. Maybe he did. "Or if you're asking about Kane it's so he won't expose the truth."

"No. Why are you doing any of this? You were the princess of the Eyrie. Even with Father's distance, he still cared for you when he could've disposed of you. You had rank, wealth, and the admiration of the nobility. I used to envy how you had all the benefits of royal lineage and none of the responsibilities."

This time a genuine smile spread across her face. "And now I'll have more rank, wealth, and admiration."

Ronin shivered. He hadn't wanted to see the truth

about his sister. He hadn't wanted to accept the darkness about her.

Oh, he'd seen her cruel actions and efficient decisions based on practicality instead of empathy. To acknowledge the darkness, though, would make it more real and somehow, he wouldn't, couldn't, turn a blind eye to it once he became king.

His sister's intelligence sparkled in her gaze as she watched him.

She knew.

Once he became king, he'd block her cruelty. He'd put an end to her games, and he'd do the one thing father was never able to do when it came to the princess—he'd reprimand her.

She nodded as if she followed his thoughts the entire way. "*Father* carried a lot of guilt for his involvement in my parents' deaths and also for thinking about killing me. He raised me as his own for over a decade, and once the truth was revealed he contemplated ending my life to save yours. I know he did. I saw it in his eyes, in his turned down mouth. Guilt haunted the king more than any ghost." She shrugged as if Father's torment was inconsequential. "He let me get away with a lot. You wouldn't. I couldn't allow you to become the next king."

"So you set me up, suggested Cora accompany me and assassinated the king. All because you wanted revenge and more power? You didn't want to see your life and current position as a gift or mercy from Father?"

"As I said at the beginning, you'd never understand." She pursed her lips again. "Originally, I intended you to stand trial and have a public execution." She tapped her finger on the hilt of the dagger strapped to her waist. "But I can't chance the old man getting to you or for you to spread the truth. Despite my lies, there are some who are not as easily persuaded. There's a pesky whiskey jack asking pointed questions. I may have to eliminate him, and that death will lay at your feet, too. You inspire a lot of loyalty, brother, and it's another reason why I've grown to hate you."

"Are you really this petty and shallow?"

She unsheathed her dagger and stepped forward. Without hesitation, she gripped the back of his head, pulling the hair and yanking his face up. With a steady hand, she brought the dagger to his throat, her yellow eyes blazing.

"Maybe, brother. But now I'm going to be magnificent."

He could surge up, try to head butt her and fight with his hands tied behind his back. He could spend his last moments agonizing over his stupidity for not recognizing his sister as the delusional sociopath she was.

He did neither.

Instead, he called up the memory of holding Cora

as they spiraled to their possible deaths in the angry ocean below. He closed his eyes and let the crisp air with floral scents and the smell of Cora wash over him.

Instead of a dagger piercing the soft skin of his neck, a strong gust of air rushed past him. Feathers slapped his face.

The pressure of the dagger on his neck disappeared.

Ronin snapped his eyes open. Another sapavian had slammed into his sister and they rolled over the stones in a heap of feathers and limbs a few feet away.

Black wings. Lithe body. God-awful attire.

Ronin blinked again.

No.

It couldn't be.

But it was. He knelt on the expensive stone flooring of the royal chamber bound and gaping like a stuffed turkey while his lover grappled with his sister. Half-sister.

The women rolled to their feet and faced off. Cora held the dagger with a hammer grip. God, she was glorious.

"Was it your mom who sent assassins to Hadren's Keep all those years ago or were you already evil?" Cora asked.

Ronin ground his teeth. He hadn't even thought of that yet, but it made sense. If Father wasn't going to eliminate the threat of Cora's family, Mother would. She knew where the cormorants were staying and tipped off her human contacts out of revenge for her dead lover and to protect Sasha. The timing was about right, the attack on the keep a mere month after Lord Gable's execution.

The humans failed, though, getting the mother and damaging Cora instead of the father. Or maybe they intended to take out the whole family.

"My mother," Sasha hissed, confirming Ronin's thoughts. She jutted her chin up and feinted, lunging in and changing her attack at the last second.

Cora dodged and countered, flipping the dagger into a reverse hold at the last moment and changing the motion. Instead of jabbing, she slashed. Unprepared, Sasha failed to block the strike and the knife sliced into her arm. Blood sprayed across the room and Ronin's face.

Sasha scowled and lunged.

Delusional. Sociopathic. And apparently immune to pain.

They circled each other, taking turns attacking and evading, but not inflicting a lot of damage. Meanwhile, Ronin awkwardly made it to his feet and waited. How could he help Cora? He couldn't stand by, bound and pathetic, and watch her die. Again.

The women's circling brought them closer and closer to Ronin. Sasha's focus was so intent on Cora, so single-minded, she didn't see Ronin move.

He struck out, slamming his foot into the back of his sister's leg.

She cried out and lurched to the side.

Without hesitation, Cora lunged in again. She blocked Sasha's flailing slash and sank her own dagger into Sasha's chest. The dagger made a sickening sound as Cora thrust the sharp blade through skin and tissue and past bone. Blood oozed around the entry site and quickly spread, saturating Sasha's shirt.

Sasha's eyes widened and she pushed away from Cora. With the dagger jutting from her chest, Sasha staggered backward, gaze frantic.

Cora's attack was a well-placed strike, one she'd practiced with him many times during their training sessions at the outpost. She'd missed piercing the heart, but she'd nicked it.

Sasha dropped her dagger. The weapon clattered to the floor by his feet. Her gaze searched the room frantically and found his. "Brother—"

His sister's eyes rolled up and she fell to the floor. Her head hit the tiles with a loud crack.

He stood beside Cora as they watched the pool of blood grow around Sasha's body.

Without speaking, Cora retrieved his sister's dagger from the floor and cut his bindings. She used her sleeve to first wipe her face and then her own weapon.

Pain rushed down Ronin's arms and he shook them until most of the prickling sensation went away. He turned to Cora. "You're alive."

"Turns out the Sea Beast is a friend of the Eyrie

and wanted to have a bonding moment." She paused, as if listening to something in the air. "His name is Darryl."

"I watched him eat you, Cora."

"I know."

"I thought you were dead."

"I know," she whispered again.

New anger rushed through his body. Hot, boiling rage rose and demanded he rush from the room and kill something.

"My mother saved him when she was pregnant with me and in return, he gifted me with his essence. He knew he'd never have children of his own and thinks of me as his daughter."

"Oh." He had so many questions, but at least the anger simmered.

"Yeah."

"So that's why you can do all that cool stuff?"

"Yeah." She looked away from him, her gaze travelling to his sister's body. She flinched. "I'm so sorry."

"For what?" She scared the crap out of him and made him feel as though his heart had been ripped from his chest, but it was hardly her fault a giant Sea Beast chose that moment to steal her away in his mouth for some parental bonding.

"For everything? You lost your father. You watched a giant sea monster eat me, and...and I killed your sister."

Oh. That.

"I think she tried to warn me, you know," Cora went on. "She came to me before we left on the trip and told me not to return to the Eyrie without you. She expected you to be killed or contained on Iom, so she'd only have to deal with our fathers." Cora glanced down at his sister's body again. "I think she tried to spare us, in her own way. Or at least give us a chance at survival." She swallowed. "And I killed her."

"She may have tried to spare us, but she would've gone through with our executions." He shook his head. His chest felt hollow. His own sister. If only she'd talked to him, confided in him...Maybe he could've prevented all this loss and heartache. Maybe Dad would still be alive.

"It's not your fault." Cora watched him, gaze too perceptive.

Instead of speaking more on the matter, he reached forward and pulled her toward him, careful not to rip her already falling-apart outfit. "It's not yours, either."

She tensed and started to argue.

"You saved me." He kissed her, pouring his entire heart into the kiss, telling her with his body how much she meant to him, how much he loved her, and how much he planned to enjoy every last waking moment of his life with her by his side.

He'd never taken her life for granted, but the scare of losing her made him realize he never wanted to go through that again. He never wanted her to be anywhere other than with him.

EPILOGUE

"Anyone can have a once-upon-a-time or a happily-ever-after, but it's the journey between that makes the story worth telling."

— CHRIS COLFER

Cora held Ronin's hands and tried to ignore the cheering crowd below. This was so not her thing. The wind whipped her hair across her face and chilled her skin through the white flying outfit made more for fashion than actually flying. If she'd had a choice, she'd wear her normal flying leathers, but after turning down numerous suggestions from the royal fashion consultants, she'd relented on this one detail.

Ronin squeezed her hands in return. He'd left his crown behind for this part of the ceremony but looked every inch the crowned king of the Eyrie in his golden armour. The light danced off the metal and made him glow. He was the sun to her night.

It hadn't taken much to convince the court and people of his innocence. She gave Marcus Jack the scoop of his lifetime. In addition to his article, her father's testimony, the communications Sasha had stashed away, the peace treaty Ronin delivered calmed the unease of the Eyrie.

After the proverbial dust settled, Ronin had a lot of questions about the Sea Beast and the underwater cavern. She shared everything with him, not wanting secrets between them.

"Ready?" Ronin asked, pulling her close, supporting her weight with each heavy wingbeat.

"This is a stupid tradition."

"And you love it."

"Okay, ready." She tilted her head up and smiled.

Ronin kissed her and a loud cheer rose from below. The low croon of the Sea Beast who'd joined the celebration added to the blast of sound.

Cora's world narrowed and focused on the joy of Ronin's mouth on hers as they cartwheeled toward the rocky shore for the entire kingdom to see.

Thank you for reading *Cormorant Run*.
Did you enjoy Cora and Ronin's story?
If so, please consider leaving a review to let other
readers know, and when you have time, check out my
website at jcmckenzie.ca for similar stories.

CHARACTERS

Aeneas: King of Iom

Ava: Cora's human contact on Iom

Cam Cormorant: Sapavian. Cormorant guard, Cora's cousin

Caleb: Gabriel's partner

Coraline Evangeline Cormorant: Cora, the main character. Did you just skip to the back? You naughty little reader, you.

Darryl: pfft, read the book! I'm not giving you this spoiler

Characters

Dax Cormorant: Sapavian. Cormorant guard, Cora's cousin

Edgar Eagle: Sapavian. King of the Eyrie

Gable: Sapavian. Eyrie lord executed for treason

Gabriel: Sapavian. Ronin's head of security, childhood friend and rival

Jacoby: Human. Ava's fiancé

Jerome: Sapavian. Called Cora ugly when they were teenagers

Kane Cormorant: Sapavian. Head of Cormorant Clan. Cora's father

Karla: Human kingswoman

Marcus Jack: Sapavian. Also known as Jack. Eyrie reporter

Phil: Human kingsman

GLOSSARY OF TERMS

Alara: Iom fishing village. Also, an acronym for "as low as reasonably achievable," used in reference to personal or environmental exposure to radiation.

Bearcat: a sciper created by merging black bear and mountain lion DNA.

Cap: Originally an abbreviation for Channel Access Point, this acronym evolved over time from.CAP to Cap and is pronounced k-ah-p instead of C-A-P.

Calandria: Iom city, site of the royal court where the king of Iom resides. Also, a cylindrical vessel that contains the heavy water reactor in a pressurized heavy water reactor.

Cetus: better known as the Sea Beast. An ichthyoid sapien, transformed as the result of scientific experimentation and the nuclear cascades. Cetodes (pl).

Cetodes: plural of Cetus.

Cladding: Iom town. Also, the metal surrounding nuclear fuel material.

Dose: Iom town. Also, the energy absorbed by tissue from ionizing radiation.

Giga: Iom town. Also, a measurement prefix for one billion units.

Hadren's Keep: Iom fortress located at the Outpost Access Point

Hunter's Quad: a group of four human hunters.

Ichthy: Eyrie Waystation. Also, a word derived from the Greek word ikhthus, meaning "fish." Ichthyology is the study of fish.

Iom: Isle of Man.

Khondros: Eyrie Waystation. Also, Greek for "cartilage." Chondrichthyes is a group of cartilaginous fish, which includes sharks, rays and skates.

MAS: Men Against Sapavians

Milling: Iom town. Also, the process for extracting minerals from ore.

Mox: Iom town. Also, an acronym for mixed oxide fuel.

Nuwaps: nuclear warped, the result of uncontrolled radiation from nuclear explosions on scipers with volatile DNA.

Oap: Originally an abbreviation for Outpost Access Point, this acronym evolved over time from OAP to Oap and is pronounced Oh-p instead of O-A-P.

Ostei: Eyrie Waystation. Also, a word derived from osteo which comes from the Greek ostéon, meaning "bone." There is a group of boney fish called Oste-ichthyes, which includes goldfish, salmon, and tuna.

Otos: short for Otolith bone, the inner ear bone found in fish.

Patagium: elastic fold of membranous skin found in sapavian wings that aid in aerodynamics.

Sapavians: Formed by genetically splicing bird DNA with human DNA, these human-bird hybrids exhibit mostly human characteristics, but are capable of flying and have some remnant birdlike tendencies.

Scipers: species created from scientific experimentation, including sapavians, unicorns, thunderbirds, and the Sea Beast.

Sievert: Iom city. Also, a unit of measurement for the biological damage caused by radiation.

Thunderbirds: nuwap scipers that scavenge the Carrion Channel. Distant cousins to sapavians.

Wap: Originally an abbreviation for Waystation Access Point, this acronym evolved over time from WAP to Wap and is pronounced w-ah-p instead of W-A-P.

Zircaloy: Iom city. Also, an alloy of zirconium used as fuel rod cladding in water-cooled reactors.

ACKNOWLEDGMENTS

First and foremost, I'd like to thank the reader. Without you and your words of encouragement, I wouldn't be nearly as motivated to keep going. If you enjoyed this story, please share with a friend or leave a review. This feeds the author soul.

I'd like to thank my editor, Lara Parker, who's just a fabulous human being. I snuck in an Easter egg for her and she spotted it right away. I'm forever thankful she squeezes me into her schedule.

A huge thank you to Anna from Eerilyfair Fair Designs. She created another incredible cover for me. Seriously though, she creates works of art.

This book wouldn't be the creation it is today without the constructive feedback from my beta readers—Karilyn Bentley, Charlotte Copper and Nicole Flockton. They're authors in addition to being readers. You should check our their books!

Thank you to Book Nook Nuts for the proofread. I always think I send you a clean manuscript and your eagle eyes still spot blunders.

And as always, a giant thank you to my friends and family for their love and support.

ABOUT THE AUTHOR

J. C. McKenzie is a book loving, gumboot-wearing, unapologetic science geek. She predominantly writes urban fantasy and post-apocalyptic dystopian fantasy with strong romantic elements. When she's not spinning tales, she's in the classroom sharing her passion for science and mathematics while secretly warping the young impressionable minds of our future to carry out her evil plans for world domination. She lives in the Pacific Northwest with her family and a feisty dog named Angus who believes rules were made to be broken.

Visit her at jcmckenzie.ca

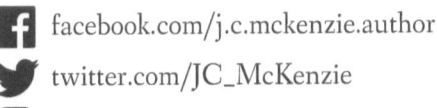

facebook.com/j.c.mckenzie.author

twitter.com/JC_McKenzie

instagram.com/j.c.mckenzie

www.ingramcontent.com/pod-product-compliance
Lightning Source LLC
Chambersburg PA
CBHW060222030726
47499CB00004B/1154